Love Without Limits

NATIONAL BESTSELLING AUTHOR
NIOBIA BRYANT

Infinite Ink Presents...

Love Without Limits
Publisher: Infinite Ink Presents...

Copyright © 2017 by Niobia Bryant

All rights reserved. No part of this book may be used, reproduced or transmitted in any form or by any means without the prior written consent of the author, except for brief quotes used in reviews.

ISBN-13: 9781521076507
First Electronic Edition: July 2017
First Paperback Edition: August 2017

For two brilliantly brown sistahs of the word, lost to this world while their creativity, thankfully, remains.

Octavia Butler
(1947 - 2006)
and
Gloria Naylor
(1950 - 2016)

I thank them for the countless hours of getting lost inside the pages of their books and for inspiring me to nourish my creative spirit.

LEXICON

Please note most of this lexicon is based on Oromo, an Afroasiatic language.

A
Abbaa—father
Abiyyuu—father-in-law
Abuturoo—ancestors
Aduu—sun
Afur—four
Alkoolii—alcoholic beverage
Alwaada—kitchen
Amaatii—mother-in-law
Ayyaaneeffachuu—celebratory cry of the Empath people

B
Baatii—moon
Badaa—evil feminine; bitch
Bara—equivalent of Earth's year
Bona—the hot season
Bwa Kasuwa—slave marketplace on Planet Kordi

C
Cabbii—snow
Chollolaattaa—chocolate
Cidha—traditional Erisedian wedding

D
Da'ee—mother
Dawaa—medical and spiritual leader
Dhiqata—cleansing room chamber; similar to shower
Diinqa—bedroom
Dhotli—animal with feathers (similar to Earth's geese)

E
Extos—a powerful aphrodisiac

G
Gaa'ila—marriage, lifelong union

G (cont.)
Gabra—slave
Galatoomaa—thank you
Ganna—the cold season
Gennii—technologist or scientist
Giiftii—Queen
Giiftiin—Prince or Princess, heir to throne
Goojjoo—log cabins in which the Empath people reside
Gumna—prostitutes

H
Hayyisa—security guards
Huccuu—material of the softest and richest quality that also adjusts to body temperature. Used for linens and clothing.

I
Illeetis—furry animal of Erised
Inaba—a fruit indigenous to Erised that is primarily used to make juice

J
Jaarraa—equivalent of Earth's century
Jaarsa—husband
Jahannam—planet of fire where evil souls are exiled
Ji'a—equivalent of Earth's month

K
Kaasuu—a lift or elevator
Komputara—display screen
Kutaa Dhiqannaa—bathroom

L
Lama—two

M
Mana—residence
Mkpuru—a sticky and sweet fruit indigenous to planet Nede
Morkii—Erisedian board game
Moticha—King, ruler of the entire planet

N
Nagaya—greeting that means both hello, goodbye, good evening, good morning, and good afternoon depending on the time of its usage
Nkume—rare and precious stones found on Planet Nede, also used as a light source

O
Ollaa—village; city developed on Planet Nede by the Empaths
Ooftuu—an automated robot chauffeur
Ow'a—the warm season

Q
Qaadhimamuu—engagement
Qoricha—illegal drug
Qorobu—damn; swear word
Qanddii—bed

R
Riti—wife
Rooba—the rainy season

S
Sadi—three
Shaanxtaa—luggage
Shan—five
Surrii—brain

T
Televiziyoona—television
Tokko—one
Torbaan—equivalent of Earth's week

U
Urjii—urjiis

W
Warqee—monetary denomination
Waqaa—god or goddess

X
Xiyyaara—flying personal vehicles

Y
Yecas—equivalent to pounds on Earth
Yeeyyii—animal of planet Nede (similar to Earth's wolf)

Z
Zwodriu—simulator room

Please note:
Masculine(s) - equivalent of Earth's man/men
Feminine(s) - equivalent of Earth's woman/women

PROLOGUE

Life is never quite what you expect it to be. It is a series of unexpected events that can send you spiraling through phases of glorious good or hellish bad. Turned on your head. Pleasantly reclined on your back. Begging on your hands and knees. Standing resilient on your feet. Knocked flat on your behind.

One solitary tear raced down the beautiful mocha face of Aja Drakar. She didn't dare raise her hand to swipe it away because more would follow. In the darkness, she felt the steady trickle of that lone tear, up until it dropped from the edge of her oval face so similar to her da'ee's. The high cheekbones, the feline eyes a startling shade of honey, the pale metallic gold moles on her chin and on her forehead that were characteristic of her people. Full lips that used to be ready to smile in a second and brown streaked hair flowed in soft waves nearly to her waist. All of it was a reflection of her.

Another tear fell.

Aja closed her eyes and fought back the instinct to release a deep guttural moan as a wave of pain radiated across her chest. Sorrow. It now ran so deep that she wondered if there was ever a moment she had truly been happy. Her people had suffered. Wounded. Dead. Enslaved.

She never expected there would be a race war.

She never expected there would be such violence and death.

She never thought she'd feel her Empath powers fade.

She never thought she'd lose her entire family.

She never thought she'd lose her freedom.

Life is never quite what you expect it to be.

I

72 hours earlier

"*Nagaya*, Aja."

At the sound of her *abbaa's* words through the curtain hanging in the entrance to her *diinqa*, Aja Drakar's eyes opened as she lay in the ebony darkness of her *diinqa*. It didn't take much to rouse her from her sleep. It had been that way since she was a child. One foot in the wake zone and the other in the slumber zone with just enough balance to keep her from being sleep deprived. Her family teased her that she was too curious to become completely inert.

"*Nagaya*," she called out to him, her voice still thick with sleep.

Moments later she heard his footsteps carry him away from her door.

She released a soft grunt as she stretched her limbs and breathed deeply, preparing herself for whatever lay ahead for the day. When it came to life in their rugged region of the planet Nede, anything was possible. Homegrown food. Physical labor. *Goojjoos* made of mud and rocks packed between the sturdy trunks of brilliant red trees. Illumination of the small windowless rooms came from stacks of glowing *nkume* stones harvested from the remote underground caves. Rudimentary cooking and eating utensils. Just one medic of increasing age to monitor the health of nearly a thousand people. One small hut to educate the children.

The basics of anything and everything.

The story of their exodus was a part of their folklore. Once the decision had been made to flee from Erised, the *abuturoos* plotted to hijack a *xiyyaara* and learn to navigate it. Thankfully no Empath was suspected. The assumption that the simple living Empaths wouldn't need such a thing worked to their advantage. With much time and practice, the *abuturoos* soon were exploring planets in the Acirfa galaxy. Upon choosing what would become Planet Nede, that lone *xiyyaara* was used to transport the Empaths and their belongings in groups of fifty. Many trips were made, and the exodus was exhaustive on the Empaths and the *xiyyaara*. Without proper knowledge of maintenance and repair of the vehicle, it soon was nothing more than a broken-down eyesore. The Empaths were isolated on Nede and every day was a struggle to survive in their new environment.

The *abuturoos* of the Empath people had left behind the technological advances of their true home planet of Erised. They'd chosen happiness and freedom over the ability to acquire even the simplest creature comforts that Erised offered. Their way of life on Nede didn't vary much from their humble life in the highlands of Kilo on Erised. That simplicity brought about the ridicule, scrutiny, judgment and harsh treatment by the ruling class of Jeynas on Erised. The Empaths desire for a slower-paced life, and their respect for nature, upon which they relied, was seen as foolish and weak. Thus, their decision to leave their planet Erised behind and start a new life for future generations.

Sighing a bit, Aja pushed aside her thoughts as the fire of anger and indignation stoked inside her at the thought of ever having to kowtow to anyone.

"Never," she mouthed as she turned over onto her side atop the large round sac of *dhotli* feathers.

Aja pulled her knees to her chest, releasing a small murmur of pleasure at the warmth of her smooth, cinnamon-brown skin-on-skin contact.

The heated body of a masculine would be fun to hold.

That thought made her smile.

As a feminine who had lived close to thirty *baras*, Aja was no stranger to sexual indulgence. She and the rest of the Empaths lived with intense, simmering attractions because of their ability to connect emotionally with anyone through physical contact of any kind.

Sex could be quite fun.

Finding a body—a warm and willing body—was not an issue. Aja was an attractive feminine. Since she'd blossomed into womanhood over ten *baras* ago, she'd seen enough long stares, wolfish smiles, lingering touches and bold requests from masculines to make her aware of her appeal.

A mate in her *qanddii*? Easy. Getting him not to linger and yearn for more? Ridiculously hard.

Men wanted more than just to couple with her. They wanted to own her. Possess her body. Dominate her thoughts. Douse her innate fire.

Aja was having none of that.

She rolled over onto her back and sat up in the middle of her *qanddii*. As always, her eyes landed on the log wall and not the window for which she constantly yearned. She would love to look out at the beautiful and vibrant world in which they lived. Walking barefoot in the purple grass was her favorite pastime, especially when she snuck away to her secret coppice and stripped herself of her attire to let the orange *aduu* deepen the brown of her skin.

'Today,' Aja promised herself, as she removed the weighty square cloth covering the bowl of *nkume* stones on the small table by her *qanddii*. Immediately, the bright light surrounded her and cast a reflection off the dull red of the logs. It could have felt like standing in the middle of a fire, if not for the chill in the air.

Her cover, made of the clean and dried hides of *yeeyvii*, fell to her lap. Goose bumps raced across her nakedness and hardened her nipples into twin tight buds that ached. She wished the *nkumes* were as useful for warmth as they were for light.

On the outskirts of the uninhabited lands surrounding the area where the Empath people had settled nearly half a *jaarraa* ago, their small exploration team had discovered underground caves with walls made of stone that glowed. The discovery of *nkumes* had transformed life for the Empaths. Her *abbaa*, Malc Drakar, was a part of the research team trying, with such limited resources, to find other uses for the stones. Unfortunately, providing heat was not one.

Aja rushed the short distance across her *diinqa* to pour water from the pitcher into the bowl sitting beside it. She bent over the small table by the doorway and splashed her face with the water. Her body tensed for a few moments in reaction to its coldness. The feel of her fingers brushing against her cheeks registered. Aja closed her eyes and pressed her palms to her face and lightly tapped her fingertips against her eyelids.

When it came to knowing the look of her face, she might as well be blind. There was nothing to view the reflection of herself. The overt ardor of masculines let her know she was pretty and the constant reminders by her *abbaa* and younger brother, Llor, let her know she was the spitting image of her beautiful *da'ee*.

Still, I would love to see me.

Pushing aside her regret, Aja finished washing up, glad for the warm bath she had taken the night before to lessen her time being surrounded by the morning chill. Soon the *ow'a* season would begin, and the heat would reign so that she would have to shed some of her clothing—which was ideal for Aja. She would prefer wearing nothing at all...if it weren't so distracting.

She reached for one of the few tunics she owned to cover her nakedness. It offered no comfort nor design. Unfortunately, it was new, and it took nearly fifty washings to soften the roughness of the plain, white cloth made by the weavers' looms. The cut was simple and square, leaving her womanly curves to pure imagination.

Men, however, seemed to be pleased when finally given a peek at the body beneath the shapeless clothing. The thought made her smile as she twisted the soft waves of her waist-length hair atop her head. She left her small *diinqa* located just off the common area of their *goojjoo*. She stopped by the doorway to her brother's diinqa and pulled back the rawhide curtain, not at all surprised to find it was already empty. The masculines in her family were complete opposites. Her *abbaa?* Brains. Her brother? Brawn.

Llor was undoubtedly helping to tend to the crops along with the other masculines assigned to farming duties, providing the food upon which their community depended. On Nede, team work was the key to their survival. No masculine or feminine stood alone fighting for his or her survival.

At the entrance to the *alwaada*, Aja smiled and shifted her eyes away from her *abbaa's* tall and firm body dwarfing her *da'ee* as he stood closely behind her and held her hips with his hands. He bent his head to whisper something in her ear. Her soft giggle told the tale of his intent.

It was that "can't keep my eyes or hands off of you" kind of love and passion she wanted for herself.

Aja cleared her throat.

They pulled apart with much reluctance.

"I'll go fetch some water," Aja said, her voice soft and husky in their native tongue.

Quickly, she moved to the red wooden door and walked outside. She knew they would use those moments alone to enjoy the very thing she yearned for that morning. *They had all night to enjoy themselves.*

As the door closed behind her, she leaned onto it and took a deep breath of air as she eyed the colorful landscape before her. Towering red trunk of trees that were more than ten times her height, with large blue-green triangle-shaped leaves, against a pale lavender sky as its backdrop. The caves and mountains in the distance were emerald green. The dirt beneath them was a dark and deep midnight blue, in sharp contrast to the thin blades of bluish-green grass that grew sparsely across the land.

The smell of nature was thick, and Aja inhaled deeply of it as she closed her eyes. It was early in the morning, with the *aduu* not yet fully set in the sky. Not many Empaths were up and milling about outside. The sounds of winged animals mingled with the heavy grunts of the masculines laboring in the fields off in the distance or those powering the crude water irrigation system.

She opened her eyes and shaded them with her hand as she turned to look down at their *ollaa*. Two rows of more than fifty dull red *goojjoos* were lined up and facing each other with some distance between them for privacy, yet still close enough for them to function as a community. The *abuturoos* believed the arrangement had been critical to their survival on the new planet.

The river was a quarter mile to the east. Close enough to serve as their primary water source and far enough to avoid flooding when the water level crested during the raining season, the *rooba*. To the north, in the highlands where the dirt was rich, the collective farm was over fifty acres. Those who were skilled tradesmen gave away their wares, as needed, at a large *goojjoo*, creating a marketplace under the shade of trees to the west. There was a communal area bordered with rocks and centered on a fire pit for large meetings or gatherings.

Aja's body jumped slightly, startled by the sound of something tumbling to the floor inside. Her eyes widened, horrified at a rather vivid image of that something being her *da'ee*...beneath her *abbaa*. Shaking her head for clarity, she quickly moved away from the door and walked the wide path up the middle of the *goojjoos*.

"*Nagaya*," she greeted everyone she met along the way.

A young child, no more than six, raced past her at full speed, his little feet kicking up dark blue dust as he ran. On impulse, she took off behind him, laughing when he looked back over his shoulder at her and picked up speed as he gave her a cocky wave.

She gave up, slowing down to a stop and bending over to press her hands on her knees as she breathed deeply. Her heart raced as a fine sheen of sweat ran down the groove between breasts. She felt exhilarated.

Aja loved life on Nede.

As she resumed her trek to retrieve water and passed the last *goojjoo,* she looked around. The clearing was ready for new growth. The fields were off in the distance, and she could see the sweat-soaked backs of the masculines as they swung their arms and sliced the air with their machetes. The trees in the background shadowed the sky.

Her steps slowed as the distant sound of methodical drumbeats filled the air. She tilted her head a bit to the left to focus on the message delivered from one of the few Empath families who had chosen to live miles away from the heart of the *ollaa.*

"A new life," Aja said with a soft smile.

"Yes."

She turned to find Pintar Neek, the *dawaa,* standing behind her. She immediately bowed her head to him in respect, a sign of his status as their medical and spiritual leader, and because he was the eldest of the *abuturoos.*

Although his wooly hair was nearly white, his bronze skin was still tight and belied his age of more than a *jaarraa.* The whites of his eyes were still bright, and although his tunic nearly dwarfed his thin frame, he stood tall with his more than six feet height. The grip on his intricately carved staff, which rose more than eight feet, was sturdy. The small gold dot between his eyebrows and on his chin, typical of the Empath people that generally dimmed with age, was still bright.

"*Nagaya, Dawaa.*"

He nodded in return.

She tilted her head to look up at him. "And Mova?" she asked of the laboring feminine.

"All is well," Pintar said, his voice gruff.

There was no doubt he was right. Pintar just knew things, just as he would have sensed if something went wrong. It was another of the ways of the Empaths, the acute ability to sense emotions, and his was the most finely honed.

He spread his thick lips into a smile and revealed his lone tooth. "Tonight, we celebrate new life," he said, in their native tongue, beating his staff against the packed dirt next to his bare feet.

Tap...tap...tap...

"Everyone will enjoy the good news," Aja said. "I will spread the word..."

Pintar's eyes flashed with a white glow that covered the brown of his irises and the gold dots on his face illuminated.

Aja blinked. It happened so quickly that she might have doubted seeing it if she didn't know better. "Is everything okay, *Dawaa?*" she asked, reaching out to lightly touch his wrist.

She gasped, filled with a surge of agony. She wrenched her hand away from Pintar and stumbled backward a step, releasing a shaky breath as she wiped away the tears that filled her ears.

Pintar frowned deeply.

Aja swallowed over a sudden lump in her throat as she wiped her hands over her eyes. "What is it, *Dawaa?*" she asked, her breathing labored.

"No worries," he said, before turning to walk away.

She took quick steps to catch up with his long strides. "*Dawaa*," she called out, her heart racing.

He didn't stop, his staff striking the ground with each step.

She reached out to touch him, but pulled her hand back at the last moment, not wanting to experience the pain again. So, she stood there, her fingers lightly resting against her chest where her heart continued to pound almost as loud as kettle drums.

The glowing of his eyes meant that he'd had a vision. What had he seen that filled him with such despair?

"Did something go wrong with the labor?" she wondered aloud as she reluctantly turned to continue her journey to retrieve water.

No worries.

She glanced over her shoulder just as Pintar entered the *goojjoo* of another *abuturoo*.

She trusted in Pintar, but she also trusted in

what she felt.

I'll tell my abbaa *about it when I get back.*

Filled with confusion, and seeking balance after encountering such an intense emotion, she forged ahead. "Ow!" Aja cried out as she slammed into someone. Her hands splayed against an undeniably hard chest.

Desire filled her, and her entire body tingled with an excitement that hardened her nipples and infused the fleshy bud between her thighs with heat.

Aja looked up as warm hands settled on her upper arms to steady her. She smiled at her brother's best friend, Juuba Huuntu. He was a skilled farmer, a well-respected leader on the rise in their *ollaa* and proponent of the Empaths advancing themselves technologically. "*Nagaya*," she said, removing her hand pressed against the opening of his tunic.

The amorous feelings subsided. They were not her own. Her touch had connected to *his* desire for *her*.

Although Juuba was a tall and handsome masculine with a muscular build that could compete with a carved statue, the feelings Aja had for him was platonic. Her power of connecting with feeling through touch had made her well aware of his feelings for her years ago, and he was aware of hers for him.

The metallic gold spots on his face glowed until the moment he let his hands drop from her arms, breaking their connection. She instantly saw the regret in his eyes through the smile he gave her.

"Where you headed?"

Aja shifted her eyes over to her brother, Llor, standing and holding a large basket filled with *mkpuru*.

He was boyishly handsome with a round face and clean-shaven head. He had inherited his shorter stature from their *da'ee*, but every bit of his rotund frame was might and strength. He was loving, charming and always quick to laugh and smile.

Aja adored him.

"Our parents were in need of some alone time," she said, with a deliberate arch of her brow.

Both Llor and Juuba groaned in feigned disgust.

She chuckled. "I'm off to get water," she said, glancing up at Juuba. She noticed him looking over her shoulder.

Aja turned to find a group of young womenfolk walking towards them. His expression was quite familiar. Juuba's feelings for her apparently didn't interfere with his lust for others. It was well known he was rarely alone at night.

"Juuba, Juuba, Juuba," Aja said, with only a slightly playful mocking as she looked at him.

His eyes shifted back down to hers with a twinkle in the depths of his gaze, before eyeing the feminines as they passed. He slapped his hand against Llor's arm and jerked his head in their direction.

Aja eyed her brother. His attention was on the young females as well. She rolled her eyes upwards briefly before releasing the knot of her thick hair and reaching for the basket of *mkpuru* to steady atop her head. "Go, you're both in heat," she teased, causing her brother to look at her in surprise.

They took off—almost as quickly as the little boy she'd chased earlier.

"*You* bring the water!" she yelled at him, taking one of the sweet, juicy fruits from the basket and wiping it against her tunic before taking a big bite.

She walked smoothly and steadily with the basket on her head. The *aduu* was now bright orange in the sky and knocked a bit of the chill off the air. Aja neared the *goojjoo* Pintar had entered. Her eyes lingered on the weathered red wood door.

No worries.

Somehow, she knew that wasn't true.

∞

The air was filled with the beating of drums mingled with the stomping of feet against the ground, and the high-pitched guttural cries of celebration as the Empaths danced around the roaring fire in the center of the pit. The entire *ollaa* was in attendance. Laughter and joy filled the air. Roasted meats and *alkoolii* were in abundance. The merriment would go on long into the night.

Every birth was celebrated and seen as a symbol of growth for their people. It was a tribute to their history and all the obstacles they overcame with the bold decision to explore and inhabit a new planet.

"*Ayyaaneeffachuu!*" Pintar bellowed at the top of his lungs, raising his staff high into the air.

"*Ayyaaneeffachuu!*" Aja and the rest of the Empaths returned the triumphant roar.

Aja was dancing, and with each person, she touched she could feel their joy and float upon it. She tossed her head back and laughed as she moved her hips and feet to the sounds of the drumbeats.

"*Ayyaaneeffachuu*," a voice began to sing in tune with the drums.

Aja turned and clapped her hands excitedly as she recognized her *da'ee's* voice. Shia Drakar beautifully sang as she stood by the firelight with the night winds lightly blowing the thick strands of her hair up into the air. The moment seemed surreal. The song she chose was entirely in their native tongue and spoke of celebrating love and family.

Aja's eyes shifted to her *abbaa* standing there gazing at his lifemate, exuding all the love he obviously had for her. The Empaths began to encircle her. Aja lost sight of her parents in the crowd even as her *da'ee's* singing continued to ring loud and clear. She climbed atop a flat rock, but as soon as she rose to her full height, the choral was drowned out by a shrill war cry that pierced the air.

The drums stopped. Shia's voice faded. The Empaths danced no more.

The air became tense as they all turned to look at Pintar.

"Danger is on the way," he roared, his eyes now glowing as he stomped his staff against the ground.

Danger?

As Aja scrambled down from the rock, amongst

her people's shrieks of fear, she thought of the agony she felt from Pintar earlier that day. Her heart raced as she looked around for her parents and brother in the melee of bodies all headed back towards their *goojjoos* for shelter.

BOOM!

The ground beneath them shook, and in the distance, a cloud rose up from a fire.

'What is this?' she wondered, her heart racing wildly. Fear was her adrenaline.

She spotted a small girl huddled by a large rock, crying, with her eyes were wide with panic.

BOOM!

Another cloud of smoke was framed by the fire from which it came. It was closer this time.

Before Aja could reach the child, another feminine paused in her flight to scoop the little one up into her arms. For that Aja was relieved.

A fiery ball shot across the dark purple skies. Moments later it landed against a *goojjoo* that instantly exploded in flames.

BOOM!

Cries of pain filled the air.

They were under attack, and their aggressor had just claimed lives.

"No, no, no, no, no," Aja moaned. Even as she continued to run at full speed, she looked around for her family members.

There was nowhere to run. Nowhere to hide. The weapons of the Empaths were spears, bows, and arrows. How could they win? How could they survive?

The agony she felt at that moment equaled that of Pintar's, and she felt weakened by it. Defeated.

Another shrill war cry filled the air.

A stream of bright, blue light shot across the air and landed on one of the masculines. His entire body had stiffened before he collapsed with a look of pure horror on his face.

Those who witnessed it, turned in the direction of the light just as a group of laser gun-toting figures in all-black emerged from the darkness.

Who are they?

Aja stopped and looked around. Their attackers encircled the *goojjoos*. The numbers were close to a few thousand. She was filled with rage and had to fight to keep from racing at one of the attackers to claw out their eyes. She clenched her fists so tightly her nails pierced the flesh of her palms. She panted hard with each breath.

Laser beams filled the air. Victims killed with ease. *Goojjoos* destroyed. Fires lit.

Time seemed to slow down as she spotted her brother. He stopped and picked up a large rock to fling at the attackers with all his might. Aja ran through the crowd towards him. "Llor!" she cried out.

A laser beam landed on the rock in the air with accuracy, and it exploded, sending the pieces down upon the heads of Empaths before landing on his chest with deadly precision.

Llor's body fell to the ground.

"No!" she roared, her mouth wide open, the veins in her neck stretching, her face twisted with rage and agony.

She reached him and fell to the ground beside him, pulling his head onto her lap. His body was limp. Lifeless. The gold dots on his forehead faded. Aja planted a kiss against his brow as she released a gut-wrenching cry.

A strong hand gripped her arm. She lifted her head like a wild animal under attack to stare at one of the invaders, his face hidden by a leather mask. She wrenched from his grasp, nearly growling as she reached behind him to hit the back of his knee sharply. His body buckled. She rose, and Llor's body hit the ground softly as she elbowed the back of her attacker's head and then punched his temple in quick-fire succession.

She was relentless. She would not go easily.

The leather-masked assailant fell flat onto Llor's body. A hand grabbed the laser gun he'd dropped. Aja looked up, and her heart burst to see her *abbaa* as he bit his bottom lip fiercely and fired off laser shots.

Aja gasped as she felt a stinging pain in her calf. She looked down to see the invader she thought she'd defeated had press a metal tube against her leg. Her body went numb before slumping to the ground. Her eyes felt heavy.

Just before they closed, she saw her *da'ee* run up to her *abbaa* as he continued to aim and strike. A laser sliced through his heart just as her *da'ee* pressed her body to his from behind.

Both their bodies had frozen before they slumped to the ground together, their bodies still entwined.

She was too numb with grief to feel pride that for at least a few precious moments, they had fought back and won.

II

Captain Anansi Nyame crossed his strong muscular arms over his chest as he stood with his legs apart looking out the window of the observation deck of the *Spaceship Infinite*. He squinted his ebony eyes in deep concentration as the massive ship orbited above his home planet of Erised. He took in the vast blue-black world surrounded by three *aduus* and a *baatii*. Soon he would be transported from the bridge of the large and powerful vessel to the comfort of his *mana*. It had been nearly six *ji'as* since last he was home. He had mixed feelings about his return—or rather mixed feelings about the reason for his return. His thoughts were troubled, and nothing soothed him.

"Worried about tomorrow?"

Anansi's eyes focused on the reflection of his best friend and first mate, Daryan Dvani, in the glass before him. He briefly looked at him over his shoulder as he slid his hands into the pockets of his form-fitting, one-piece, military uniform. "It's not every day that a masculine meets his lifemate," he answered, his deep baritone voice tinged with sarcasm.

Daryan grunted in agreement.

It was the wish of Anansi's *abbaa* and the ruling council that Anansi and *Giiftiin* Oduda Diasi of the planet Kordi meet and spend some time together before the official announcement of their *cidha*. They wanted the pretense of it being anything but what it was...an arranged union. Oduda was scheduled to arrive at Erised tomorrow.

Daryan bit back a smile. "I wouldn't mind having *Giiftiin* Oduda as my lifemate. She's beautiful, rich, powerful and sexy as can be. Uh...no disrespect."

Anansi smiled slightly at his friend. "None taken. She's all that you said and more. But if I had a choice, she wouldn't be my lifemate."

"But you are, aren't you?" Daryan asked, his

tone as resigned as his friend felt.

Anansi eyes focused on an *urjii* shooting above the ship. "The gaa'ila will ensure the signing of the peace treaty ending the war between the Kordis and the Empaths, securing the freedom of the Empath's *gabras*," he said, before releasing a sigh heavy with the weight of his obligations. "There's been enough senseless killing over something as immutable as race. Yes, yes, she will be my lifemate."

They lapsed into silence.

For the last two *torbaans*, Oduda's *abbaa*, Kyl Diasi, the ruler of the planet Kordi used all of his might and power to invade, bully and wipe out thousands of Empaths on their planet Nede. His intent was twofold. The Kordi's disdain for the simple living Empath people on the neighboring planet of Nede was well known. Their desire to live humbly, even with technological advances overtaking other planets in the galaxy, was ridiculed. Their primitive culture made the Empaths an easy target. The Kordis exploited that weakness and only their desire to claim the valuable *nkumes* found on the small rural planet topped their hatred of its inhabitants.

In truth, the Kordis were not the only ones in the galaxy looking at the *nkumes* with a longing. Outside of their use for illumination and as an energy source, they were valuable for their rarity.

Anansi was willing to acknowledge the irony of those with a steadfast alliance to bucolic living moving to a planet that contained a rare energy source. Through their surveillance, the discovery that the Empaths were barely scratching the surface to the varied uses of the *nkumes*, made it a bit sad. It was a waste. He shook his head a bit at the thought of it.

Anansi did not share the Kordis disdain for Empaths, but he didn't understand their resistance to change and their abhorrence to advancement.

As the direct heir to the throne of Erised, Anansi was well aware of the history of Empaths on his home planet. They faced ridicule and harsh treatment because of their empathy and healing powers. He agreed that the ruling powers of the planet all those years ago—his *abuturoos*—did nothing to help protect them.

His eyes filled with regret and then determination.

It was time to fix that.

The Acirfa Galaxy was home to nearly fifty planets governed by The Council, an intergalactic sovereign body comprised of the leaders of the seven largest planets. Kordi nor Nede were members of the alliance, and neither fell under the protection or rules of The Council. With their history of animosity for Erisedians—the ruling planet of the galaxy—the Empaths had never sought inclusion in the coalition, while the Kordis' attempts at joining were consistently refused because of their tendency towards violence and corruption. With the invaluable *nkumes* now in their control, the Kordis had major leverage.

"It's a lot on your shoulders, Anansi."

He briefly glanced over his broad shoulder at Daryan, nodding in agreement. "The Council wants to end the senseless violence and mayhem of the Kordis against the Empaths," he said, his look becoming pensive. "Especially with the Kordis using Empaths as *gabras*."

"Disgusting," Daryan spat.

"That's not a strong enough description for it," Anansi said, his tone grave and dark. "It has to end. Such heinous behavior will not tarnish the legacy of the Acirfa galaxy."

Daryan came up to stand beside his friend. "Are you resigned to your role in it all?" he asked, giving him a brief sideways glance.

Anansi remained quiet.

The negotiations between The Council and Kyl Diasi had been lengthy, but the terms had been set. The proposed treaty with Kordi would free the hundreds of Empath *gabras*. Both Kordi and Nede would join the coalition, bringing them under the governing laws and protection of The Council and open up the rare *nkume* stones for commodity trade. The Kordis would receive their membership in the coalition and wealth from the trade of the *nkumes*. The Empaths would win their peace, their freedom, and the right to live as they pleased on their planet. The Council would strengthen its control of the galaxy and benefit from the trade, as well.

Win-win-win. Right?

Wrong.

Two *torbaans* later, Anansi learned the role he would play in all of it. He released a heavy sigh. The treaty, the trade agreement, and the freedom of the *gabras* all hinged on the success of his union to *Giiftiin* Oduda Diasi.

My life has never been my own.

He was the son of Hwosi Kan Nyame, the *moticha* of planet Erised and the Supreme Principal of The Council, making Anansi heir to a very influential throne. He had been raised his entire life to fulfill his obligations. To lead. To sacrifice. To do what's best for the greater good of his planet and the entire galaxy.

I have no choice.

Anansi was also the Captain of the *Spaceship Infinite* for the coalition's military forces. A champion and victor just like his *abbaa* and many generations before him. It was in his blood.

"It is all for the best, Anansi," Daryan said, reaching up to pull the waist-length twisted locs that were characteristic of all Erisedians masculines back from his square and handsomely rugged face.

Anansi smirked. *What would have been best was if my abbaa respected my life and my wishes enough to consult me before I was traded away like chattel.*

As close as he and Daryan were, Anansi would never verbalize his annoyance. Even in the face of trying times, Anansi had more respect than that. *Moticha* Hwosi Kan Nyame was a great leader.

Anansi squinted. "What of your mission?" he asked, changing the subject.

"Connect live feed," Daryan said into the wireless communicator on his wrist.

They turned as the glass monitor on the far wall illuminated, and the room darkened. The crystal-clear image of a round blue and green planet appeared before zooming in on a busy urban landscape with buildings tall enough for the tips to touch the vibrant blue skies.

Anansi crossed his arms over his solid chest as he eyed the bustling movement of the planet's inhabitants. "I'm always so amazed that we are from two different worlds, yet we don't look that different," he said, as he studied the images on the *komputara*.

"It will make our assignment on Earth easier," Daryan said. "The makeup of their atmosphere, climate and weather patterns is intriguing."

"And the transition to its environment is safe?" Anansi asked.

"Yes, we have undetectable nostril filters to breathe safely of their air, and the ear buds to translate their language," Daryan said with pride, having led the planning of their exploration to Earth for the last *bara*.

"And the physical characteristics of our people?" Anansi asked, referring to the Jeyna people's solid black eyes and the markings on their arms.

"The eye covers replicating that of earthlings is complete, and the markings on our arms resemble what they call tattoos."

Anansi nodded as he turned away from the *komputara*. "I wish I could join you."

"Your mission is just as important," Daryan reminded him.

Anansi grunted. "A lifelong union should be about love. Not a mission," he said, turning back to the window to gaze at the *urjiis*. "Right?"

At Daryan's continued silence, Anansi looked over his shoulder. His face filled with curiosity as he watched his friend walk closer to the display and tapped it.

"Zoom target," Daryan stated.

Moments later the image of a beautiful dark-skinned feminine earthling appeared. She made quite an impression striding up the middle of the street with large kinky curls blowing in the wind, wearing a beautiful crimson suit that made her stand out in the substantial crowd.

Daryan tapped the monitor again. "Zoom target," he repeated, the varying colors from the images playing against his black eyes.

Her face filled the *komputara*. She was gorgeous, and the oversized spectacles she wore did nothing to hide that.

Anansi's eyes went from the face of his friend to the earthling and back again. "Stay focused on your goals, first mate," he said sternly, quickly slipping back into the role of his commander and not his friend. He came over to slap him soundly on the back.

"End live feed," Daryan ordered, before awkwardly clearing his throat.

The images disappeared.

"Distraction can lead to destruction," Anansi reminded him.

"And she would be a distraction," Daryan agreed with a nod.

Anansi moved away from his friend again and released a heavy breath, feeling the weight of the worlds, he was forced to save on his broad shoulders. He spent the majority of his time aboard the ship traveling the vast galaxy, but at that moment he had never yearned so badly for the peace and luxury of his sprawling *mana*.

His arranged first meeting with *Giiftiin* Oduda meant taking a temporary leave of his command of *Spaceship Infinite*. He hadn't been in need of a break, but he planned to enjoy the one forced on him.

He just couldn't stand the public spectacle he was to make of himself. Both The Council and Kyl Diasi wanted to give the impression that the heir to the Erised throne had fallen for the Kordi *giiftiin*, in hopes of unifying the races across the galaxy after the signing of the treaty. The coalition would say, their love led to the truce, instead of the reverse.

"Be safe, my friend," Anansi said as he stepped onto the circular transport dock of the observation deck.

"You too, Captain."

The glass enclosure sealed around Anansi like a cylinder.

"Transference requested," the automated feminine voice echoed inside the chamber. *"Identify yourself."*

"Captain Anansi Nyame," he said, as the tube filled with a greenish-blue light that came and went like a flash.

"Voice, retina and fingertip scan complete. Identity confirmed. Body prepared for transference. Destination?"

"My *mana* base," he commanded.

"Transference confirmed."

Anansi gave Daryan one final brief nod of his head just before he blinked. When his eyes opened, he was in the *diinqa* of his *mana*. He patiently waited a moment for his body's homeostasis to return before the glass enclosure automatically opened.

He had docking stations throughout his home but preferred the one in his *diinqa* for when he left his ship. It was the most convenient because most times he was weary and just wanted to sleep.

Anansi barely took the time to take in the rugged design of his circular suite. His *mana* was lavish. The heir to a throne would have nothing less. The walls were padded and covered in black leather. On one section of the wall was a massive fireplace of ebony stones. The plush rugs covering the polished black floor were made of the hides of a thousand *illeetis*. His bedding was made of the finest *huccuu*, smooth enough to caress the worry from a masculine's body and technologically designed to maintain that body at the perfect temperature.

With three *aduus* that cast the giant planet almost continuously in brilliant light, every bit of the design was both a luxury and necessity, including the window coverings that blocked out the light so that Erisedians were able to sleep under the pretense of darkness. The blackness of night only reigned nine times in a *hara*.

"*Welcome back, Giiftiin.*"

That was the masculine voice of XR-2, the virtual reality servant programmed to fulfill his every wish— whether spoken or unspoken. XR-2 handled everything including his meals, cleaning, and security. When he hosted events at his *mana*, he had a legion of like-like automatons ready to be programmed by XR-2 to do his bidding.

One of the things that made the Erisedians so powerful among the galaxy was their nanotechnology advancements. XR-2 and the automatons barely scratched the surface of the science they manipulated to their advantage. *Gennii* on Erised had developed the neurotechnology ages ago and it was now commonplace to use brain imaging to personalize lifestyle and health habits.

He stripped off his black leather jacket and then unzipped his all-in-one form-fitting uniform before he kicked off his knee-length black boots. He removed everything and dropped it to the floor. It all immediately disappeared. XR-2 was hard at work.

He enjoyed the feel of the plush fur-skin rugs underneath his large feet as he strode his bronze frame to the opposite end of the large expansive *diinqa*. He twisted as much of his thin locs as he could atop his head as two hidden doors quietly slid open when he neared them. He entered his *kutaa dhiqannaa*. Everything was black and uncomplicated in design because for him it was about the bare necessities.

Anansi stepped his eight-foot muscled body into the *dhiqata*, a glass-enclosed cleansing chamber. The door automatically shut behind him as he closed his beautiful ebony eyes and stood still with his well-toned arms at his sides. A mix of steam and cleaning solution filled the chamber. The vapors pressed against his sculpted frame easing the ache from his bones and dissolving away the dirt and bacteria from his body minimizing the waste of water on their planet.

He was relieved when the cleansing cycle ended, and the steam completely evaporated. When the door slid open, Anansi's body was completely dry as he stepped out of the *dhiqata*. The slight draft from the door closing caused a "swoosh" of air to brush against his firm buttocks and the back of his muscular thighs.

He yawned as he walked back into his *diinqa*. His *qanddii*, a solid black base with a plush air mattress atop it, rose from the floor and drifted over to him. It hovered.

It was a *qanddii* made for pleasure, be it sleep or sex. There was nothing better for Anansi than burying his hardness into the walls of a voluptuous feminine as it floated around in dips and waves that intensified each deep and delicious stroke.

His muscle stirred between his thighs, lengthening and widening a bit, as he down. He pulled the *huccuu* sheet over his naked form and buried his head deeply beneath the many feathered sacs.

"Make love to me, my Anansi."

He didn't need to open his eyes to know "Sasha" lay in his *qanddii* beside him. Every inch of the skin covering the curvaceous frame was golden. Her round and full breasts, with taut and teasing nipples, were an even deeper shade of gold. Her hair was bright ivory as it flowed in waves to her perfectly formed buttocks. Her eyes were hazel and in sharp contrast to her skin. Her beauty was limitless. Her desire to please him was endless. Her abilities to sexually and sensually drain him were sublime.

A lifelike virtual reality lover generated from the very erogenous zones of his brain would be nothing less.

He felt her plush breasts pressed against his strong back as her leg moved atop his and her hand slid down to grasp his stirring member just the way he liked it. "I feel like going for a ride, my Anansi," she whispered in his ear with a saucy suck of his lobe.

"Sasha off," Anansi ordered without opening his eyes.

She disappeared in a flash.

Tomorrow he had so much on his plate to handle, but tonight he wanted nothing—absolutely nothing—but sleep. Just as his deep-set eyes drifted close, the window covers lowered bathing the *diinqa* in total and complete darkness.

∞

Every moment Aja Drakar spent huddled in the corner, surrounded by darkness, with furry rodents brushing against her as they scurried past, the more hatred and the need for revenge consumed her.

She tried to summon her empathic powers, but nothing. No telepathy. No premonition dreams. No taking on the emotions and feelings of those she came in contact with when they brought her food and drink. Nothing.

Aja tilted her back against a stone wall. She could only guess that she had been entrapped for two *torbaans*. No *qanddii*. No light. No windows. She didn't even know where she was being held. She awakened from her drugged state laying on the cold floor of her prison. She didn't know who her captors were and that was important because she had every intention of killing them the first chance she got.

Anguish filled her. *My family is dead.*

Violent and painful images were her only distraction. She couldn't escape them, even in her sleep. Memories of her family being vaporized by laser guns filled her nightmares. Friends and neighbors being imprisoned or killed left her sleepless.

The attack had been so sudden. So unexpected and destructive. Even if there had been a warning, it was a war the Empaths had no chance of winning.

Aja pulled her knees to her chest and hugged them tightly as she rocked her body back and forth a bit, seeking comfort.

What does life hold for me now?

The door to the room opened and a stream of light reflected on the floor. It widened. The shadow of two masculines filled the doorway. These were not the thin *gabras* that had brought her food and then scurried away. These masculines were warriors. That was evident from the outline of their towering size. Fear gripped Aja even as her hands balled into fists. She would never back down from a challenge or a fight, even when she knew the odds were against her.

They stepped inside, and each grabbed her roughly by the arm and jerked her up onto her feet. Aja fought and struggled against them as they tugged her towards the door, causing the top of her toes to drag against the cold stone of the floor. She barely felt the pain of that as her heart pounded with force and she felt panicked. She had never been taken from her prison before, and she had no idea what awaited her beyond that doorway.

Aja hollered out roughly as she summoned up as much strength as she could to lift her feet, bring her legs forward and swing them up to spread and then kick back towards their stomachs.

Their grips tightened until sharp darts of pain radiated up her arms. She bit her bottom lip to keep from screaming out.

"Where are we going? Where are you taking me?" Aja demanded in her native tongue.

They ignored her.

Her questions halted once they stepped into the light. Her face swung back and forth between them. They were tall and muscular, covered from head to toe in leather armor. Just like those who attacked Nede. She would recognize them anywhere.

Aja instantly straightened her spine, and her beautiful face became stoic. If she were to die at their hands, she would do so without begging or crying to be spared.

As they moved, she looked at the wide violet-colored palatial hallway with gilded trim and moldings. Everything from the furs lining the floor to the tint of the walls was a shade of purple. Aja found it garish.

What is this place?

They climbed steps to a set of double doors with pillars flanking them. The doors swung open with far too much grandeur to reveal a *diinqa* as large as four Nede *goojjoos*, with a *qanddii* almost as large in the center of it.

A nude and curvaceous feminine with skin as deep as *chollolaattaa* sat astride a prone and equally naked masculine, her hips moving in a rhythmic motion while his hands deeply grasped the flesh of her quivering buttocks.

Aja's eyes hardened.

The feminine glanced back at them, her hips still working her lover as he raised up to suck at her breasts. "I'll just be a moment," she said, before turning back to grasp her lover's long blonde hair roughly.

Aja closed her eyes to the spectacle. Her mouth twisted in disgust as the lovers both cried out hoarsely as their sex came to an end. The heat and scent of their bodies were thick in the air.

"Welcome, *gabra*."

Aja flinched at the word, knowing enough to comprehend what being called that meant.

She opened her eyes to find the feminine now standing before her with her nakedness still exposed by the sheer robe that hung open at her sides. Aja could not deny the beauty before her. Her body was entirely devoid of hair, and her smooth skin was dark brown with eyes that were brilliantly violet. The smoothness of her bald head only enhanced her high cheekbones, full lips, and deep-set, wide eyes framed by long thick lashes.

"I am Oduda Diasi, *giiftiin* of Planet Kordi," she said as she circled Aja and the stoic guards slowly.

Aja stiffened.

Kordi.

Aja remembered from history lessons as a child that the Kordi planet was the nearest to Nede, but still too far for them to travel to with their rudimentary lifestyle.

Hatred for the feminine and her kind burned the back of Aja's throat.

"What is your name, *gabra*?" Oduda asked, revealing that the tip of her tongue was slightly forked as she licked her bottom lip.

"Aja Drakar," she answered with pride, her glare unflinching.

"Strip her," Oduda ordered, placing her hands on her hips as she stood before them again.

Aja gasped in shock as her short tunic, now dirty and torn, was ripped from her body like it was nothing but paper. She struggled to have them release her arms to cover herself, but she was no match for the strength of the guards. She dropped her head to hide her shame and embarrassment. It jerked up when Oduda reached down and lightly stroked the soft curly hairs covering Aja's plump mound at the top of her thighs. In a flash, Aja lifted her left foot and roughly kicked Oduda's hand away from her.

Just as fast, violet eyes had flashed before she delivered a wicked backhand slap across Aja's cheek that echoed like a whip to flesh.

"Aah," Aja cried out. Her face stung, and she tasted blood inside her mouth.

Oduda laughed cruelly.

Aja lifted hate-filled eyes to her captor. "Do not touch me again," she warned in a hard voice.

Oduda slapped her right cheek, sending Aja's head swinging to the left. "Do not tell me what to do," she returned disparagingly. "Be glad I have use of you, or you would be dead, *gabra*."

"Be happy for your guards," Aja lobbed back with boldness.

Oduda cocked her bald head to the side and batted her lush lashes at Aja before she gave her a wicked yet beautiful smile. She reached out quickly and pressed a small silver tube to Aja's neck.

The effect of the sedative was all too familiar, and Aja remembered nothing after that as she slipped into a deep unconsciousness within moments.

∞

Oduda watched Aja's naked body go limp between the masculines. "Drop her," she commanded sharply in her native Kordi tongue.

When the first round of imprisoned Empaths arrived at the *Bwa Kasuwa* Oduda had been there to handpick those she wanted to possess personally. On first sight of the unconscious Empath lumped on the floor of the filthy *xiyyaara*, Oduda could not deny her appeal. She was too beautiful to be a servant and draw the eye of one of Oduda's many suitors, but Oduda couldn't see letting a gem like her slip through her fingers. She had almost forgotten about the Empath locked in one of her underground rooms.

I knew she would come in handy one day. Yes, this gabra *will be just the distraction I need.*

"Leetoo," she called out, even as her eyes continued to take in Aja's smooth brown naked frame.

A small-framed feminine in a hooded cloak walked in, bowing in servitude and fear as she approached Oduda. "See that she is bathed, shaved thoroughly and that her hair and make-up are done."

Leetoo Waizee averted her doe-like eyes away from the nude and curvaceous form of the feminine on the floor. "What to dress her in?" she asked, her voice barely higher than a whisper and filled with the constant terror in which she lived.

Oduda's eyes pierced her docile and obedient servant. "Nothing. The work she will do for me will be well suited for her ... nakedness."

The medicine she infused into Aja's blood was her own concoction. She had no doubts about its efficacy. It would ensure the *gabra* would not awaken during the short journey she was to make and fill her with the lascivious desire of one hundred *gumnas*.

Oduda turned as the guards picked Aja up and followed Leetoo. The sheer ends of her robe drifted up in the air behind her as she made her way back to her *qanddii*. She licked her full lips and stroked her hands softly over her bald scalp—it was the most potent erogenous zone of all Kordis.

She had been scheduled to meet her soon-to-be lifemate, Anansi Nyame, on his planet tomorrow, but her plans had changed for the better once she met Huung. She had been in her private booth at the *Bwa Kasuwa* when she spotted the blonde-haired, tall and brawny *gabra* broker moving through the massive crowds. His confidence was evident, and the way he moved through the crowd with a cocky wide leg stride like his member was too big to do otherwise intrigued her. The more she watched him, the more her curiosity won out. She had to know if her instincts were dead on and instantly discharged one of her guards to summon the trader to her.

They did so immediately.

She had cleared her private booth, made quick work of the introductions and then ordered him to lower his pants to see if he lived up to the name Huung. He had.

As the auction carried on, he mounted her from behind with her face and breasts pressed against the glass of her booth. The one-way glass shielded them and her rough cries of passion.

Oduda was no innocent to passion, and he impressed her. She wanted more of him, but he was on Kordi handling business for only one *torbaan* before he was to return to his planet of Zheen in the distant Acirema galaxy.

Her invite for him to spend that time in her *qanddii* was readily accepted.

Huung kicked off the *huccuu* sheets and spread his muscular thighs as he began to massage the full and thick length of his dick. It was already stirring to life in his hand. His name suited him *so* very well. Unfortunately, it was his greatest attribute. He was no great beauty or intellectual. Still, he—or rather *it*—served its purpose.

Oduda crawled onto the *qanddii* between his open legs and took his length into her mouth, sucking and licking him until his rod hardened and glistened.

She could please her *abbaa* and his grand ambition for power and respect or satisfy herself with the first masculine in a long time that had the skill and the tool to match her voracious sexual appetite. For her, there really was no choice, particularly when the last she saw of her betrothed, he was every bit of three hundred *recas* or more. Hardly on the level of the physically sculptured and sexually aggressive masculines with whom she coupled.

As the *giiftiin* of Kordi, and the next in line to rule, her *abbaa* wanted her to become the lifemate of Anansi Nyame of Erised and she would, but this one last *torbaan* was hers to do as she saw fit. Anansi, her *abbaa*, and the entire coalition could—no, would—wait.

"Aaah," Huung cried out hoarsely, his narrow hips writhing as she took him deep into her mouth and throat with vigor, causing her cheeks to cave.

"Say my name," she whispered against his thick hardness as she stroked him tightly and with speed.

"O-O-du-du-du-da-da-da-da," Huung stammered.

Her eyes locked on his sweaty face and pursed lips as he shivered in reaction to her. She felt power and desire flow through her like a drug.

III

The planet Erised was a paradox. The flat lands and towering reddish-brown mountains were picturesque and beautiful beneath the glowing red, orange and yellow *aduus* and white sky. Amid that calm beauty stood towering metal and glass oval-shaped *manas* of varying heights and scale, atop metal cooling towers encasing *kaasuus*, that seemed cold and out of place against the warmth of the land and skyscape. Even in the distance, the range of mountain formations against the backdrop of the *manas* seemed to compete for dominance. The more prominent and wealthy the Erisedian, the higher the residence soared off the ground, some reaching as high as the skies.

Anansi looked down on it all from the tinted windows of his office. His *mana* stood the tallest in this northern region of Erised. The expectations for him were just as lofty. Tension crept into his neck at the thought of Oduda Diasi. Erisedian nuptials were lifelong and only ended with death. There was no law allowing for separation once the traditional *cidha* was performed. The moment he completed the ritual of placing the heavy gold band with his family's seal around her ankle, he and Oduda would be united endlessly.

Forever.

Anansi frowned deeply as the word seemed to reverberate inside his head like an omen.

He met *Giiftiin* Oduda many *baras* ago—possibly more than ten—and it was hard to forget the striking bald beauty with skin as deep as sweet *chollolaattaa*. Nor could he overlook the indifferent manner in which she had regarded him.

Anansi turned and studied his reflection in the glass of the window. 'What will she think of me now?' He wondered, taking in his masculine features and sculptured frame in nothing but low-slung sleep pants. His physique had been hidden beneath seventy *yecas* of weight. His military service and rigorous exercise had taken care of the weight that had plagued him since his youth.

"Giiftiin, *there is a request to transmit a prerecorded message from Oduda Diasi.*"

Anansi's rock-hard abdomen clenched. "Transmit," he ordered XR-2.

A full-sized transparent hologram of Oduda appeared. He had to admit that the violet robe she wore with an elaborate hood was a perfect complement to her haunting eyes. He was sure that any masculine that loved her would dream of those eyes. But he felt no such adoration.

"Captain Nyame, let me first say that I am honored at your request to join our families and our people. My *abbaa* and I are positive that this union will lead to a long and fruitful treaty for us all—"

Anansi snorted in derision. "*My* request?" he drawled, moving over to sink down into the leather chair behind his clear acrylic desk.

The hologram repopulated with every shift in his line of vision and now played in front of his desk. For a moment, he allowed himself to wish that Oduda's bulky robe did not hide her body from him. He was a masculine. He could admit he was curious.

"Some unforeseen business has arrived here on Kordi, and I will not be traveling to Erised for another *torbaan*." Oduda smiled. "I have some...*business* to attend to. I'm sure you understand."

Anansi thought he saw a rather mischievous glint in her eyes as she saucily licked her lips at the mention of her business. She was not arriving that day as planned. Initially, he felt relief, but that was soon replaced by annoyance. His square jawline clenched. Her *abbaa* had plotted and schemed for this union, and now *she* was postponing their first meeting as if he was at *her* beck and call.

"I have a little *something* for you, a gift to show how deeply I regret not keeping our appointment." Oduda turned her head and stated something in her native Kordi language. "I'm sure the gift will be to your intense liking and will keep you occupied until we both are able to meet face-to-face."

Her provocative image disappeared.

Permission requested to transfer.

Anansi leaned back in his chair and steepled his fingers under his square chin. He was used to being in control when it came to feminines. Although he liked feisty bedmates, Oduda was proving to be quite a challenge already. "Transfer," he demanded softly, lifting one bare foot to press into the seat of the chair.

His look of nonchalance transformed to confusion as the shapely form of a nude feminine suddenly appeared atop the width of his desk. She was laid out before him like a feast, and suddenly he felt starved. His eyes started from her feet, up long shapely bronze legs that showed her fitness, to curved hips built for the grip of strong hands. Her plump mound was cleanly shaven and taunting beneath a flat stomach that had to be shaped by a million sit-ups. Her breasts were full and heavy with large aureoles and plump nipples that were the color of midnight, instantly making his mouth water to tease one—or maybe both—with his tongue.

Long before his eyes rested on her face, his dick swelled and hardened until it throbbed and ached between his muscled thighs, but the beauty of her face indeed pushed him over the edge. Her smooth, unmarred complexion, the highness of her cheekbones and the slant of her eyes above a pug nose drew him in until he felt he could sit there and stare at her endlessly. The flat gold moles positioned between her brows and on her chin let him know she was an Empath and probably Oduda's own *gabra* of war.

Anansi wiped his eyes with his hands. What type of game was Oduda playing? Her words replayed in his head. *"I'm sure the gift will be to your intense liking and will keep you occupied until we both are able to meet face-to-face."*

He looked up to find the beauty rousing from her sleep as she arched her back and stretched her arms above her on the desk. She turned her head and looked into his eyes. He felt lost in swirling depths of hazel flecked with gold. His heart swelled a bit.

"I am Aja," she told him huskily, before smiling and wickedly licking her lips as she lowered her hands to cup her own breasts and spread her legs. "And you are?"

"Anansi Nyame of Erised," he answered, his eyes intense as he stared at her.

"You are one fine masculine, Anansi Nyame of Erised," she returned as she studied him.

His thin and long dreadlocks were pulled back from his face with a leather band emphasizing the thickness of his slashing brows and the lushness of his almost feminine lashes. High cheekbones and a square jawline gave his looks a regal air. Both of his eyes were entirely ebony and seemed infinite. His lips were kissable.

And his body.

Aja chuckled softly as she bit her bottom lip.

He was tall. Very tall. Eight feet. Like a giant. Broad shoulders. Well-toned arms with black tribal marks. Square chest and abs. Muscled thighs that seemed ready to run a million miles with speed and ease.

Anansi Nyame of Erised was built to satisfy.

His breath caught in his chest as she licked her fingers before teasing her own nipples with a purr. "What the..."

Aja sat up on the desk and opened her legs before him. Her smile was tempting as she slid one of her slender fingers inside her warmth. She pulled it from her core, and it glistened wetly as she then slowly slid it into her mouth.

He gasped in a mixture of surprise and pleasure as rose and worked his sleep pants over his hips and let them fall into a puddle around his ankles and feet. He wanted to be inside Aja. To have her. To feel her. Her heat. Her moisture.

The window covers lowered, and the lights came on at a seductive level. The soft sounds of sultry music filled the air. One tray with *alkoolii* and two flutes appeared on the corner of the desk. Another tray of erotic toys and oils appeared beside it. It was the perfect setting for seduction, compliments of XR-2.

She picked up the bottle of *alkoolii* to lightly pour over her chest as she flung her head back. The golden liquid rained down her breasts, dripping from her hard nipples.

He swallowed over a lump in his throat.

"Thirsty?" she asked, as she lifted her head to look at him.

Yes, suddenly he did feel parched.

She rose to her feet atop the desk, dancing in front of him as she circled her hips. "You like?" she asked with a sultry giggle.

Anansi licked his dry lips as he eyed her. "Of course," he assured her as he stepped forward to grab her hips and pull her body forward towards him. He cupped her buttocks as he bent his head to the side to lightly bite her clean-shaven plump mound. He inhaled her sweet scent as he felt the shiver race through her body, clouding his head with desire for her. What little fight he had left dissipated. "I want you," he said, tilting his head back to look up at her.

"And I want you," she said, consumed with an urge to fill herself with him, from the thick root to the throbbing smooth tip. She wanted to glide up and down on his hardness until he came inside of her and went soft. "Sit."

He did as she ordered, his eyes never leaving hers.

Aja moved down off the desk to straddle his lap. The motion caused the chair to spin slowly. Beneath the weight of his locs, she locked her hands behind his neck as she tilted her head back until the ends of her hair tickled the top curve of her full buttocks. "Touch me," she whispered into the heated air. "Please."

He splayed his hands on her buttocks as the chair came to a slow stop. Her skin was smooth and warm perfection.

Aja shivered from the feel of Anansi's touch against her skin. She looked at him, lost in eyes as black and endless as the night, before dipping her head to hotly lick his bottom lip. They kissed slowly. Deliberately. Passionately. Her heart pounded. Her pulse raced. Her core ached with a desire to have him inside her, while her senses begged for her to wait and enjoy their exploration of one another.

Anansi planted soft bites along her jawline before capturing her lips with his own again as Aja leaned towards him, causing his chair to tilt back with the weight of their frames. The move made her body inch forward a bit on top of his, pushing her breasts against his face. Anansi allowed himself to nuzzle his chin against her soft flesh. His body ached for her as he turned his face sideways to stroke the deep valley between her breasts with his cheek before he planted a kiss to each one. Her sigh of pleasure pushed him to draw more from her.

"Hold on," he warned, just before he leaned back in the chair and grasped her waist to ease her body downward until he was able to capture one brown nipple in his hungry mouth.

Aja felt tiny jolts of pleasure and electricity course through her body, even outweighing her concern that because they leaned backward at such a precarious angle that her body would soon slide forward over his head and onto the floor. She closed her eyes and gasped as he brought one hand down to play in between her thighs as his arms locked around her buttocks like a band of steel, securing her safely in place. Passion and power. He was those things and much more. Her desire for him surged.

Anansi enjoyed the feel of her nipples and the little trembling of her body as he enjoyed the feel of them hardening beneath his eager touch. He felt lightheaded. Was it his desire for her or his backward position in the chair? He didn't know. He didn't care. He was completely lost in her. Lost in the feel of her skin, the taste of her nipples, and the tightness of her walls surrounding the finger he slid inside of her.

She extended her arms to press her hands against the walls as she bent her legs, pressing her knees against the arms of the chair and propping her buttocks high up in the air. As Anansi began to stroke inside her with his middle finger, Aja gently thrust her hips back and forth as well. "Yes," she sighed into his dreadlocks as he ended each thrust with a gentle stroking of her clit with his calloused thumb. "Yes, yes, yes."

Unable to resist any longer, Anansi let his head fall back and looked up into her face with his mouth slightly ajar. His breath was bated. He replaced his finger with his hardness. Inch by inch. He thrived on the transformation of her face from an initial jolt of surprise to a slight wince and pout before intense pleasure.

Wanting more of him, she pushed off the wall and gripped the armrests as she lowered her buttocks, easing more of his inches inside her.

Anansi's mouth widened, and he moaned loudly in pleasure.

Their eyes remained locked as they thrust their hips in unison, sending the remaining base of his thick and hard length in and out of her. She bit her bottom lip before lowering her head to lick hotly at his mouth in between them both breathing in the heated air in that small space between them. Her eyes widened a bit as she felt his dick harden even more inside her, pressing against her walls, leaving no doubt that he was near his climax.

And so was she.

Anansi kissed her, capturing her tongue in her mouth to suckle deeply. She jerked her head back, freeing herself as she laughed at him softly, playfully. Using the tight muscles of her walls she clenched and released his dick several times.

He could only shake his head in wonder before bringing one hand up to grasp her hair tightly as he gripped and massaged one of her butt cheeks with the other. He lightly bit her chin before he kissed it. "You're the best," he swore to her.

"I only get better," she told him huskily before swatting his hands away and standing to her feet.

"So do I," he said, righting his body in the chair and then rising to stand before her. "All I need is a little more room."

Anansi looked up as the doors to his office slid opened. In floated his *qanddii*...just like he craved.

Aja looked over her shoulder, her eyes widening in surprise at the movement of the *qanddii*. She climbed up onto the desk and then jumped from it onto the middle of the cushion. "Ooh, it feels so good. Come, Anansi," she said with a bend of her finger. "I've never mated on a floating *qanddii*."

Slowly he walked around the desk, his intense ebony eyes locked on her, before he climbed onto the *qanddii* atop of her, pressing her body into the softness of the mattress as he grasped her face and sucked the tongue she offered him.

Her legs rose to wrap around his waist, the heel of her foot resting against his firm buttock as he ground his length against her.

"Your body feels so good," Anansi told her, his words whispered into her mouth.

Aja grasped his shoulders and pushed him up from her. He rested on his knees, the air lightly breezing against his wet and hard shaft as she slowly turned over onto her stomach. She did a frontward split before him and began to vibrate her hips until her buttocks moved in a thousand different directions as she pretended to sex the *qanddii*.

"Whooooaaa," he said, drawing it out as he looked down at her in amazement. She bent her legs and began to back her body his until she lowered her throbbing core onto his hardness with ease.

Aja looked over her shoulder at him, working her lower back so that her buttocks popped as she rode him. Anansi cried out, shifting his hands up over his head as she worked him. She opened her legs wide across his thighs and began to slowly work her hips side-to-side, each movement sending her tight core up and down as many inches as she could take before she circled her hips to tease the tip and then slide down upon his dick again.

Anansi couldn't hear from the pounding of his heart, his loins, and pulse. He reached down and grasped her hips to stop them as he felt his nut swell the tip. He backed out of her heat.

Aja wiggled her bottom for more, reaching back to slap her own bottom. "Hurry," she moaned as if she would die from not having his dick planted inside of her.

"Turn over," he whispered.

She did so and opened her legs to him without hesitation.

Anansi looked down at her. She lightly licked her lips and his hawk-like eyes locked on her mouth as he bent his body to replace her tongue with his own. He lay down atop her, his hardness pressed against her stomach.

Time halted for them as their eyes locked. They deeply breathed in each other's quintessence.

Anansi felt confused by the emotion that squeezed the very breath from his chest as she raised her hand to caress his cheek.

"Who are you?" he whispered, his heart wildly pounding in unison to hers.

"I am whatever you want me to be," she answered before raising her face to lightly kiss his chin in a decidedly intimate fashion.

His brows furrowed. *Something's not right.*

Anansi pressed his open mouth to hers briefly but sweetly, before he moved away from her with the most reluctance he ever felt in his life.

"No. No," Aja moaned in regret, sitting up to follow Anansi's nude frame with her eyes as he jumped down from the *qanddii*.

Anansi turned from her because the sight of her tousled hair and bare curvaceous frame caused a battle deep within him.

"Scan her, XR-2," he ordered as he fought to ease the need to sex her until her voice was lost from calling out in the pleasure and satisfaction he knew he could bring her.

The fine hairs on the back of his neck stood

one end. Anansi looked over his shoulder, and he found her walking over to him, her hard nipples poking through the wavy strands of her hair. Looking away from her again, he dropped his head onto the padded wall as he struggled to find the strength to resist her. He nearly hollered out in anguish when she pressed her body against his back with a purr, massaging his wide muscular back with her plush breasts as she slid her arms down the front of his hard physique to wrap both her hands around the length of him. She stroked it downward.

"Please...no," he begged for mercy.

He turned and roughly grabbed her shoulders, standing nearly three feet over her. He shifted his hands up to grasp her face. "You test my ability to resist you, Aja of Nede," he admitted.

"Then why deny yourself?" she asked saucily, before lowering her body to kneel before him to take his dick into her hand again.

He shivered when she boldly met his eyes as she licked the length of him hotly before taking the tip into her mouth, she circled it with her tongue. A fine layer of sweat covered his body. His knees buckled. Blindly he reached back for the wall to steady himself.

"It tastes as good as it feels," Aja cooed, her words breezing against his dick before she took him deeply into her mouth again. Her lips surrounded him as her cheeks caved with each sucking motion. His juices and her spittle drizzled down his dick to race across his balls as she imbibed him with vigor and drew the strength from his knees.

"*She's has a large dose of* extos *in her system and her Empath powers have been blocked as is customary for Kordi gabras.*"

Anansi swore at the mention of the powerful aphrodisiac. With *extos* in her system, Aja would be hard pressed not to mate an animal in such a highly aroused state. He tried to step back. Her hands rose to tightly clutch his buttocks as she drew his rod deeper into her throat. He cried out, his mouth forming a circle as he fell back against the wall.

Soon his seed would fill her mouth.

Anansi pressed his hand against her head and successfully stepped back this time. Still, she held on with a deeper sucking motion. His hand gripped her hair, and his hips lightly rocked back and forth as he flung his head back and whimpered.

"Hmm, so good," she moaned, her mouth full and her words muffled.

"No," he cried out, releasing her hair to press his hand to her forehead again. His rod slipped from her.

Anansi moved away from her, but Aja was right on his heels across the room. He reached the desk and picked up his sleep pants as Aja climbed across the desk like a tiger. Calmly he opened the top drawer of his desk and removed a small rod, setting on stun.

When Aja climbed off the desk to fling herself at him, he caught her and allowed himself one small kiss before he pressed the small metal rod to her fleshy bottom. Instantly her body softened against him.

Anansi swung her up into his arms with ease. He walked out of the office, deciding against having XR-2 transfer her to one of the guest rooms to sleep. He wanted to place her in *qanddii* himself, but that walk away from her would be the longest one of his life.

IV

Aja's eyes felt heavy as they opened and there was a bitter, metallic taste in her mouth. She felt lost in time and place as she slowly turned over onto her back in the middle of the plushest *qanddii* she'd ever felt. She frowned at the crisp feel of the *huccuu* sheets against every inch of her skin. She lifted the material and looked to find she was indeed unclothed. With a jolt, she sat up and clutched the sheet to her chest. She winced and grunted softly as her head began to throb at the sudden movement. Her heart raced, and her stomach was a pit of nerves as she looked around at her surroundings. None of it was familiar. Not the thickness of the fur rugs covering the floors or the stark whiteness of the décor, which made everything feel surreal.

It was very different from the barren and filthy room where she had been held captive or the *goojjoos* in which she was raised. Different and better, by far, but still not her home. Aja wanted to be back on Nede. Free.

With my family.

Tears filled her eyes at the difference of her life in comparison to two *torbaans* ago. Life had been so simple. Family. Friends. Freedom. All of it was gone.

Aja dropped her head into her hands. "Where am I now?" she asked, surprised by the hoarseness of her voice.

She rose from the *qanddii*, wrapping the *huccuu* around her shapely body. The room was an odd circular shape and filled with brilliant light from the large windows. Every inch of the walls beneath the windows were covered with light and airy drapery that gave the room a feeling of decadence. She had to admit the surroundings would be comfortable under different circumstances.

A prison is still a prison, no matter how eye-catching.

Aja reached out and touched the transparent

layers. The drapes suddenly drifted to the left. Startled by it, she jumped back, the sheet slipping from her fingers to the floor. The curtain drifted back close.

Her heart hammered as she leaned a bit to the side to see if someone had made the drapery move. She was afraid she was not in the room alone. Long moments seemed to pass until her heart finally settled back to a normal pace.

Aja bent to pick up the *huccuu*, wrapping it around her frame before she took a tentative step forward. The curtain opened.

A step back. The curtain closed.

Oh.

She moved forward and even peaked her head beyond the curtain when it opened again. Her eyes widened a bit at the entry to an equally luxurious *kutaa dhiqannaa*.

Curious, she moved behind the hangings and the entire floor of the room illuminated. Aja gasped in surprise and jumped back. The light remained. Biting her bottom lip, she eased one foot ahead and tapped the floor lightly with her heel. The light dimmed. She tapped again. The light dimmed further. One more tap and the lights went out entirely.

She stepped into the room, illuminating the floor lights again, and made her way to a large oval-shaped tub in the center of the chamber. It looked inviting, but now was not the time for indulging in luxury. There was no time for anything but obtaining her freedom.

Aja turned, the edges of the lavish *huccuu* dragging behind her. The panel drifted open again as she neared it. She continued her inspection of the *diinqa*. The contraption with fancy glass containers holding different colored liquids she assumed to be *alkoolii*. A large clear square box that was thin hung on the wall. Most of it was foreign to her. The way everything in the room was automatic as if pulled by strings by some unseen source.

The *abuturoos* often spoke of the advances they

left behind on Erised, but beyond her imagination, Aja had never seen such things. She felt lost. Out of place. Only the discovery that yet another curtain concealed clothing and footwear was of some comfort. Her nudity was a weakness she would rather correct.

Aja reached for an all-in-one, form-fitting jumpsuit of shimmering lavender and matching thigh-high boots. She looked around before she dropped the *huccuu* and quickly dressed. It took her a moment to figure how the metal zig zag parts worked, but soon she pulled up the ones on the jumpsuit and thigh-high footwear with ease.

She had just rose from sitting on the edge of the *qanddii* when the panels on the far wall fluttered slightly before opening wide and revealing the hall beyond the room. Her heart slammed against her chest, and fear made her pause for just a second before she dashed for the opening.

Just before she stepped into the hall, a tall, masculine figure stepped in front of her blocking her exit. Aja collided into firm muscle and strength. Hands rested on her waist to steady her, and she began to thrash wildly at his touch. "Let me go," she screamed in her native semantic.

As soon as he released her, she flew across the room and reached passed the panels to pick up one of the glass bottles holding the liquids. Ready to fight for her life, Aja broke the glass against the edge of the square steel shelves and whirled around. Her eyes flashed as she took a battle stance with the jagged edge pointed towards him.

"This is quite a change from the last time I saw you," he teased, his voice rich and warm.

Anansi head tilted back a bit to take in his face. The masculine was nearly three feet taller than her. His eyes were entirely black, but somehow, she was able to detect humor in the ebony depths.

"And what is so funny?" Aja snapped, switching her impromptu weapon to her other hand.

The white short sleeved shirt and pants he wore pressed against the hard contours of his steely frame as he crossed his arms over his chest. "I am Anansi Nyame—"

"—of Erised," Aja finished softly in sudden enlightenment, her honey-gold eyes widening.

Hot flashes of scenes that seemed like a dream played in rapid succession in her head. Her nude body sprawled across a desk. An *alkoolii* shower. Spinning chair. Similar shades of bronze flesh pressed together. A floating *qanddii*. Her hips and backside working like crazy. A stiff dick working her like crazy. Her knees pressed into fur. The feel of his hardness against her tongue.

Heated touches. Loud moans. Deep kisses. Intimate caresses. Mind blowing strokes.

"I only get better."

Her own words floated back to her.

Aja's eyes locked on him. She saw his eyes leisurely stroke her body in the form-fitting clothes she wore. She felt naked and violated.

With a cry of outrage, Aja raised the crude weapon above her head and went barreling towards him.

∞

Anansi frowned at the pure rage and hatred in her eyes as she came towards him at full speed. He stepped towards her to effortlessly grab her around the waist with one strong arm before tightly gripping her wrist with his free hand. He applied just enough pressure to it until she dropped the broken bottle.

"I am not your enemy, Aja," he told her softly as he looked down at her, his eyes searching hers as his body registered the soft feel of her breasts pushed against his chest.

"Erisedians and Kordis are now the same in my book," she countered coldly, her breathing heavy as she futilely tried to wriggle free of his hold.

"My people never enslaved yours," he reminded her firmly.

Anansi loosened his hold on her when he felt the stirring between his legs in response to the feel of her body against his. A heated vision of her mouth surrounding his member sent a jolt of electricity through his body. He shivered.

"No, you just sat back watched for sports as the Kordis violated innocent people," she spat, her full mouth twisted in anger.

"Once your *abuturoos* left Erised, your people never wanted the protection of The Council, Aja—not even in the more recent *baras*. It was a risk that your people took." Anansi looked down in her eyes before his own gaze dipped to take in the slight part of her soft lips. He yearned to taste her kisses again and was ashamed at the regret he felt that he did not finish their mating when she had been so willing.

"Release me. Or did you plan to force yourself on me...again?" Aja asked, freeing herself of his touch before moving to sit on the edge of the *qanddii* with her arms crossed over her chest.

Anansi tilted his head to the side as he looked over at her. The brilliant light of the room made her all the more beautiful, and he found himself distracted by that fact. Shaking his head slightly for clarity, he walked over to stand before her. "More like you forced yourself on me. I had to stun you to get you off me, Empath."

She leaned back to be able to angrily lock her stare with his. "Liar," she spat.

He just chuckled lightly. "I'm many things, but a liar isn't one of them."

Aja gave him a withering look as she eyed him from head to toe. "I would never willingly mate with an Erisedian, much less beg him to mate with me."

"Trust me, you wouldn't have had to beg, *but* you did," he chided her.

Their eyes locked. Stormy honey ones to his unflinching black.

Anansi looked away first and turned his head to eye the shards of glass and spilled *alkoolii* now staining the white fur throws. In a flash, the mess vanished, and a new white rug appeared in its place.

Aja gasped in horror and scrambled back on the *qanddii* until she was at the center of it, looking over at him with accusing eyes. "What is this place?

Where am I?" she snapped, her voice cold and successfully concealing her fear.

"This is modern times, Aja, and nothing to be afraid of," he began, coming around the *qanddii*. "The *mana* is programmed with XR-2, a virtual servant."

Suddenly she scrambled off of it and moved away from him. "Why am I here? What role does Oduda Diasi play in my being here?" she asked, abruptly switching the subject.

Anansi hesitated, rubbing his chin, as he continued to eye her intently. "I thought you might be hungry. If you promise to retract your claws, I will explain everything that I know over our meal," he said, turning back to the entrance. The panel swayed to the side, opening for him.

"Am I free to leave?" she asked, hating the hope in her tone.

A question he knew she would ask. He crossed his hands behind his back as he turned to look at her briefly with a serious expression. "Unfortunately, not. I'm sorry."

Aja pressed her hands to her hips and tilted her chin up a bit in defiance. "Then you and your meal can go to *Jahannam*."

"Then the truth of your being here will go with me," Anansi countered dryly, even as he inwardly admired her spirit. Her life force was strong. Bold. Defiant.

Certainly not that of a *gabra*.

He said nothing else and turned to leave the *diinqa*. He smiled when he heard Aja's reluctant footsteps behind him.

∞

When Aja stepped out of the *diinqa*, she expected to see guards. She was wrong. There was nothing but the view of Anansi's broad back as he slowly led her down a long wide hallway. She detested that he was so confident that she would not strike out at him again. Childishly, her hands literally itched to dig into his long waist length locs and tug at them with her fists until he fell backward.

Smug bastard.

Instead, she took in everything about her surroundings as she followed her newest captor. She did not allow herself to be distracted by the opulent surroundings, even if his calm demeanor had erased a tiny bit of her trepidation. She was alert for the earliest opportunity to either claim her precious freedom or a weapon to take his life—whichever came her way first. She paused at a large entryway to her right leading down to a large diamond shaped great room in shades of brown that was masculine yet sensuous all at once. On the other side of the room were double doors that had to be an exit.

She chanced a look at Anansi to find he was still headed down the hall before she turned and raced across the great room. The plush fur rugs covering the floor blanketed her footsteps as she moved as quickly as she could to the doors. Her heart pounded with pure adrenaline and a desire to finally be free again. She pulled on the handles with a grunt. Nothing budged. They were sealed shut. She saw a scanner near the panel and ran her hand over it. The doors remained closed. She even pushed her fingers into the thin slit between the doors and tried to pry them apart until frustration brought tears to her eyes. Nothing.

Giving up, she dropped her head to the door and banged her fist against it.

Aja never considered herself a fragile feminine, but she'd never felt so vulnerable and defenseless in her life. Of course, her freedom would not be as easy as walking through open doors, and she felt foolish for thinking so. She didn't even know what awaited her on the other side of the door if she had made it out. She was completely powerless.

"I know it doesn't seem like it, but you're safer in here. You'll have more freedom in here. I can protect you...*in here.*"

Aja turned, pressing her back to the doors as her tears flowed down her cheeks. She watched him. He was across the room leisurely leaned against the archway with his arms crossed over his broad chest. He didn't have a care in the world, including concerning himself about her escaping.

She used the side of her hands to wipe away her tears. "Lately, my life has been in the hands of other people—my enemies at that. I am so tired," she admitted, allowing her true emotions to show for a moment "*But* I will reclaim my freedom even if I must take a million lives to do so. Including yours."

Anansi walked down the stairs and crossed the room to stand before her. "I am not your enemy, Aja."

"Then release me," she requested solemnly.

Anansi frowned deeply and stared at her with those limitless eyes of his as he shook his head, denying her. "You are still a *gabra* and until...things change you can be legally claimed by anyone. Let me protect you until the time comes where you are free."

She looked up into his eyes. "Then *you* are my master," she stated sarcastically. She could hardly believe people had the audacity to claim ownership of another.

Anansi reached down and held her face in his hands. His thumb lightly stroked her cheek. "I would like to be many things for you. Your friend, your protector, your lover, but never your master, Aja of Nede."

A shiver of pure awareness raced across her body, and she hated herself for it. "I can tell by the look in your eyes and the feel of your arousal against my thigh that you want to mate with me. I am your *gabra*. If I resist will you punish me?" she asked, meaning to be crude, even as she registered the warmth of this touch against her skin.

"I would never make love to you against your will, Aja. If that were the case, then I would have allowed you to continue your seduction of me last night." He rubbed this thumb against her lower lip. "And trust me I have never been seduced so well."

Aja's eyes dropped to his mouth as he lightly licked his bottom lip. She beat down her growing desire for him, even as her nipples tightened and her clit throbbed like a rapid heartbeat. "That will never happen again," she swore, although she clearly remembered the feel of his thick inches deep inside of her. Stroking her. Pleasing her.

"That is your choice," Anansi said, stepping back from her with a slight bow of his head.

A polite captor?

"If you remember I invited you to eat with me so that I could explain why you're here." Anansi offered her his arm.

This masculine presented hospitality that was nothing like the horrible *torbaans* she'd spent in Oduda's cold, damp and dirty room with rodents. Was it a front? A cruel joke? Would his politeness be jerked from her just as she felt comfort? Would she ever be free?

She lightly placed her hand in the bend of his arm, a guise to give her a chance to see if their contact would give her insight into the masculine. It didn't. Her powers were no more. She would have longed picked up on the sincerity of his words through his emotions. She felt at a disadvantage. Nothing about her life was her own anymore.

∞

Anansi watched Aja over the rim of his cup as she sat at the opposite end of the table with her arms across her chest. "How is your meal?" he asked, although it was evident her food remained untouched before her.

"Information makes me hungry," she countered with an arch of her brow.

"Good sex does the same for me," he said around a tender piece of meat.

Anansi saw anger flash in the depths of her gold-flecked eyes. "Okay, *Giiftiin* Oduda of Kordi presented you to me as a gift...a carnal gift. There were large amounts of *extos* in your system. Once I discovered that your amorous reaction to me was drug-induced, I gave you a sedative so that you would sleep until all of the *extos* was out of your system."

Be glad I have use of you, or you would be dead, gabra.

Aja remembered Oduda's last words to her right after she had been stripped naked.

She lowered her eyes from his.

Anansi saw the shame in them before she did. He let down his utensil. "I apologize for my role in it."

She looked up and stared at him for long moments before looking down again. "I'm sure you know that we Empaths can be very sexually liberal, but choosing someone to mate with and having someone forced upon you is an entirely different thing," she murmured.

Anansi thought of how she worked her hips backward until she lowered her wet tightness around his length. *Extos* worked only to release inhibitions not to teach sexual tricks that would weaken a masculine to his knees. Still, it was her choice and not something to be induced by a powerful aphrodisiac.

Anger and disgust at Oduda burned his gut.

He looked down the table at her just as she raised her eyes to look at him. For long moments, their gazes remained locked. Pure awareness shimmied over his body, and he fought an urge to walk across the top of the table to get to her. His dick hardened with ease. He felt the smooth round tip slide against his thigh as it lengthened.

Anansi felt shame. His arousal was the last thing she needed.

"You say you apologize for your role in Oduda's sick game, but do you have the same remorse for holding me here against my will?" Aja asked, never once looking away from him.

His ire was sparked. He couldn't help that. "I offer you nothing but hospitality and respect here in my *mana*," he said, fighting to keep his tone and his composure calm.

"And you believe there is respect in being considered someone's property?" she countered fiercely, as she pounded her fist against the top of the table, causing the tableware to rattle against each other.

Anansi's hand slashed the air. "There is no guarantee of your safety even on your own planet. The war is not over. If a Kordi— or anyone else for that matter—captured you, he could sell you or keep you at his will to do whatever he pleased with you. You'd rather risk that uncertainty than remain here in safety and comfort? Don't be foolish!" he roared, flinging his utensil onto the table.

Aja jumped to her feet so quickly and abruptly that her chair fell backward to the floor. "I am no one's fool and no one's *gumna*."

"Until the practice of owning *gabras* is officially abolished you are whatever I wish you to be," he said, his voice cold and unrelenting.

Aja nodded her head and smiled bitterly as she raised her hands to applaud him. "The truth has been exposed."

Anansi rose to his feet in exasperation at his poor word selection. "I detest the use of *gabras*. Our research of the planet Earth revealed that the European Earthlings enforced this same brutality against Africans *jaarraas* ago. And here we are, far advanced beyond our wildest dreams, and yet we follow them in such barbarities," he said, before releasing a heavy breath. "I only meant to say that legally I own you, but I am not treating you as my property. You are my guest, Aja."

She picked up her plate and flung it. It shattered against the wall sending shards of glass and food everywhere. "I'd rather starve to death than be owned by *anyone*."

"The choice is yours." Anansi's temper snapped as he dropped back down into his seat. "XR-2 transfer my guest to her *diinqa*."

"*Of course*, Giiftin."

He watched as she dashed to pick up a shard of glass. Before she could reach it, her body faded and then disappeared. He knew she was safely in her *diinqa*.

Anansi roughly pushed his plate of food away. Should he return Aja to Oduda? That thought did not set well with him. His intended had filled the Empath with an aphrodisiac and presented her like a *gumnas* from the infamous Planet Whoor. Under Oduda's control, who knew Aja's fate?

As angry as the sexy Empath made him, Anansi wanted nothing but to keep her protected until the *cidha* was completed, the treaty signed, and the *gabras* were officially emancipated. Then she was free to return to Nede without fear of enslavement again.

He rubbed his eyes with his fingers before pinching the bridge of his nose and releasing a long sigh.

Perhaps once she knew the entire story of his own sacrifice to bring about peace, Aja would release some of the anger she felt for him. The question was, why did he care?

V

Aja paced the oval-shaped *diinqa* until her feet ached, but hatred and a need for vengeance fueled her on. She wanted nothing more than to be free so that she could work to get her hands around Oduda Diasi's neck until the bald headed *badaa* died at her feet.

She could hardly believe the shrew presented her to Anansi as nothing more than a *gumna*. As time passed more and more of her scandalous behavior with Anansi came back to her. She felt her face warm with embarrassment, and she pressed her hands to her cheeks with a tiny whimper from the back of her throat. They were strangers, and now he knew her intimately.

She shivered in abhorrence.

Although it was evident Anansi was a handsome and virile masculine well-equipped to deliver hours upon hours of pleasure, he was unknown to her.

She clenched her fist and punched the air with swiftness and strength.

Her mood swung like a pendulum between rage and shame.

"*You test my ability to resist you, Aja of Nede.*"

Her brows dipped as she recalled him fighting her off as the *extos* caused her to behave like a sex-starved nymph. He could have easily ridden her until he was spent, but he resisted. That spoke to some semblance of honor on his behalf. For that, she gave him credit.

Still, he refused to set her free. Thus, he was nothing more than her enemy no matter how appealing the cell.

"But I'm a guest," she remarked sarcastically with a bitter laugh.

She sat down on the *qanddii*, fatigued and weary. Her stomach grumbled at its emptiness. She wanted to take off the boots and maybe take a bath but felt that would be giving in to the comforts he offered and thus accepting her fate. She didn't want to forget her status here. She was a captive. Nothing more.

Still, I can't remember the last time I bathed...

Aja rose and walked across the *diinqa*. The drapes leading to the *kutaa dhiqannaa* opened. In the face of her family's death and the Empath's near extinction through death or enslavement, it felt selfish to enjoy such luxury. She did not want to be rewarded in any way for the tragedy of her people.

'I have to wash,' Aja reasoned, remembering the time at Oduda's where cleaning had not been an option.

And the scent of our sex is still on me.

Shaking off her reservations, Aja undressed. Nude and admitting that she loved the feel of the plush fur between her toes, she tried to figure out how to turn on the water. She bit her bottom lip but saw nothing but a circle of medium sized holes around the base and a long narrow slit at the head.

"XR-2?" she called out softly, following Anansi's lead.

Nothing.

"XR-2?" she called out again.

Nada.

"It's only programmed for my usage."

Aja whirled around to find Anansi standing in the doorway, now dressed casually in all black. The effect of it with his locs, ebony eyes and the dark patterns on the skin of his arms was impressive. She regretted her immediate awareness of him.

His eyes drifted lazily across her body, and she remembered she was naked.

"Do you molest all your guests?" she snapped bending over with an arm barely across her breasts and her hand futilely covering the warm triangle at the top of her thighs.

Anansi smiled as he turned his back. "I've seen and tasted it all."

"Well, I hope you have a good memory."

He laughed. "Good memories of damn good things, Aja."

Her body warmed as she let her eyes shift from

his broad shoulders to his firm buttocks in his pants. "Can I help you?" she asked coldly.

"I will be holed up in my office all day, but you will have free reign of my *mana*. Again, you are my guest. I've had XR-2 ensure you cannot get into too much trouble."

Aja remained silent.

"I brought you a meal. Hopefully this time it will wind up in your stomach and not on my walls."

Aja said not one word.

"To turn on the water just voice your command."

Aja's eyes dropped to the tub.

Anansi sighed. "Water on," he ordered, glancing back over his shoulder for just a moment.

Pale pink water began to pour from the holes in the sides of the tub, and the slit was actually a waterfall faucet.

"Normally we use *dhiqatas* to conserve water, but I understand how much a bath must mean to you right now," he said.

Aja bit her tongue to keep from asking him what a *dhiqata* was. In fact, she had many questions about the way of life on Erised, but she would not let her curiosity get the better of her. Instead, she slipped into the tub. The warm water felt wonderful. "Hmm, so good," she moaned.

Her eyes popped open just as Anansi quickly turned to meet her eyes. Long seconds ticked by as their gazes locked. She had cried the exact same words as she sucked his dick deep into her mouth.

Her cheeks warmed.

Anansi cleared his throat and turned away. "Enjoy."

She said nothing.

As soon as he walked past the curtain panel and it closed behind him, she closed her eyes.

The Empaths were told stories of the evil Erisedians who had made their lives almost as torturous as being banished to Jahannam because of their prejudice. Never in a million *baras* did she imagine she would feel the least bit attracted to an

Erisedian. Of course, she had been full of a potent aphrodisiac.

Still, she had to admit that her system was now free of *extos* and she found everything about him sensual. His long locs. Those brilliant black eyes. His smile. That cocky stride. His confidence.

That body.

Tall and muscular frame. Rigid abdomen. Strong thighs. Hard buttocks. Long and thick dick.

Certainly, she was no innocent, but any of her former lovers would be hard pressed to compete with Anansi Nyame's prowess.

Even as her core warmed, Aja thought, 'Too bad every delicious inch is attached to an Erised.'

As the water warmly caressed her body as if it was a smooth hand, it was hard to forget the way he had made her body feel.

She slid her hands down between her legs and palmed her flesh, shivering as she squeezed it lightly. "Too bad indeed."

Aja arched her back in the water with a moan as she opened her plump thick lips to lightly tease her swollen bud. Her hips began to circle against the base of the tub as she lifted her legs and placed them both over the rim of the bathtub. Water dripped from her feet onto the floor, but she didn't care as her bud swelled and became sensitive to her touch.

She licked her lips as she increased the pressure. The tips of her taut nipples poked through the edge of the pale pink water as she arched her back. It felt good to feel something other than grief. "Hmmm, Anansi," Aja moaned.

Her eyes popped open. She sat up straight in the water. Her hand slid away from her core. The waves of her climax retreated.

Aja cursed herself for calling out his name.

∞

Anansi turned his chair towards the *komputara*, a transparent flat monitor, taking up a major portion of the left sidewall of his office. His parents' images soon appeared. He pressed a button, and their full images suddenly appeared as four-dimensional holograms inside his office. His deep-set eyes rested on his *da'ee*, Mondi Nyame, and he wore the hint of a smile at how most of his looks came from her. Often, they were told she was as beautiful as he was handsome, and there was no doubt that they resembled one another.

"Welcome back, Anansi," Mondi greeted him, a smile already at the corners of her mouth.

"Yes, welcome back," Hwosi Kan Nyame added.

Anansi bowed his head in deference to both. "Thank you."

"Please let *Giiftiin* Oduda know that I look forward to meeting her in person," Mondi said, looking regal in the metal floor length coat she wore over an equally long black dress with her locs piled high atop her head.

"She did not arrive as planned, but I will let her know as soon as she does," Anansi admitted, his deep-set black eyes shifting to the left to take in his *abbaa's* reaction.

As expected Hwosi's square face immediately formed into a frown.

"Okay, the way Hwosi is looking I know that means it's business time, so this is where I say I love you and I'll see you soon. Right?" Mondi asked, arching a brow.

"Right."

She winked and blew him a kiss before lightly stroking her husband's cheek as she took her leave. Her image disappeared leaving him alone with the imposing holographic image of his *abbaa*.

"What's the deal, old one?" Anansi asked, picking up a pair of small metal balls from the desk to work between his fingers.

Hwosi laughed, his ebon eyes sparkling. "You wish to look this good when you get my age, young one."

"If it's left up to my future lifemate, I might look like I am your age a lot quicker," Anansi mused. "Not only did she skip our first meeting she sent me a *gabra* doped up on *extos* and more than willing to please."

Hwosi frowned. "That's quite a gift."

Anansi thought of Aja backing her fleshy buttocks towards him until her core fit his dick like a sheath. He shivered. "Yes. Yes, it is."

"I won't ask how your night went," his *abbaa* quipped, shifting his stance so that his hands were locked behind his massive back.

Anansi grabbed another ball and began to juggle them above his head as he casually leaned back in his chair. "Actually, I slept quite well. *Galatoomaa*."

"And where is your ... gift?"

"She is here as my guest under my protection until the treaty is signed and her freedom secured." He caught the three balls in one hand with ease.

"Will that sit well with your lifemate?"

"Lifemate to be," Anansi corrected. "And the choice is no longer hers."

"Life with Oduda will certainly be fascinating." Hwosi shook his head and lifted one hand to massage the long silvery beard on his chin. "I understand that although Kyl Diasi is a brute, he assured me that she is well educated and genteel, making her the proper candidate for a lifemate."

Anansi snorted in derision.

"Son, I respect your willingness to accept your duty as my successor and go through with this union."

Anansi shifted his eyes away from his *abbaa* as he swallowed a rather large—and sudden—lump in his throat. "I will admit that the thought of joining lives with a stranger is no easy thing for me. I am used to being in control, and at times this entire situation feels completely out of my hands."

"You know there is no other way to bring about this treaty. The rest of The Council and I have debated this issue and weighed the risks and the gains."

Anansi shrugged a bit as his face became pensive.

"Arranged *gaa'ilas* used to be the custom of our

people. You know that is how your *da'ee* and I came to wed. Look at us now. I'm sure you and *Giiftiin* Oduda can have the same type of happiness."

Hwosi reached out as if he could touch his son.

Anansi closed his eyes as the warmth of his *abbaa's* hand was replicated against his cheek. "Perhaps," he said, sounding anything but sure of that.

It was evident Anansi had his doubts. A feminine that would willingly fill another person with a powerful aphrodisiac and then present her to her future lifemate as a sexual gift did not bode well for a friendly, compassionate, and loving feminine like his *da'ee*.

∞

Aja was laying on her side on the *qanddii*, her thoughts full, when she heard the soft shift of the curtains at the entrance to the *diinqa*. She closed her eyes just as she saw Anansi come to stand in the ingress. Sleep offered her no solace as Aja dreamt of everything lost to her, so she rarely succumbed to it. Thus, she lay awake, her heart pounding and her pulse racing, as she feigned sleep under Anansi's watchful gaze.

Although it was just a few moments, it felt like an eternity because of her nerves.

Long after he took his leave, she wondered about his thoughts as he observed her. Did he remember their mating as she did at odd moments of the day? As much as she fought them away, the recollections of their heated passion returned. Constantly. Consistently. Taunting and teasing her.

Looking for a diversion from her scandalous thoughts of Anansi, and an escape from her prison, Aja quickly rose. There were no lamps or lanterns to fully illuminate the room, but soft lighting filtered through the draperies adorning the walls. It was enough to reach the closet, and she chose something dark.

As Aja pulled on form fitting pants and long-sleeved cropped top that exposed her belly, she briefly wondered to whom the clothes belonged. She assumed Anansi had no lifemate, was she wrong?

She looked pensive and then shook her head as if to remind herself of her hatred of him.

Nothing about Anansi Nyame is of concern to me.

Aja approached the entrance to the *diinqa*. The curtains swung open wide, and she forged ahead, even as her heart pounded wildly in her chest. Her stomach rumbled in hunger, but she ignored it. Her primary objective was to continue exploring for an escape.

There is no guarantee of your safety even on your own planet. The war is not over. If a Kordi—or anyone else for that matter—captured you, he could sell you or keep you at his will to do whatever he pleased with you.

Aja frowned as she remembered Anansi's words of warning.

It was true she had no idea what awaited her outside of his mana, but she could no longer sit back and have her freedom denied. She had to try.

As she had yesterday while he was locked away in his office, Aja explored Anansi's *mana*. It was sprawling, large enough to comfortably contain a third of her *ollaa* and tried every possible outer door she could find—only to discover they were all locked. She hadn't been surprised by that.

I won't give up.

Under the cloak of darkness, she moved swiftly, pressing her hands against the cold walls to guide herself. She felt the seam between doors, and suddenly they spread opened. Bright sunlight flooded her from inside the chamber. She swore as she closed her eyes until they adjusted to the sudden brightness.

Aja stepped further into the room, blinking her long and lush lashes as she looked at the surroundings.

The walls and floor were made of some transparent material and were devoid of furniture giving her first real look at the world around her. It was majestic, and she was in awe.

Metal structures rose from the side of dark purple mountains against the backdrop of bluish lavender skies and three brilliant *aduus*. "Three?" Aja murmured in wonder.

She had never seen such a thing in her life.

Normally we use dhiqatas to conserve water...

Anansi's words came back to her as her golden eyes shifted from each *aduu* to the other. The need to save water made since in the face of what had to be blazing heat. Still the sight of them glowing with the sky as their backdrop was picturesque.

She looked down beneath her feet and frowned. Below her was exotic flowers and lush greenery that was picturesque but in total contradiction with the idea of a drought. The floor gave her the feeling of walking on air in a backyard that was a tropical playground, replete with a waterfall that filled an impressive pool of water. It was as if Anansi had his own personal paradise. *Is it real?*

Aja walked further into the room and pressed her hands against the transparent wall. Far in the distance, barely distinguishable, the tops of *manas* built up from mountains were numerous, and flying vehicles soared through the sky like giant birds. Down at the base of the mountains the bustling activity of Erisedians crowding the street was so different from life on Nede. Life on the planet Erised moved at full force.

Filled with longing for her life as it used to be, Aja turned away from the view and left the room to continue her exploration.

The heels of her footwear clicked against the smooth granite floors of the hallway as she approached a door. It slid open as she neared. Her face became a mask of confusion at the black walls and floor. They were as dark as Anansi's eyes.

What is this for?

Aja didn't spot a door and turned to leave. She walked right into a strong wall of muscle and became surrounded by the warm spicy scent of a masculine. She jumped back as if electrified as she looked up at

Anansi's handsome face and those limitless black eyes.

His strong hands rested lightly on her hips to steady her. The pants were low-slung on her waist and exposed her to the heat of his hands. "You can release me now," Aja snapped even as her nipples hardened and a shiver raced through her body.

Anansi smiled. "Same goes for you," he smirked, pointedly looking down at her soft hands splayed against his chest.

She was grateful for the shirt that served as a barrier from his warmth.

His smile widened.

Aja hated the way it made her heart leap in her chest. She immediately stepped further back from him, removing her hands from his chest. "What is this room, a sex chamber?" she asked sarcastically.

"I'm sure you remember that I don't need a particular place to bring out the freak in a feminine," he countered, his intense eyes resting on her as he slid his hands into the pockets of his pants.

"Especially with the use of aphrodisiacs," she flung back.

Anansi dropped his head, causing his locs to float down and partially cover his face, as he bit back a smile and cut those eyes up to look at her again.

A sexy move without even trying.

Aja shifted her eyes from him as her pulse betrayed her and raced.

"This is my *zwodriu*, Aja."

She shivered at the sound of her name slipping with ease from his mouth. Almost against her will, her eyes shifted back to him and fell on his lips. His very supple, full, and completely kissable mouth. Aja admonished herself as she diverted her eyes again. "And a *zwodriu* is?" she asked dryly, turning her back to him to look around the black room again.

"A fight simulator," he explained, stepping past her to enter. "Power on. Level five."

Aja turned, her eyes taking in his tall sculptured physique. She gasped when the room was transformed, and they stood in the middle of a battlefield, as a bloodthirsty crowd roared from the stands at the large, half-masculine, half-creature of nearly ten feet which came charging towards them with a large weapon posed above its head. He roared, and its breath pushed their clothes to press against their bodies and Aja's hair to fly up in the air behind her. She could smell its horrid breath as saliva dripped from its green pointed teeth.

Aja screamed at the top of her lungs and turned to run straight towards Anansi, jumping up to wrap her body around his tightly as she buried her face into his neck and squeezed her eyes shut.

"Power off," he calmly stated as his arms came around to tightly wrap around her waist.

Her heart hammered against her chest. She clung to him like her life depended on it. The soothing circles he rubbed against her back calmed her.

"It's off. I'm sorry. I should have warned you," Anansi said speaking softly into her ear as he rubbed his cheek against hers. "I wasn't thinking. Are you okay? Huh? You alright, Aja?"

He lightly brushed kisses against her cheek and Aja instinctively held him closer.

On planet Nede, Empaths were encouraged to have the greatest respect for emotions, and thus sex could at times be given very freely as her people acquiesced to their feelings of desire and passion. At that moment, as she felt her body pressed against Anansi, and as she recalled the heated lust they shared in his office, her desire for him was high. Her primal instinct was to mate him until they both were sweaty and sated.

She held her head up and looked into his face. Her eyes locked with his and she felt a current pass between them that caused her breath to catch in her throat. She desired him, and in her head, she could clearly see how she wished the scene would play out...

∞

"If you were not my enemy and my captor, I would ride your dick until I made you scream my name, Anansi of Erised."

He turned and released her body just enough to press Aja's back to the shiny black wall. He locked his eyes with hers. "Then let's pretend I am your lover," he whispered as he lowered his head to crush his mouth down upon hers with a moan filled with his hunger for her.

Aja brought her hands up to grasp his face as his tongue slipped between her lips to lightly tease the tip of her own. The only sounds in the room were the combined deepness of their breathing, their heads shifting from left to right as the kiss deepened.

Aja felt high from their desire and gave into it, locking her ankles behind his back as she ground her hips against him, bringing the moist and soft lips of her core against the hard length of him.

Anansi's shifted his lips to kiss a heated trail down her jawline to the sweet hollow of her neck, nuzzling his heated lips right at the vee of her shirt where her cleavage tempted him to distraction. He inhaled deeply of the soft scent of her body before he lightly sucked the flesh until a round love bite was left. He shifted over to the tops of her other breast with ease to do the same.

Aja cried out in sweet torturous pleasure. She ached to feel his tongue against her hard nipples and longed to have him suck as much of it as he could into his hot mouth. Arching her back she reached up to grab the edges of the thin shirt to tear the material and free her breasts for his liking.

Anansi moaned in pleasure and lifted his hands from her buttocks to cup each luscious globe into his warm hands as he lowered his head to lightly circle the nipple until it was glistening wet. He leaned back to look at her body exposed to him. Waiting for his touch. His kisses. His licks.

Her aureoles were large brown circles with thick

nipples that made his dick harden and drip for her in his pants.

Wildly, almost like an animal, he licked at each breast. Back and forth. Nipple to nipple. Quickly. Slowly. Quickly again.

"Taste them," she ordered softly, her eyes closed as waves of pleasure like nothing she had ever experienced before coursed through her body.

Anansi gladly took one breast into her mouth and sucked it as his hands sought and found the torn edges of the top. With one quick movement, he opened his arms wide bringing the sides of the shirt with him until it ripped in half and fell to the floor.

He grabbed the waist of her pants and inched them down around her hips. She pressed her back against the wall and raised her hips to help get them over her round buttocks. With one firm grip and pull he tore one of the legs of her pan. Her body jerked with the move, but his body pressed her against the wall securely. Flinging the material behind him, Anansi spread her legs wider to reach between them and sex her with his fingers, making swift upward motions that rubbed against her swollen clit.

"Make me cum. Please. Make me cum, Anansi," Aja begged, biting her bottom lip as she teased her own taut nipples with trembling fingers.

He leaned back to watch her, his face intense and his black eyes gleaming as he enjoyed the feel of her ridged walls throbbing against his two fingers. He used the tips to stroke her before sliding them in and then pulling them out again. Her heavy lids barely opened, nearly blocking the sight of her eyes clouded with desire. Blood rushed to the tip of his dick, and he felt near spilling his seed. "Cum for me," he ordered thickly as he brought his thumb up to deeply circle her clit as his fingers continued their up and down motion inside of her.

Aja cried out as a feeling of anticipation coursed through her. She brought her hands up above her head as her hips began to jerk with the first fiery explosion. "Aaaah," she cried out roughly, *pulling at her own hair.*

Anansi felt her climax dampen his fingers and drew them from her. "Look," he demanded.

Her breathing was ragged as she cracked her eyes open to watch as he sucked her juices from his fingers. "Good?" she asked boldly, her chest heaving.

"You tell me," he said, lowering his head to kiss her.

Aja cockily met his ebony eyes as she sucked his tongue until it was juice free. She ended with a kiss on his lips and a moan of pleasure. "Damn good," she told him huskily, answering her own question.

With her legs still wrapped securely around his waist, Anansi lowered his hands to jerk his pants down. They fell into a pool at his feet, freeing his dick. He stroked every bit of the curved eleven inches.

Aja loosened her legs, and let them fall to her side. She pushed her hand against Anansi's chest to force him to move back enough for her to stand on her shaky feet. On wobbly legs, she encircled him. Playfully she slapped his firm buttocks.

He turned to face her again, still massaging his own dick and squeezing the thick and smooth tip as he watched her through hooded lids. She kicked off the footwear and removed the rest of the tattered pants to stand before him naked

"I want you," he admitted, totally caught up in her.

Aja dropped to her knees before him and flung away his hands to take his dick into her mouth, looking up at him as she tried to suck the life from it. Anansi's knees buckled as he roughly cried out. She continued to suck him even as his hands tangled in her hair to hold her head between his knees.

"Qorobu!" he swore, his hips jerking as a bit of his own juice coated her tongue.

Anansi's body weakened, and he slid down the wall to the floor, looking down at her in amazement as she lowered her body along with his and kept him planted in her hot mouth.

Aja used her tongue to circle his dick from the base up to the tip until he shivered like he was freezing. She raised her hand to push against his chest. Anansi dropped to his buttocks, opening his legs wide. She gave him one last suck before pulling her body up to rise to her knees and crawl onto his lap.

Kissing him, she used one hand to hold his curving dick up straight. "Ready," *she teased and the other to twist in sweet-smelling locs.*

"Hurry," *he countered, letting his head fall back against the wall.*

"One good climax deserves another," *she told him hotly before sliding down onto his length in one fluid motion.*

"Aaaah," *they both cried out.*

Anansi's hands rose to cup her buttocks as Aja began to ride him, and with each movement of her gyrating hips she pulled on the length of him and teased her swollen clitoris. "I needed this," *she admitted into his open mouth as she placed her hands above his head on the wall.*

"Me too. Me too."

They both laughed a little, sharing a deep and passionate kiss before Anansi raised his hands to massage her soft breasts and tease her thick nipples.

"That will make me cum even faster," *she told him with a long moan as she flung her head back and continued to work her hips.*

"Oh yeah?" *Anansi asked, tilting his head to look at her.*

"Oh, yes."

He increased the pressure of his fingers against her nipples. "I want you to cum all over this dick."

Aja felt the first delicious wave rising fast as she licked her lips. "Your...y-y-your wish is my...my...my...my command."

Her body jerked with each convulsion as she continued to work her hips, sliding up and down the length of him as her walls clutched and released him in a wicked rhythm. Her cum coated him making the sounds of sex echo in the room.

Anansi grabbed Aja's buttocks, roughly bringing her cheeks up and down, sending his shaft deep up inside her as he hollered out with the first explosion of his release. The world around him became a kaleidoscope of colors with each spasm of his hard dick propelling his hips up from the ground. Their mingled juices drizzled down to coat their thighs.

Aja collapsed against his chest, the fast beating of his heart echoing in her ear as she waited for her own pulse to return to normal. Her throat was dry. Her body was shaking. Her legs wouldn't have the strength to hold her up. She wanted nothing more than to lie atop Anansi and succumb to sleep.

He stroked Aja's sweaty back, his rod still implanted deep within her. He grunted as another shot of his release filled her as her walls continued to convulse against him. "That was good," he admitted, shaking his head in wonder at what they just shared.

"I know," Aja said as she lifted up her head to look up at him...

∞

"Aja? Aja? What's wrong? What are you thinking of?"

She blinked, and her eyes focused back on Anansi's handsome face. She was still in his arms, her body entwined with his, their clothes in place, the passion just a dream. A sexy wet dream, but a dream none the less. "I'm okay. *Galatoomaa*," she said.

Anansi reached up to tweak her chin playfully. "I thought you were going to climb over my head," he teased.

"I don't scare easily, but that monster nearly stopped my heart."

They laughed a little as Aja jumped down to stand on her feet before him.

"What can I offer you to set me free?" she asked.

Anansi's face hardened as he looked down at her from his towering height. "You have no *warqee* or anything of value to offer besides your body. Are you used to trading yourself for what you want?" he asked coldly.

Aja reached up to slap him. Hard. It echoed.

His hand came up quickly to tightly grip her wrist as their eyes locked.

She hated to admit that his words stung her far harder than the slap could have hurt him.

Aja snatched her arm from his grasp and strutted to the doors. They barely opened before her as she left the *zwodriu* to make her way to the *diinqa* he assigned her. She wished for a traditional Nede door to slam.

VI

Oduda moved her body to the sounds of the pounding music as she looked down at the gyrating bodies from her position above, in one of the floating private balconies of Xion. The lights hanging from the ceiling shifted from one color to another in a frenetic pace. The air was filled with heat, the strong fumes from the *alkoolii* that flowed freely, and the thick stench of the *qoricha* being smoked in abundance.

"Your order, Oduda."

Cloaked in her robe, she looked over her shoulder at the waitress, an automaton whose upper half was the replica of a nude feminine and the bottom half was a glass bubble showing her robotic components. "Thank you. Just add it to my tab," Oduda said reaching into the hidden pocket of the wide gold belt surrounding her sheer white dress. She winked at the automaton as she poured a small dose of liquid *extos* into each of the eight glasses on the tray she held. She used her fingers to gently stir each one before using her damp fingers to lightly circle one of the automaton's permanently erect nipples. "Uhm, very lifelike. Now be gone."

The waitress floated away.

With a small gesture to her four armed guards, they closed the heavy *huccuu* drapes around the entire moving balcony.

Oduda took the tray and turned to face Huung and the rest of her guests sitting around the edges of the *qanddii* that was the centerpiece of the elaborately decorated private balcony. "Here's to good friends, good times, and good sex," she said as she handed each one a flute.

She slid onto Huung's lap, watching over the rim of her own glass as the other three masculines and four feminines sipped deeply. *Won't be long at all before the* extos *kicks in.*

Oduda rose and stood at the foot of the *qanddii* even as her guests began to lightly touch one another while the music pulsated around them. She pulled off the hood of her gold robe exposing her bald head and her face elaborately decorated with pure gold dust makeup. Next, she slipped the straps of her sheer white gown down her smooth round shoulders. It fell to the floor with her robe exposing her nude body to their hungry eyes. She tingled in anticipation as she turned and fell backward onto the center of the *qanddii*.

"Let the entertaining began," she whispered into the frenzied air as different hands began to massage her legs. They spread them to play in her moist folds. Numerous tongues began to lick off the edible gold dust lightly coating her body. She opened her arms wide as two separate mouths latched onto her aching nipples to devour them wildly.

Oduda purred as all the hands pushed her legs up and held them open wide as eager tongues licked her from her buttocks up to her clit. When a hard and throbbing penis was pushed deeply inside of her, she didn't even open her eyes to see just who was stroking her to a shattering climax.

∞

"So, the Kordis are abiding by the temporary halt on collecting *nkumes*?" Anansi asked as he studied the hologram of the *morkii* board game before him. He positioned his finger above one of the board pieces carved of precious gems. It lit up. A flick of his finger sent the piece floating to his desired new position with the goal of blocking one of his opponent's rare metal pieces onto an emerald square and thus ending the game.

"In fact, there has been no movement in the last couple of days. Oh, and good move," Daryan Dvani's image said from the *komputara* showing him in his private quarters above the *Spaceship Infinite*. "But not quite good enough."

Anansi watched as Daryan's piece slid across the board next to his. He smiled broadly. "Good enough to trap you," he said in satisfaction, waving his finger in quick movements to shift five pieces forward to efficiently block Daryan from moving anywhere but backward into the emerald green square.

"I give," Daryan conceded, laughing and shaking his head. "One of these days I will increase my record beyond just thirty wins out of more than a hundred games."

"Perhaps," Anansi teased, swiping a button inside the control panel of his desk to remove the hologram of the *morkii* board that was floating in the air above it.

"The *giiftiin* won't arrive for another *torbaan*—"

"Or more," Anansi added.

"Are you returning to the ship?" Daryan asked, his dreads pulled back from his dark-skinned striking face with a thin strap of leather. "We could use you on the upcoming mission to survey Earth."

Anansi shook his head, thinking of Aja keeping her distance from him in her *diinqa*. "Actually, I have other personal business to attend to anyway. Since I have the leave, I'll just use it. I'm sure you will handle everything just fine without me."

"Of course," Daryan assured him.

"Be careful. Those Earthling feminines can be very distracting—"

The doors to his office opened, and Aja strolled in.

This was the first she had left her *diinqa* since their argument this morning in his *zwodriu*. All of Anansi's senses focused on her. His eyes devoured her from head to toe. The faint scent of her bath oils reached him first, and he inhaled deeply. His hands ached to touch her. His mouth watered to taste hers. His ears were tuned into every step she made that drew her closer to him. He felt sensory overload.

"May I speak with you, please?" she asked, standing before him with her hands on her hips, her nipples piercing the attire, the soft mound of her womanhood quite evident as the thin material clung to her plump lips like a second skin.

"I thought you said the *giiftiin* postponed—?"

Anansi sat up in his chair. "I'll get with you later, Daryan."

"But—"

"Bye." Anansi hit the button ending the communication and causing the *komputara* to disappear. He looked up as Aja crossed her arms over her chest.

"How long will I be forced to stay here?" she asked.

"A little over a *ji'a*," he answered quietly.

Aja's face was quizzical as she looked down at him. "Why in a *ji'a* and not now? What will change in a *ji'a*?"

Anansi leaned back in his chair and eyed her. "I cannot go into details, but your safety will not be an issue at that time."

"You say that I am here to protect me from being captured and sold as a *gabra* again?"

Anansi nodded his head.

"So next *ji'a*, it doesn't matter?"

"No next *ji'a*, it will be safe," he repeated, his tone firm. "I cannot discuss this with you in detail."

"And what am I to do here? Roam around all day playing dress up in another feminine's attire?" she asked, her tone snide.

His eyes roamed over her body leisurely.

"Please get me more clothing than this," was all she said, before turning to leave his office. "I feel like I am dressed to sell my wares on Planet Whoor. And regardless of what you think, I mate for pleasure and nothing else."

"Yes, pleasure is a word I would associate with you."

Aja paused a step as the doors to the office opened before her.

"What about me, Aja?" he called out, sitting up in his chair to watch her. "How do I rate?"

Aja turned to face him before she walked back towards him. "Insecure?" she asked boldly.

"Curious," he countered, rising to come around the desk and stand before her.

Aja looked him up and down.

Anansi pointed briefly towards that fleshy vee at the junction of her strong legs. "I know what those lips said, but I'm curious what these lips will say," he told her now pointing briefly to her mouth.

He didn't miss the way she pressed her thighs closer together, or how her nipples hardened further before she crossed her arms over her chest.

Aja opened her mouth, but he held his hand up.

"Remember the Empaths are known for their high moral standards and a firm belief in emotionally based thoughts and actions," he reminded her.

"Since I lack my powers perhaps I am no longer held to that standard," she told him softly.

He didn't miss the flash of pain in her eyes. And he wondered just what those eyes had seen to fill them with grief. The war was one of the most brutal ever, and he could only imagine the carnage.

"There are actions in place to officially end the war and the ownership of *gabras*," Anansi admitted to her, reaching out to take her hand as hi chest literally ached for her.

Hope filled her eyes only to be replaced by doubt. "How would you know such details? Has there been a report of this? How do you know this?" she asked, her questions almost running together even as she eased her hand out of his grasp.

Anansi wanted to take hold of it again and entwine his fingers with hers. He was pleased with the glimmer of hope he saw in the depths of her honey-gold eyes. "There are classified things that I cannot discuss. I've said more than I should have already."

Aja stepped back from him and paced a bit, every so often stopping to cast a look in his direction, before she went back to pacing again.

"Listen, you have my word that you will one day be free," he swore.

Aja came to stand before him and reached up to grab his square chin with her hand. "Who are you?" she asked huskily, her eyes searching his. "I do recognize this is a question I should have asked before we mated like beasts in your office, but I am asking now. Who...*are*...you, Anansi?"

"I am *Giiftiin* Anansi Nyame, Captain of the *Spaceship Infinite* for the coalition of Galaxy *Acirfa* and heir to the throne of Erised."

His eyes measured her reaction.

Aja frowned. "You are the *giiftiin* of Erised?" she asked in amazement. "This is all so confusing."

"*Komputara* on," he ordered, not once taking his eyes off her as the large transparent monitor on the far wall of his office brightened with a flash of turquoise light. An image was displayed on it, and he waved his hands towards it.

Aja had glanced at him before she moved closer to the display. The light from it reflected in her eyes. In time, the color began to fade from her face as a nude Empath masculine was raised from the floor on a platform in the center of a circle of laughing, cheering and applauding people. Aja's eyes turned cold as an electronic ticker above his head showed the highest bid amount, while he was circled and paraded about like nothing more than a brute.

She soon recognized the strong masculine. "Juuba," she gasped, instinctively reaching out towards the image him. Tears flooded her eyes for the shame he knew he felt and for the predicament of their people.

He had been a friend of her brother and a frequent visitor to their *goojjoo*. Now she watched him emasculated and ridiculed. Naked and exposed. Still, his handsome face was stoic, and nothing of the raging emotions he had to feel was revealed.

"This is the *bwa kasuwa* on Planet Kordi. This is how the Empaths and others who have been enslaved are sold off. Those in attendance or bidding online may win him. And then he is the winner's to do as they see fit," Anansi explained solemnly from behind her.

"This is barbaric," she told him angrily, her eyes blazing.

"This is what I want to protect you from," he countered. "That could very well be you on that block. I'd rather keep you here than have you go through that."

Aja met his long measuring stare over her shoulder. "*Do* something," she stressed, fighting back the tears built up her from her anger.

Anansi shook his head, his black eyes filled with his regret. "I do not agree with any of this, but right now I am powerless to stop it."

Aja looked back at Juuba's face. "For a person as powerful as yourself to accept the gift of a *gabra* from that Kordi *badaa* and then lock that *gabra*, namely *me*, within your *mana* is not a ringing belittling of the practice. In fact, it speaks to the very nature of it."

"Aja, you are my guest—"

"I want to believe that because you have been kind to me, but how do I know I won't get comfortable, and then you dope me up and pass me on to your friends as sport."

"Because you're not locked in a cell being fed bread and water only to be released to do my chores, *that's* how!"

Aja laughed bitterly as she faced him again. "Another reminder of your power over me."

Anansi threw his large hands up into the air. "You infuriate me. You are the most stubborn feminine I have ever had the misfortune of being around."

"And did you feel this misfortune last night in your office?"

"Luckily then, you had a mouthful, and I didn't have to hear your complaining."

"Go to—"

"XR-2 transport Aja to her *diinqa* and lock her in it like the prisoner she craves to be," Anansi ordered, turning to look out the window with his hands behind his broad back.

The last thing he saw of her was her expression of aghast before she disappeared into thin air.

∞

Aja hated that Anansi could dismiss her from

his presence with nothing more than a voice command. A command she had no power to ignore or fight since his *mana* was programmed to fulfill his every whim.

Of course, he's the giiftiin.

When his *zwodriu* nearly scared her witless, and she jumped into his arms, her undoing came when she looked into his eyes. Something inside of her said, "Go for it. Have him."

And in her imagination, she did. Shamelessly. Wildly. Impulsively.

And it had been so good.

One look and a little back rub from him and she had dreamt of coming out of her clothing quicker than a finger snap. Come out of it? More like torn out of it.

She could hardly believe she was in the *mana* of the masculine first in line for the most important position of power in the entire galaxy.

Aja sighed as she flopped down onto the middle of the *qanddii* and tried to busy herself thinking of anything but Anansi. Anansi and his hurtful words. Anansi and his good loving. Anansi and his hospitality. Anansi and his power. Anansi and his hold over her freedom. Anansi. Anansi. Anansi.

In all honesty, she knew her situation here could be worse—much worse. She'd seen none of the ridicule and scorn of the Erisedian that Empaths had been taught since childhood. And he promised that he would free her. Further exploration had proven fruitless. There was no escape. All she could do at this point was wait and see.

She didn't like the thought of not being free to come and go as she pleased, but she shivered at the thought of being displayed at the *bwa kasuwa*.

Like Juuba.

Aja forced herself to think of better times—life back on Nede where things were simple. Growing their own food. Making their own clothes. Working together to build their own *goojjoos* and communities. Following their own rules and way of life. Living without ridicule or judgment.

But that simplicity had ultimately been their downfall against the Kordis. The Empaths had been in no way prepared to fight off the Kordi's with their technological advances. They never had a chance to win, and ultimately the Kordis slaughtered a huge portion of an entire race of people with ease.

Her family and countless friends were gone. Aja didn't even know if their bodies were buried with respect.

"I miss them so much," she whispered aloud as snapshots of precious moments that she'd shared with her family replayed in her mind.

Tears filled her eyes as the breath was squeezed from her chest by pain. She didn't want it to hurt. She didn't want to miss them so much that she sometimes wished she had died with them. She didn't want to feel so alone.

But what choice did she have when there was nothing she could do to bring them back.

Nothing at all.

∞

It was late at night. The window covers blocked off the constant rays of the *aduus*, and his *diinqa* was in total darkness. Silent. Peaceful.

Still, sleep eluded Anansi. He tossed and turned on the *qanddii*, kicking the *huccuu* covers from his body. With one strong arm, he swept the plush feathered sacs to the floor.

Suddenly the lights dimly lit up and Sasha his golden animated virtual reality lover appeared, naked and alluring as she knelt on the *qanddii* between his open legs and tried to take his flaccid member into her eager mouth.

"Sasha off," Anansi ordered roughly, glad when the animated beauty with the reality-defying, gilded body disappeared.

Nothing would satisfy him but to give in to his desire to check on Aja. *Is she still mad at me? Is she sleeping?*

A digital display of Aja's room appeared at the foot of the *qanddii*. Anansi sat up. His heart pounded like battle drums. The light from the picture was reflected on his handsome face. His chest ached to see her body curled into a tight ball in the center of her *qanddii*. His body stilled at the sound of her tears and the slight shake of her shoulders.

Anansi instantly flew into action and jumped his nude frame from the *qanddii*. He grabbed the *huccuu* pajama bottoms that appeared at the foot of the *qanddii*. He had barely jerked them up on his narrow hips when XR-2 transported him directly inside Aja's *diinqa*. The lights in her room powered up to a soft glow.

He paused for his eyes to readjust to the darkness before he moved towards her. The sound of her crying echoed, and for a moment Anansi felt he was intruding. He couldn't override his desire to hold her, comfort her, and shoulder some of her pain. "Aja," he called out softly.

"Go away, Anansi," was her muffled reply as she lay on her side with her back to him.

He came to stand beside her *qanddii* and crossed his arms over his chest to keep from reaching out for her. "XR-2 off," he ordered sternly.

The last thing he needed was XR-2 fulfilling his every wish—spoken and unspoken. Even an involuntary thought of seducing Aja would lead to a scene set for seduction.

"Okay let's try this again," Aja said, turning over to lie on her back and look up at him with red-rimmed eyes. "May I humbly request that I am left alone, *Giiftiin* Anansi?"

He ignored her sarcasm as his heart tugged at the evidence of her obvious sorrow. "Have I made things so unbearable for you here, Aja?" he asked softly, moving to sit down beside her and use his thumb to gently wipe away the tracks of her tears.

"Believe it or not there are things in my life that I miss even more than my freedom," she admitted even as her lips quivered with renewed despair.

Aja shut her eyes. Tears raced from beneath her closed lids and Anansi instantly lay beside her to draw her body to his, resting her head against his bare chest. Anansi felt warmed when she leaned her face into him. "Tell me what is making your cry," he requested huskily as he kissed the top of her head and tried to breathe through the surprising emotions squeezing his heart.

"My family was killed during the war. I miss them and my life on Nede so much," she admitted, her voice barely above a whisper.

Anansi nodded as he used his hands to massage her scalp. "Tell me about your family."

Aja was silent for a long time, and he assumed she wasn't going to speak at all.

"After twenty *baras* of *gaai'la*, my parents thought they would never have children and then came me," she began. "They adored me, and I felt nothing but loved and cherished by them, but I was lonely. Most families had three or more offspring. And for the longest time, it was just me...until my brother, Llor, was born six *baras* after me. Finally, I wasn't alone anymore."

Anansi frowned and held back his thoughts of how Erised was disease-free, and there were no medical issues that could not be addressed and defeated. He couldn't imagine an Erised feminine waiting for twenty baras to have a child. Nearly half a *jaarraa* ago, when the Empaths fled Planet Erised to set up their own colony on the planet they named Nede, they began their lives from scratch and were even further behind technologically than they had been on Erised. *Perhaps with the treaty and the Empaths joining the coalition, they could improve their quality of life.*

He considered his role in the deal but immediately pushed those thoughts away as he refocused on Aja's words.

"And now," she released a shaky breath. "Everyone and everything I cherished is gone. Now I am all alone."

Aja became quiet.

Anansi tilted his head up from one of the feather sacs to look down at her. Her eyes were distant and glossy as she stared at one of the curtain covered walls.

"Tell me about life on Nede," he requested, wanting to distract her.

Aja smiled a little, but it didn't reach her eyes. "Nede is—*was*—beautiful," she began.

He didn't miss the way her voice broke, and he squeezed her a bit tighter. As she began to tell him about her life, he knew her head and her heart was elsewhere. But he lay there, and he held her, comforting her as best as could as he listened to her memories.

VII

Aja stretched her body against the warmth and strength of Anansi. Although she knew it had to be early in the hours of the next day, the window covers continued to block the *aduu's* light from the room, and they lay entwined in the darkness. His body framed hers from behind. Her head rested in the crook of his arm as the smooth hairs of his chest lightly tickled her back as he breathed deeply in sleep. His other arm rested on her hip while their feet were entwined beneath the covers.

She didn't even remember falling asleep, but it had been one of her best rests since the war. She didn't know if it was the comfort of Anansi's arms or the pleasure she received from talking about her life back on Nede. It had been so good to remember the better times. For a few precious hours, she had forgotten the sadness and the pain.

For that, she was grateful for Anansi's ear and his arms. Last night he felt more like her friend or her mate than anything else. And she couldn't deny that there was chemistry between them that nearly burst into flames whenever they were within feet of each other.

Should I trust him? Aja wondered as Anansi snuggled closer to her in his sleep. *And why does it feel so right lying in this qanddii beside him?*

Aja closed her eyes and soon felt herself fall back asleep.

She awakened hours later with a jolt. She was surprised to find she was alone. She gave in to the urge to roll over onto the feather sac to deeply inhale his warm spicy scent. She admonished herself, pushing the pillow and memories of his warmth away.

"*Nagaya*, Aja of Nede."

Aja frowned as Anansi's voice echoed in the *diinqa*. She sat up, pulling her hair back from her face. "*Nagaya*," she answered, wondering if he was looking at her via surveillance and hating that she cared.

"Would you like to eat in your room or do you care to join me today?"

"Do I have a choice?" she asked, searching for her anger towards him.

She jumped in surprise when he suddenly appeared in her room. He was dressed in comfortable a short-sleeved brown shirt and pants that only emphasized his warrior good looks. His locs were loose and accentuated his high cheekbones and deep-set black eyes.

"*Giiftiin*, you say I'm your guest, but you pop in and out of my *diinqa* at your whim. May I request that you knock or ask my permission to enter?"

Anansi bowed his head slightly. "If you wish. But there is nothing about you that I haven't seen."

Aja flushed with warmth. Had it only been two days since they coupled like it was the very last moments either would share alive? "Neither of us can deny this chemistry between us, but I think sex will only complicate things. So being platonic is best."

Anansi's black eyes were on her as she rose from the *qanddii*. "Any other requests?"

She bit back a smile. "That's the only request I have that I *think* you will grant me."

As he grinned his teeth flashed against his bronze skin, making her heart flutter. "You're very smart."

"I do have some questions."

"Ask them."

"Will you answer them?"

"Depends."

The curtain swung open as Aja walked towards the *kutaa dhiqannaa*. The floor lit her path to the *dhiqata*. "How does it work?" she asked.

"Just step inside *after* you undress," Anansi said. "Keep your eyes and mouth closed."

Aja nodded her head, as she walked back into the *diinqa* to rejoin him. She waved her hand for him to be seated.

Anansi sat on the edge of her *qanddii* with his

hands folded in the air between his legs

"Ready?" she asked, amazed that she felt playful and flirty.

"For whatever you have for me."

She cocked her brow at his possible double meaning and then ignored it, even as he laughed. "You are the *Giiftiin*, but I don't see any guards or servants. There is nothing but you and your precious XR-2. Do you always live here alone?"

"Planning to execute me in my sleep?" he asked, tilting his head to the side a little as he looked up at her.

Her eyes met his. *I couldn't kill him if I wanted to*, she admitted to herself as she studied him. "I thought I was asking the questions?"

"XR-2 is all the servant and guard I need," Anansi said. "I have a suite at my parent's *mana*, and when I stay there, I get all the grandeur I can stand. I'm hardly here enough to hire a staff. Plus, I like my privacy. My little *mana* suits me just fine."

"Little?" Aja balked.

Anansi said nothing, although the twinkle in his limitless eyes revealed his amusement.

"You say there is an imminent end to the war and a treaty to be signed that will free the rest of my people and me?" she asked, as she looked down at his striking face. It suddenly became guarded.

"True."

"I don't know whether to hate you for keeping me here or be grateful for the protection and the hospitality you offer...*except* when you're banishing me to this *diinqa*," Aja admitted, accepting the conflicted feelings creating turmoil within her.

"Then do neither," he offered. "I do not want you to hate me, Aja."

She looked away from him, unable to bear the intensity in those eyes. *And I can't seem to hate you, even though I want to*, she thought, before turning to the closet. The curtain swung open when she neared. "Whose clothes are these?"

"The clothes are new and never worn," he said.

Aja turned slightly to eye him over her

shoulder. "And?"

Anansi's eyes shifted a bit, before refocusing on her. "And they are yours to have."

Aja faced him completely. "Who were they *meant* for?" she asked.

"A friend of mine who is a clothier," he offered, rising to his feet.

Aja released a mocking grunt as she selected an outfit. With a neutral expression, she reentered the *kutaa dhiqannaa*. "I have no more questions...for now."

Anansi said nothing.

Aja was confused by the jealousy burning her gut as she stripped bare. Sunlight filtered through the sheer draperies and warmed her body as she opened the door to the *dhiqata*. She peeked her head inside, before slowly stepping in.

She was nervous. There was no denying it. With the way Anansi could appear and disappear throughout the *mana* or call on XR-2 to give him his every desire, she had no idea what was about to happen. Here on Planet Erised, she was out of her element.

Aja squeezed her eyes and mouth closed as the door automatically closed, sealing her inside. She reached up and twisted her long hair into a loose topknot. Within moments, steam filled the chamber. She felt it swirl around her body and coat her skin like sweat.

Aja had to admit that it felt invigorating, and soon she tilted her head back and relaxed her nude body, allowing herself to enjoy yet another little piece of Anansi's advanced world.

She felt regret when the steam disappeared, and the door opened. By the time she stepped out of it, her skin was moisture free leaving no need for a drying cloth. She raised her arm to her nose to smell it. There was no scent at all. She pulled a few loose tendrils of hair from her top knot and sniffed them as well. It also was devoid of any smell.

Aja thought of the exertion needed to retrieve water on Nede and how a device like the *dhiqata* would alleviate a lot of that.

But then the joys of a warm bath would be missed.

On Nede after a hard day's work, a hot bath was a luxury.

Aja still felt in need of a drying cloth and began looking behind the curtains. She jumped in surprise when another feminine looked back at her.

She was sure she was in the *kutaa dhiqannaa* alone. Was this another of the tricks of Anansi's *mana*?

"*Nagaya*," she said, her tone unsure.

Tilting her head to the side, Aja leaned in closer. And then closer.

As did the other feminine.

A looking glass?

It's me.

Her heart raced. The *abuturoos* had spoken of such, but Aja had never seen one for herself. *I've never truthfully seen myself.*

Aja smiled a bit as she stepped closer to her reflection. Her gold-flecked eyes quickly took in everything. Some things she recognized. Her brown streaked hair and her nude frame. Other things were new to her. Her gold-flecked honey eyes and the slight sprinkling of tiny brown spots at the top of her cheeks.

She stroked the flat pale metallic gold moles on her chin and forehead that were characteristic of her people. Her eyes saddened. Would she ever see them light again with the use of Empath powers?

She turned from her reflection and continued her search and found shelves loaded with folded drying cloths. She clutched one in her fist and stroked it with her thumb. *It's so soft.*

Aja wrapped one around her body, remembering the rough texture of the woven tunics worn on Nede. It would take a hundred washings against rocks to finally soften the material.

When she left the cleansing room, she was surprised to find Anansi still in her *diinqa*. He stood by the far wall, the hangings floated to the side as he looked out the window. She allowed herself to take in his profile. He was magnificent.

"Doesn't someone of your power and prominence have more to do than staring out a window?" she asked, moving to the closet.

He looked at her over his broad shoulder. His black eyes took in the cloth wrapped around her shapely frame. "I was just thinking how beautiful my planet—"

"*Your* planet?" she teased.

Anansi smiled. "You know what I mean."

"Yes, oh great *Giiftiin* Anansi Nyame, heir to the throne of Erised, I know exactly what you mean," she quipped.

He stepped back from the window and the curtain floated close. "Do you find humor in everything, Aja?"

"Sometimes you make yourself laugh to keep from crying, my *Giiftiin*," she said with uncomfortable honesty, before selecting a pale-yellow outfit.

Aja turned and walked into the *kutaa dhiqannaa* to maneuver her curves into the form-fitting jumpsuit. She moved over to the curtain shielding the looking glass. It swayed to the right, and she saw her reflection. Her eyes widened. *I might as well be naked.*

The one-piece garment fit like second skin and revealed her hard nipples, full breasts, and the warm "vee" atop her thighs. There was no way Anansi would not be affected by it all.

Aja released her hair, raking her slender fingers through the waves before pulling the long ends forward over her shoulders to cover her breasts as best she could.

She walked back into the *diinqa*. "Your friend has interesting taste, my *giiftiin*," she said, casting him a sly look.

He crossed the room to tower over her.

Aja's entire body felt electrified. She bit her full bottom lip to keep from gasping in awareness of him.

"If I promise to buy you a whole new wardrobe will you promise to call me Anansi?" he asked, his voice deep and low.

She trembled. The distance between them was almost nothing as she studied him with her eyes. "Are you sure you what to pass up on seeing me in this ensemble?" she asked.

Anansi's black eyes smoldered. "Are you sure you want to stick to the no-sex rule?" he asked thickly, pushing his hands into his pants pocket.

Aja licked suddenly dry lips. "Positive," she lied.

"Then the jumpsuits *have* to go."

They stood there. Aja looked up at him. Anansi looked down at her. Their eyes were locked. Time stood still. Chemistry was ablaze. Anticipation and want pressed between them.

Aja released a shaky breath and looked away first. "I'm hungry," she said softly, swallowing over a lump in her throat as she walked to the entrance.

"For?" he asked, his tone serious.

She looked back to find his eyes watching the movement of her buttocks in the shiny, clingy material. She warmed. "Food," she lied.

His eyes shifted up to lock on her.

She saw his disbelief in the black inky depths of his eyes.

"Nourishment won't feed the hunger I have," he warned, pointedly directing his eyes down to his thick erection pressed intimately against the soft *huccuu* of his pants.

Aja turned from him and closed her eyes as she released a long breath through pursed lips. He proclaimed to be her protector, but who would protect her from her desire of him?

"XR-2," Anansi said.

Aja blinked.

They were transported to the dining hall. The large metal table was already set, and the *aduus* brightly shone through the windows casting the room and all its grandeur in warm light.

"What do you have against walking?" she asked,

with an arched brow.

Anansi chuckled, placing a hand on the small of her back to guide her to a seat.

Aja tried to hide her frown as Anansi held her chair for her.

Bowls of fresh *inaba* and nuts awaited them.

"Do you prefer something else?" he asked walking to the other end of the table to take his seat across from her.

"On Nede our work days are long, and sometimes we don't have a midday meal, so I'm used to starting the day with a large one," she explained.

Anansi cast a charming smile. "You can have whatever you wish, but I am very careful about what I eat."

Aja used her fingers to pick up the sticky sweet fruit of the deepest shade of red. "What for?" she asked.

"I used to be overweight," he admitted before taking a swallow from his cup of tea.

Aja checked her surprise as she raised her own cup. "Here's to losing it in all the right places."

"You're tempting me, Aja," he told her, playfully scolding.

"Me? A temptress?" she asked innocently.

"Yes, and you're playing with fire," Anansi warned as he leveled those eyes on her.

"Should I be afraid?" she asked, before sucking the juice from the *inaba*.

Anansi tossed a few nuts into his mouth and chewed as he leaned back in his chair. "Only if you want to continue avoiding having me deep inside you. *But* if you keep teasing me I'm going to give you just what you are looking for."

Aja pressed her thighs together under the table as she felt the room warm considerably. "You tempt me at times as well, Anansi," she admitted.

"Not intentionally."

"I feel guilty for wanting you," she told him, her eyes meeting his. "But sometimes you make me forget it all. And the break from it is good. Selfish...but needed."

They fell silent and looked away from each other, focusing on their meal.

"Are you afraid of me, Aja of Nede?" he asked suddenly.

She met his eyes again and shook her head slightly. "No," she confessed. "I may discover I'm a fool but you have been nothing but good to me, Anansi of Erised, and in a different time I might just give you what *you're* looking for."

Anansi cleared his throat and leaned forward to take a deep sip from his cup.

Aja bit back a smile.

∞

Oduda stretched her bare frame in the center of the *qanddii*. She lifted her bald head, surprised to find she was alone. Nothing but the scent of Huung and their sex surrounded her.

Still yawning, she sat up and reached behind the headboard to push a button. As she leisurely settled herself amongst the many luxurious feather sacs adorning her *qanddii*, the wall above the fireplace lowered revealing a second wall of nothing but *komputaras*. Each one showed the activity of her servants and guards. Small undetectable cameras were all over her mana, and also unknowingly followed each one of her personal staff and security twenty-four hours a day, never leaving the presence of their assigned target.

Her violet eyes widened a bit at the heated sight of one of her guards pumping away between the open thighs of one of her servants, Kinye, against the wall of a small clothing chamber. They thought they were hiding from her eyes. "Fools," she muttered even as her lips pursed when the guard's buttocks began to quiver with each upward thrust as he sucked deeply at the ample breasts spilling over the top of her nightgown. They knew she didn't allow the mating of her servants and guards...unless she was a part of the fun.

Deciding to deal with them later her eyes shifted from *komputara* to *komputara*. Servants sleeping. The cold *cabbii* covered grounds outside were quiet and undisturbed.

Her brows rose slightly as she recognized the broadness of Huung's back on the next display. "Increase number five," she ordered. The image magnified into one large image across all the displays. Her eyes hardened at the sight of Huung sweaty and grunting as her usually humble, quiet, and skittish personal servant, Leetoo, was on her knees hungrily sucking the tip of his long erection.

"Badaa!" Oduda swore, jerking up in her *qanddii* as she balled one of her hands up into a fist that pressed her sharp nails into the flesh of her palm.

With each suck of Leetoo's lips to his dick, Oduda's anger steeped. With each of Huung's groans and the tightening of his square buttocks, Oduda's jealousy soared. She didn't love him or even desire him beyond the time he was scheduled to be on Kordi, but she didn't want to share him. It was a trait she had never acquired. She got what she wanted when she wanted it. Always.

With one last glance at her lover and her servant's sex play on the display, Oduda took several calming breaths and smoothed her quivering hands over her scalp to soothe herself. For Huung to leave her *qanddii* to find pleasure with another feminine? For her servant to dare betray her?

She screamed until the back of her throat ached.

"Think," she muttered, climbing from the *qanddii* and reaching for her sheer robe to pull on. The ends flew up around her thighs each time she turned and paced the floor.

Huung's shuddering moans filled her *diinqa*.

Oduda strode to her table next to her *qanddii* and reached in the drawer to extract a small black case. She blew a stream of her breath into the tiny hole atop it to identify herself. It opened automatically to reveal five metal rods ready to imbue a body with drugs she fashioned herself.

She picked up the third bar and closed the case.

Like the rest, it was no larger than her palm. Her hate-filled eyes locked on the servant as she pressed a buzzer connected to an implant in Leetoo's nape. She smiled snidely as Leetoo jumped back from Huung guiltily. His member bobbed from the sudden movement as Leetoo scrambled to her feet and wiped her moist mouth and chin with her hands.

"Oh, isn't that sweet," Oduda snapped as she watched them share a brief kiss before Leetoo scrambled from the room.

She pressed another buzzer to summon the guards on duty.

Oduda watched as the supposedly obedient servant walked in bowing to her. "Rise," she ordered harshly, walking forward to roughly grab Leetoo's chin in her hand.

She forced the servant to look to the *komputaras* and enjoyed the fear fast rising in her eyes as the monitors reflected Huung.

The guards entered the room, and Oduda motioned for them to detain Leetoo. "Since you love dick so much let's see if you can take endless hours on your back and your knees working on Planet Whoor."

The servant's eyes filled with fright and horror at her fate of life on the dark and dingy lawless planet that serviced the worst of the worst of the galaxy. "No? *Giiftiin* Oduda, *please* forgive me."

Oduda slapped her soundly twice, silencing her words and drawing blood from her lip.

"Drop her in the center of Planet Whoor," she ordered, before turning away from the guards carrying Leetoo away, her frantic cries echoing.

Oduda looked up at Huung peeking out of the thin wooden door of Leetoo's little *diinqa* before easing into the hall. "You're next," she mouthed, stroking the silver rod. With one press of it to his neck, it would draw the one drop of blood needed to mix with the brew inside. It would ensure that he delivered every bit of his twelve inches of hard goodness to her and no one else—even once he returned to his home planet.

The camera she assigned to him showed his movements throughout the *mana*. She fingered the rod as her anger-filled eyes watched him make his way back to her.

∞

Anansi had been gone all day, and Aja had to admit that she missed his company. Although her surroundings were far more lavish than the hole where Oduda had stuck her, she still felt alone and lonely. Her thoughts and worries were constant. She couldn't erase the images of her family's death or the vivid memory of Juuba on sale as a *gabra*.

With Erised having nearly constant daylight, she missed the Nede nights were the ebon sky would be overflowing with *urjiis*. When she was small, she used to lie on the roof of their *goojjoo* and foolishly try to count them. Once she was full-grown, she found nothing more arousing than mating on soft grass as the *urjiis* lit her sexual passion.

Anansi said that the Erised nightfall was spectacular. Aja didn't know if it truly was extraordinary or if the Erisedians thought so because they only saw it nine times per bara.

She sighed. She was bored. Sitting around wishing for Anansi's return was futile.

The Erisedians and the Empaths shared the same language, but Aja decided it was not the time to read from his extensive library. She left her *diinqa* and made her way to the *zwodriu*.

"Okay, here goes," she said, wiping her hands on the legs of the bodysuit. "Fight simulator. Level one. Power on."

She struck a fight position and steeled herself.

Nothing happened.

She frowned. "Fight simulator. Level one. Power on," she repeated with a louder tone.

Still nothing.

Like XR-2 the *zwodriu* would not follow her command.

"Anansi," she snapped.

"Yes."

She whirled around. Anansi stood behind her. She squinted as she studied him. He smiled. It looked like him and sounded like him, but she wasn't quite sure it was him. She moved close to him and reached to touch his chest. Her hand slid right through him.

She gasped and jumped back from him.

Anansi held up both hands. "Aja, it's okay. It's a holograph."

She dropped her head in her hand as she breathed deeply. "Another of your technological advances?' she asked, cutting him a side glance.

"Yes," he agreed.

"You're not even in the *mana* are you?" she asked.

He shook his head.

"But you can see and hear everything," she said, her voice resigned.

"Yes."

She fell silent. Then her exploration of Anansi's mana in search of escape was not her secret.

"Aja—"

She held up her hand to stop him. "Can I use this?" she asked, waving her hand around the room.

"XR-2 allow Aja use of the *zwodriu*," he ordered.

"Thank you," she said begrudgingly.

His image disappeared.

Aja released a heavy breath. "Fight simulator. Level one. Power on," she said.

The black floor and walls transformed to the lavender skies and she stood on a cloud. She took a fighting stance.

A six-foot feminine with white scaly skin with a face made up of nothing more than a lone eye on her broad chin and a thin ponytail atop her head came running towards Aja. The scowl on her face was enough. Add on biceps that were bigger than Anansi's, and Aja swallowed the lump of fear in her throat. Adrenaline sent her heart racing.

"Wow this is so real she even smells as terrible as she looks," Aja said aloud as she ducked the arm swung at her and came up with an uppercut to her opponent's rock-hard belly.

She heard applause and turned her head to see Anansi standing amongst the clouds watching them. The real Anansi. There was a warmth in his eyes that was missing from the holograph.

Seconds later something connected with her chin and she went floating head over heels into the distance, landing on a cloud. Her adversary came running at full-speed towards her, her large feet breaking up the puff of clouds into dust.

"Fight simulator, pause," Anansi ordered.

Aja's opponent froze with her foot in mid-air just as she was about to level a roundhouse kick to the side of Aja's head. "Thank you," she sighed, rubbing her bruised jaw just as Anansi came to stand above her. "You never said the blows felt real."

He knelt down beside her on the cloud. "As soon as the simulator is powered off, the effects of the blows immediately disappear."

Aja frowned as she sat up. "Well power off."

The simulator scene vanished, and the *zwodriu* was back to its normal state. The pain in her jaw immediately disappeared.

Anansi laughed as he rose and held out his hand to help her up. "I shouldn't have distracted you," he admitted.

Aja slid her hand in his and allowed him to tug her to her feet. "Next time I won't be caught off guard," she said but then immediately regretted the words. There was no reason she should be planning for any type of future here at his *mana*.

"Would you like to try again?" he asked.

Aja shook her head and remained silent as she freed her hand from his. Her hand still tingled from his touch. Aja tried to ignore the chemistry that surged between them.

They stood there for a few awkward moments.

"Have you eaten?" he asked.

"You already know the answer to that," she chided.

"I am just trying to look out for you," he

explained. "The *mana* can be tricky for someone not accustomed to our advances."

"And will I be here long enough to get accustomed?" Aja asked, looking up at him in question.

"For as long I need to protect you."

She gave him a sad smile before she turned and walked out to the entrance of the *zwodriu*. "I am appreciative of your hospitality, *Giiftiin*," she said over her shoulder.

"You promised to call me Anansi," he called over to her retreating figure.

Aja stopped. "You promised me less revealing clothing," she countered.

He remained quiet.

She turned.

The *zwodriu* was empty. Anansi was gone.

Aja made her way to her *diinqa*. She was surprised to find Anansi awaiting her with a beautiful feminine draped in a flowing gown of silver. "*Giiftiin*?" she asked in question as she eyed the feminine, surprised by the jealousy that burned her gut.

Another gabra *gift?*

"Anansi," he corrected as he came over to stand beside her. "This is an animated model who will display outfits for you. Just tap the one you want and swipe to the next."

Aja looked up at him in surprise, before walking over to the model. She quickly noted that she was able to detect the real Anansi from his life-like holographic image, but wasn't able to do so for the model.

"XR-2 has taken your measurement and sent them to the clothier," Anansi said, coming to stand before her.

"Your *friend*?" Aja asked, with an impish smile.

"No."

She chuckled as she circled the image. Her eyes widened when she was able to view the back of the dress on as well. "This is too much. I would never be able to wear this on Nede," she said.

"I'm sure there's simpler clothing as well," he said. "Chose whatever you like."

Aja glanced back at him. "Thank you, *Anansi*," she stressed.

He nodded before he walked away.

Aja turned to watch him leave, her eyes taking in the broad square set of his shoulders and the hardness of his buttocks. That gentle sway of locs as he moved. His long stride that spoke to his confidence and strength.

And when he was gone from her sight she felt the loss of his presence. Her regret was intense.

Sighing, she recalled her dream when Anansi had filled her with his heat. She sighed softly, shaking her head and fanning herself at how badly she wanted to...to...

Touch him.

Feel him.

Kiss him.

Taste him.

Suck him.

Lick him.

Ride him. Fast and hard. Then slow and easy.

She wanted to feel his clever tongue on her nipples and then her clit—in no particular order.

She wanted to feel every hard and throbbing inch pushed and stroked against her walls until his dick was shiny with her juices.

She wanted to make him scream her name.

She wanted to sex him so deliciously that his mouth twisted as he climaxed.

And then she wanted to squeeze the last of his cum from him with her walls as she lay on his sweaty chest praying she didn't have a heart attack.

"Whooooo," she sighed again, pressing her thighs together and brought her hands up to her own breasts.

Anansi's mana was massive in size. But when it came to the underlying tension between them—which they were supposed to ignore and deny—the place felt as small and steamy as a *dhiqata*.

∞

Anansi's eyes pierced the image as he watched the emotions flitter across Aja's beautiful face—a face that at that moment was even more alluring and tempting because of the emotions he could clearly define. Lust. Desire. Want. Frustration. *Sexual* frustration.

His dick ached as it rose between his thighs, poking through the opening in his drying cloth to lightly tap against the underside of his desk as it pulsed. He felt a tremble race over his body. Although his form was nearly nude and he was fresh from his *dhiqata*, he knew the chill was about nothing more than how badly he wanted to be with Aja. *On* Aja. *In* Aja.

"*Whooooo.*"

He leaned back in his chair and wiped his mouth with his hand as Aja's voice echoed in his office. When her hands slid up to squeeze and tease her own nipples through the thin material of her jumpsuit, he jumped to his feet sending his chair flying backward.

Anansi ended his surveillance of her and walked away from his desk, trying to come up with a million excuses why he shouldn't go to her and give her what they both understandably wanted. Of course, there was his pending lifelong *gaa'ila* to Oduda. Their *qaadhimamuu* had not been officially announced, and he had no real obligation to a feminine he'd once met in passing, but it wouldn't be fair to Aja to start something he knew he could not finish. For the good of The Council, the coalition, and the peace treaty, he would join for life with Oduda.

Additionally, he couldn't ignore the fact that, whether he liked it not, Aja was a *gabra* that he now owned.

Or that her desire for him was only topped by the disdain for the ruling Jeynas of Planet Erised was bred in her.

Or that until her freedom was secure, he should offer her nothing more than his protection and accommodation—not long, hot nights in his *qanddii*.

Long, hot, sweaty, steamy, down-and-dirty nights.

'I am hungry for her,' he admitted, his face pensive.

His virtual reality concubine, Sasha, was built and programmed to satisfy his every sexual appetite. Nothing was off limits, but he had to admit that the chemistry with Aja had far surpassed his trysts with Sasha.

Anansi's thick dick poked through the drying cloth around his waist, leading him as he paced the length of his office with his hands on his hips. He stopped and jumped up and down a bit, trying to shake off his desire to have Aja. He paced some more. Jumped some more. He took a fighter stance and pummeled the air with his fists, trying to put box his dick into submission.

His erection was strong, long, and hard as ever.

He swore, looking down at his heated length. The tip seemed to wink at him playfully.

Or was it mockingly?

Not even bothering to turn on XR-2, Anansi strode out of his office and straight into his *diinqa*. Not once did he pause in his long strides until he was inside the *dhiqata*. The door sealed behind him. "Cold water," he ordered, trying hard not to think of Aja in her *diinqa* pleasuring herself.

Her legs spread wide.

Her back arched.

Her fingers on her clit.

Her cries of passion filling the air as she climaxed.

The first spray of water shocked him a bit, but it did the job in defeating the hardness. He leaned forward and pressed his head against the glass, breathing a sigh of relief.

VII

Anansi was avoiding her.

Her meals were prepared like clockwork with XR-2 announcing their availability in the dining room. But for the last six meals, she had eaten alone.

He'd given her the space she craved, and now she regretted asking it of him.

Perhaps he is with his friend?

Thoughts like that plagued her often. Jealousy was unfamiliar to her.

Until Anansi.

Aja yawned a little as she rose from her spot on the floor of the room with the transparent walls. It was the closest she could feel to being outdoors, and she missed the feel of the *aduu* backed packed dirt under her bare feet or the cushion of grass as she lay on her back and stared at the sky.

Will I ever see Nede again?

As a *xiyyaara* flew through the sky in the distance, Aja rose to her bare feet and walked out of the room. She paused to look down the long curving hall leading to Anansi's diinqa. She'd seen every bit of his mana except his private space.

She was curious about where he spent so much of him time.

I am curious about Anansi—everything about him if I'm honest.

As she took slow steps down the hall, she reached out and touched the wall. Her steps paused when her handprint was illuminated. She frowned a bit as she removed her hand and continued on until she stood before the door.

"What am I doing?" Aja asked herself, turning to walk away. She made it just a few steps before she stopped and looked over her shoulder.

On the other side of that massive metal door awaited pleasure. *Extos* or no *extos*, she could not forget the passion they shared in his office the first day of her unexpected arrival.

Everything about Anansi Nyame did something to her: the handsome face, the long lashes framing those black eyes, the bronze caramel of his skin, and the long and thin locs that made him even more striking. And that body. His towering eight-foot height with a sculpted physique. Those broad shoulders and toned arms. His large hands with fingers that were made to touch a feminine and make his presence known. His buttocks provided just enough cushion to enjoy slapping them during sex play. And that dick. That thick, long, muscle that hung from his body like a third leg and had a wicked curve, smooth round tip, and veins that were engorged when hard. His member was dark in color, like *chollolaattaa*, and was just as tasty.

Aja moaned a little as she bit her bottom lip and briefly cut her eyes up to the 20-foot ceiling of the hallway before she looked back towards his door.

She had no doubt in her mind that all she had to do was stroll in there and make a move. Not even a big, bold move, just something as simple as climbing into Anansi's *qanddii* and he would be on her—and in her—quicker than she could blink an eye.

She should hate him, but she didn't.

She vowed to kill him, but she wouldn't.

She wasn't supposed to trust him, but she did.

She wasn't supposed to like him and enjoy his company, but she did.

She wasn't supposed to want an Erised, but she did.

She wasn't supposed to be outside his room dreaming of sexing him until he would need an entire day in *qanddii* to recuperate, but here she was.

Aja had no pretense of a serious relationship. She hoped to return to Nede one day, and he would go on with his life here on Erised. It was very possible she would never see him again once she left. But that was then, and this was now.

Aja walked back to his door.

Here she was.

She took one deep breath and stepped closer. The doors opened, and she stepped into Anansi's space for the very first time since she'd arrived. She looked around at his private chambers. The entire room was luxuriously decorated in black. Her feet nearly disappeared among the plush fur rugs covering his floors. The ceiling was domed and high enough to fit an entire second level. Her eyes shifted to his *qanddii* and memories of their heated moments on the floating apparatus made her flush with warmth.

Aja frowned in curiosity at the large circular glass chamber in the corner. She started towards it but paused at a noise from behind her. It came from beyond an expansive entry into what she assumed was his *kutaa dhiqannaa*. She turned in that direction and paused at the entrance.

Anansi was in his *dhiqata*. Nude.

The breath she released was shaky. Her pulse raced.

She swallowed over a lump in her throat as her eyes took in the sight of him as the steam swirled around his naked form.

With her eyes locked on his figure, Aja slowly undressed of the red bralette and short skirt she wore to walk straight to the *dhiqata*. She pulled the door open, and the steam escaped, surrounding her and teasing her body as Anansi turned to look down at her in surprise.

Aja felt his eyes take in her nude form and she smiled as his dick hardened before her very eyes. "Here I am, Anansi," she whispered huskily before she stepped into the *dhiqata* and closed the door. It sealed.

Anansi seemed in a daze as he watched the steam coat her body. "Aja, we can't—"

"Yes. Yes, we can and we will. Right now," she told him, taking one step forward in the small space to press the length of her body to his as she rose up on her toes to dip her head and stroke his hard nipple with her agile tongue.

She suckled the nipple deeper. He shivered.

She drew her teeth across it. He moaned.

She blew on it. He gasped hotly.

Aja leaned back a bit to look up at him. "I can't resist you any longer. I...I...want this so...so badly."

Anansi brought his hands up to deeply grasp Aja's fleshy buttocks, massaging the cheeks as his eyes bore into hers. "I want it just as bad as you," he admitted, his heart thundering in his chest as Aja traced her hands up the sides of his strong muscled legs, to his arms, then his shoulders and his neck to lightly grasp his face. "I can't make you any promises, Aja."

She hotly licked at Anansi's chest. "And I'm not asking for any. This is what it is, and nothing more."

He lifted her body up with ease and pressed her lower body against his hard-to-miss erection as she wrapped her legs around his waist. He shook his head for clarity as Aja leaned back just a bit to rub her thick and taut nipples lightly against his chest as the steam coated the valley of her breasts. "Aja," he whispered thickly, using one strong hand to her nape to jerk her closer to him.

She wrapped her arms around his neck and buried her face in his neck to suckle him. His pounding pulse beat against her lips. It matched her own.

He stepped into the clouds of steam that filled the *dhiqata* and pressed her back and buttocks to the wall. "This could go on all night long," he warned, before burying his face in the valley of her full heaving breasts.

"I'm up for it...if you are." Aja lifted her hands above her head, sighing and trembling as Anansi traced a path with his tongue to one of her taut and thick nipples. He circled it slowly with a deep guttural moan as Aja brought her hands down to hold her breasts for him.

He suckled the nipple deeper. She shivered.

He drew her teeth across it. She moaned.

He blew on it. She gasped hotly.

Aja gasped and arched her back as Anansi hands replaced her own to hold her breasts together as he sucked, licked and circled both her nipples. "Yes. Oh yes," she sighed. "Yeeeeessssssssssssss."

Her words, her moans, her shivers and her hands on his body made Anansi suck harder. He had to fight the natural urge to push his dick up inside the tight, moist core he knew existed.

This night wasn't about rushing. If it was the only one they were to share together, then he wanted to savor every single moment so that they would both remember it long after they went their separate ways.

Aja slid down to stand on her feet and pressed Anansi back against the wall as she slowly lowered to her knees. Through the fog of steam, her mouth sought and easily found his hard dick. She closed her eyes with a moan as her tongue circled the smooth tip before her lips sucked him deeply.

Anansi pressed his buttocks to the wall of the *dhiqata* and arched his back as he shivered uncontrollably. The steam blocked Aja from his view, but there was no doubt of her actions as she licked a wet trail from the base of his dick up to the tip to suckle twice before working her way back down again. Back up again. Suck. Suck. Back down again. Suck. Suck. Slowly and methodically she offered her own tribute to his dick until every inch of him knew her tongue well.

"Aah," he cried out, as she sucked him deep into her wet mouth, the thick swirls of soothing steam began to evaporate as the drying cycle started. He was grateful because he wanted to see his hardness surrounded by her lips.

Aja moaned deeply as she worked her mouth and tongue rapidly up and down his shaft, taking in as much of the thick inches as she could while she squatted before him. Her nipples ached as her breasts bobbed against her chest with each motion of her head and neck.

She felt her womanhood moisten in desire and shifted her free hand down to play in the wet folds between her thick thighs. She sought and found her swollen clit, lightly stroking it and jerking at the feel of her hand against the ultra-sensitive flesh.

Anansi's dick hardened as he felt it throb and his nut surged to the tip. "I'm...gonna...cum," he murmured his voice a mixture of excitement and regret.

Aja released him with one final kiss to the tip before she rose. "You're not getting *off* that easy."

The door to the *dhiqata* unsealed. As soon as it swung open, Anansi carried Aja out of it and pressed their bodies down onto one of the fur rugs covering the floor. Anxious, he lowered his body between her open legs until his face was just above her wet core.

"Open your legs wide," he ordered her gruffly, his bated breath fanning against the moist lips of her womanhood.

Aja did so with one swift movement of her legs and arch of her back. "Hungry?" she asked saucily with an arch of her brow as she raised her head from the floor to look down the length of her body at him.

"Feed me," he whispered, cutting his black eyes up to lock on her face.

Aja released a soft moan and used her hands to expose her throbbing clit to him, anxious for him to taste her. Please her.

Anansi inhaled deeply of her unique feminine scent with a guttural moan before he pressed an intimate kiss to the fleshy bud before he sucked it deeply between his pursed lips. His dick jumped as Aja's hips flexed up against his face.

With deliberate slowness, Anansi sucked the bud into his mouth in a one-two motion that made his chin moist from her juices. Aja squirmed like she wanted to back away from him, but Anansi locked his arms around her thighs keeping her in place as he kept up his wicked one-two motion.

Her entire body tingled in pleasure as she gasped and pulled at her own hair. Her breathing became ragged, uneven, and anxious. Sweat coated her body as she bit her bottom lip. There was no denying the warm prickling of her feet, the flutter of her heart or the pulsing of her clit. This was white-hot passion. It was better than the high from *qoricha*. Aja was intoxicated. "Yes, Anansi, I need this," she moaned as the first waves of her climax exploded in her core, sending a rush of pure adrenaline to her heart, tapping into the pleasure center of her brain, bringing her renewed life.

Anansi felt the first of her sweet release coat his tongue, and he deepened his sucking motion so much that her buttocks lifted and then lightly hit the floor with each of his tongue's thrusts. He wanted more. He was thirsty for it and eager to please her. He moaned as her scent rose in the air around him. He shivered as he felt each wave and convulsion rack her body. He cut his eyes up to see the dazed glassiness of her eyes as her mouth gaped open.

"Ooooooohhhhhhhhhhhh," Aja exhaled, sure he was going to push her into madness. He was relentless.

In one coordinated movement, Anansi shifted from laying between her quivering thighs to sitting between them. His dick was so hard for her that it ached. There was only one way to ease it. He grabbed legs to jerk her body closer to him, before lifting her up by her waist. He felt her weakness, but he wasn't done with her.

As she continued to tremble and whimper from her release, her head on his shoulder, Anansi eased her hips down, sliding his dick up into her core. She fit him like a glove. Tightly. Wetly. Perfectly.

They both cried out roughly.

Aja leaned back to grab his face and lick his mouth as she stared into his ebony eyes. "I feel you. I feel you against my walls. Pressing against me. Filling me. Anansi, I *feel* all of you," she whispered thickly into his open and panting mouth.

Anansi tilted his chin up to capture her mouth with his own for a brief kiss before pressing his head against her luscious brown globes as he felt his dick literally throb against her walls. "Don't move," he begged, his restraint almost broken as he felt her core hold and then release him. Over and over. In sync with her pulse.

Anansi breathed slowly, fighting for composure so that he didn't cum an inexperienced masculine who couldn't control his seed.

Aja dropped her forehead to his before she entwined her slender fingers in his locs. She planted a dozen or more kisses to his faces before her lips landed on his. They moaned in unison as they opened their mouths and deepened the kiss, their tongues slowly dancing in that small heated space between them. Aja offered him her tongue as she felt his large hands come up her smooth back, one lightly grasping her nape beneath her blanket of hair. She grunted as she tugged at his locs and gently bite his bottom lip. "Ready?" she asked him.

Anansi shook his head and tasted her sweet mouth. "Not yet," he said.

With effort, Anansi rose to his feet with Aja's body locked securely against his with one strong arm. "XR-2 on," he ordered as he walked out of the *kutaa dhiqannaa*.

His *qanddii* already awaited them, hovering in the air.

They fell forward together onto it. Slowly it rose towards the ceiling.

Aja sighed at being sandwiched between the hardness of Anansi's body and the softness of his *qanddii*. "Touch me," she begged unevenly. "Please, Anansi."

He shifted his body to the left of her, lying on his side to lift her leg over his hip. He looked down into her face as he traced a path from one thick nipple to the other. "Beautiful," he whispered as they stared intensely at one another.

She was amazed that although his entire eye was an inky blackness, she was able to detect emotion in the depths. Be it anger, humor, or desire.

Aja shivered even as she worked her hips up and down a bit in anticipation. "Galatoomaa," she said softly, warming under his praise.

Anansi's finger made its way down the valley of her breasts continuing down to eventually trace delicate circles around her flat navel. "Your skin is so soft."

Aja shifted her hand to stroke his erection with a wicked smile. "And you are *so* hard."

Anansi's mouth formed an "O" as Aja teased the tip of his dick with just the right grip. He trailed his fingers over her smooth V-shaped mound, spreading her lips and lightly flicking the bud before slipping his entire finger deep inside her. "It's so wet," he moaned, enjoying the way her eyelids fluttered like butterfly wings.

Aja panted, tightening her hold on his dick as she opened her legs wider—an invitation for more.

The *qanddii* began to circle the room high above the floor as Anansi slowly pulled out his finger, then sucked it deeply with a satisfied smack of his lips. "Would you like to cum again?" he asked, before following an impulse to lower his head down to kiss her.

Aja nodded as she continued to look up into his magnetic eyes. "Yes, please," she answered with mock sweetness even as she opened her legs wider and guided his warm, calloused hands back down between her legs.

He cupped her intimacy, rubbing the base of his palm against her clit. "Can we cum together this time?" he asked, enjoying their light sexual banter.

Aja's eyes drifted close a bit as she brought her hand up to grasp his face. "Yes, please," she sighed.

Anansi pressed his body atop hers, finding it far more soft and plush than his *qanddii* as Aja drew his tongue deep into her mouth. He wrapped his fingers as best he could around the base of his hardness to guide it inside her inch by delicious inch.

Aja's back arched and she dug her fingers into his shoulders as the *qanddii* dipped, sending Anansi's thickness deeper inside of her. She reached down and put one hand on his rigid abdomen. "Easy. Easy," she moaned, needing time to adjust to the feel of him again even as her juices drizzled down her buttocks.

Anansi began to pump his hips, looking down at the sight of his stiffness sliding inside of her. The lips of her core gripped him as every stroke sent him a bit deeper until another inch of his hardness was coated with her juices making its deep brown length shiny. He walked backward a bit on his knees until just the tip sat cozily between her lips. The sight of it made him heady. Her intimacy was beautiful. Her passion was unchecked.

Will once be enough?

Aja brought her hands up to squeeze her breasts, pressing them together playfully so that they clapped before she pushed them up close enough to lightly tease her firm nipples with her tongue as she worked her other lips to gently kiss the thick tip of his dick.

"Aja," he said in wonder.

She panted. Never had she felt so energized. So alive. She had experienced nothing like it before and doubted she ever would again.

Anansi shook his head in amazement before he used his hand to lightly tap the tip against her clit.

Tap-tap-tap.

"Uhmmm," she purred.

Tap-tap-tap.

"Oooh," she moaned.

Tap-tap-tap.

"Aaaah," she sighed.

He slid every delicious inch back inside of her with one thrust and grabbed her legs to push them above her head causing her buttocks to lift off the *qanddii.*

He bit his bottom lip as he got up on his toes and squatted with his knees on either side of her buttocks to stroke deep down inside of her as his hands held her legs in place. He used his strength and stamina to deliver powerful and steady strokes that sent them both over the edge.

He felt like roaring like a wild beast.

Aja could do nothing but enjoy his sex as his thighs slapped against her buttocks causing the flesh to jiggle in a thousand directions. She stared at him, lost in him and the passion, as she felt her excitement be stoked like a flame to an inferno. Her release was near. She could feel it rising. She craved it like a drug. She wanted it to burst inside her like an explosion. "Yes. Do it. Do it. Do it. Yes," she cried, feeling blinded as her walls convulsed with each spasm of her white-hot release. "I'm cumming."

Anansi's face shifted and became intense as sweat dripped from his body to coat her breasts and thighs. He lightly slapped and then squeezed Aja's buttocks as he began to slowly roll his hips causing his rod to circle her walls. Driven by the pleasure he gave her, he quickened the pace of his pumps until it matched the rapid beat of his heart. His face twisted and that fire that began in his gut exploded within him. "Look up at me," he told her thickly as his hips jerked and his buttocks clenched with the first jolt of his seed spilling against her walls, easing his thrusts.

The *qanddii* dipped and soared around the room intensifying each stroke and deepening each movement of his hips as they came together. Both were lost and unaware of time or place as they swirled in that zone where nothing or no one else mattered at all.

IX

Aja awakened the next morning disappointed that Anansi was already out of his *qanddii*. She stretched her body leisurely as she sat up, causing the *huccuu* covers to fall to her waist. Even after their sexual sessions had lasted long into the early hours of the morning, she smiled as she envisioned mating with Anansi as they floated nude in the center of outer space.

But their one night was over.

Her smile faded.

She winced at the tenderness between her legs as she climbed from his *qanddii* naked and left his *diinqa*. Her first instinct was to search him out, but instead, she headed to her *diinqa* longing for a long bath that would hopefully soothe her muscles.

Aja's steps faltered as she spotted the new additions to her wardrobe laid out on the *qanddii*. She came closer to look over it all. It was everything she ordered plus more. Leather overcoats, tunics, flowing dresses, fancy footwear, body oils and elegant accessories.

It was hardly the wardrobe of a *gabra* or a young feminine from the small rustic area of the planet Nede.

Aja touched the obviously expensive garments. Guilt plagued her. She was the quasi-guest of the *giiftiin* of Erised, her *diinqa* was more sizable and luxurious than anything she could've ever imagined living in, and now she had the kind of wardrobe she believed a wealthy feminine would possess.

Aja backed away from it, withdrawing her hand as if it was burnt by the fires of Planet *Jahannam*.

Her family was dead. Some of her people were enslaved.

She flinched as she remembered the shame Juuba must have felt at being paraded naked before people vying to purchase him.

And how many feminines from Nede had also been filled with *extos* and presented as a sexual toy?

Although she and Anansi had just shared a night of explosive passion, she still didn't feel comfortable thinking she was lucky Oduda had sent her to him and not anyone else. Being treated as someone's *gumna* was never lucky no matter how attractive the masculine.

Aja pushed thoughts of strangling Oduda Diasi from her mind—for the moment—and tried to come to terms with her own guilt.

It's not right.

Although everything was exquisite, she decided to pass on the fancier garments, jewelry, shoes and perfumes. She picked a navy-blue tunic dress, the most plain of the wardrobe.

After a long, steamy hot bath that soothed the lips of her intimacy, Aja brushed the kinks from her waist length hair. As she pulled it back and secured it with a band of leather at the top of her head, she tried not to think of how beautiful her hair would be with one of the delicate and expensive hair pins.

With one last look, she closed the case holding the jewelry and accessories, placing it on a floating glass shelf in the closet before she quickly dressed.

"*Nagaya*, Aja."

Her heart hammered at the very sound of his deep voice echoing inside her *diinqa*. She looked around. He was nowhere to be seen, but he knew she could see her from wherever he was in the *mana*. She wiped her suddenly moist palms together as her heart beat a wild and crazy rhythm in her chest. "*Nagaya*, Anansi," she Said, looking down at her bare feet.

"If you're not busy I would like a word with you."

"Okay. I'm on my—"

Aja looked around and wasn't surprised at all to find she was back in Anansi's *diinqa*. "Way," she finished with a roll of her eyes.

The hairs on her arm and neck stood on end, and she turned, already knowing Anansi was behind her. "Is that your uniform?" she asked, as her eyes took in all of him, from the waist-length locs and handsome face to his uniform and matching leather jacket. It suited him well. He looked devastatingly handsome.

Anansi nodded.

"Very nice, Captain," she said, with a nod of her own in salute to him.

"I see you found your new garments," he said, his eyes coursing over her frame. "I assumed you would have worn something more luxurious."

"This is suitable," she told him, shielding the truth of her feelings about her new wardrobe. "But I am appreciative of everything. You truly have been very hospitable to me, and I appreciate that, Anansi."

He crossed his hands behind his back and cast her a serious look. "I wish there was more that I could do."

Aja's eyes met his, but she looked away and said nothing of the freedom she yearned for.

"I would like for you to accompany me today," Anansi said, lightly squeezing her hand as he moved past her.

"I get to breathe some new air," she joked, her eyes dropping to watch the motion of his buttocks in his pants.

"Something like that," he said, sounding vague.

Aja arched a brow as he held out his hand to her. "What now?" she asked, sliding her hand into his with ease.

Anansi led her to the glass chamber that she had been curious about the day before. Aja's steps paused. He looked over his shoulder at her, his expression showing he was curious about her hesitation.

"What is that?" she asked, raising her chin towards it.

"It's a transference docking station," he explained, his black eyes amused.

Aja frowned deeply. "Transference to what?"

"Wherever I want to go."

She nodded slowly. "And where is it you want to go right now?"

Anansi lifted his hand to lightly stroke her cheek. "Trust me, Aja."

"I hardly know you, and I was raised not to trust in you."

He continued to gently stroke her face. "But do you?"

Yes. Yes. A million times, yes. "Maybe," she answered with a soft smile, fighting the urge to lean into his touch.

He shook his head and chuckled, turning to lead her into the docking station. The glass sealed around them as Anansi and Aja faced each other.

"Transference requested," the automated feminine voice echoed inside the chamber. *"Identify yourself."*

"Captain Anansi Nyame and one guest."

"Voice, retina, and fingertip scan complete. Identity confirmed. Bodies prepared for transference. Destination?"

"Ship base," he said, smiling down at her.

"Transference confirmed."

Aja allowed Anansi to pull her into a tight embrace just as their bodies faded. With a flash of blue light, they reappeared inside another glass enclosure.

Shaken a bit by it all, she rested her head against his chest.

"All safe and sound," he whispered into her ear, patting her back warmly.

Aja shivered as she inhaled the warmth of his scent deeply and tried not to let his nearness cause her legs to give out beneath her. "I feel a little light-headed," she admitted.

"It will disappear in a moment."

"Transference complete."

The chamber's door opened, and Aja reluctantly moved away from Anansi's embrace to step down into a room that was entirely gold. There were no furnishings—not even a *qanddii*—and her *diinqa* at Anansi's *mana* was twice its size. "May I ask where we are now?" she said, turning to face him as he strode across the room to pull down a section of the wall to reveal a hidden sofa with plush ivory cushions.

"We are aboard the *Spaceship Infinite*, and these are my private quarters."

An actual spaceship.

Aja's mouth gaped open a bit before she could catch herself as she moved to take a seat on the sofa. She had to stop herself from sighing in pleasure as she felt the cushion perfectly form to the shape of her bottom. "Oh, this feels so good," she sighed, making a face that was comical as she laid down flat on the sofa.

Anansi watched her carefully as her eyes rolled back in her head and she moaned in pleasure.

"I might have an orgasm. Seriously."

"Uhm, Aja?" Anansi called over to her.

"It's like lying on a very naughty cloud," she sighed, stretching her arms high above her head as she buried her bottom deeper into the cushion.

"Aja."

"I wonder if it feels as good against the front of my body?" She promptly flipped over onto her stomach, and the cushion framed her breasts and thighs with ease.

"Aja!" Anansi said sharply.

She lifted her head from the cushion and turned to look up. She was surprised that he had crossed the room to stand above her. "Huh?" she asked innocently.

"Moaning, groaning, sighing, and wiggling everything that is soft and tempting on your body while speaking of orgasms is tempting me." Anansi slid his hands into the pocket of his pants as he looked down at her.

Aja cleared her throat as she rolled over and sat up. "Something as innocent as my enjoyment of your sofa turns you on?"

He cast her one last look before turning to walk away from her. "Keep going on, and I'll show you just how turned on I am," he advised her, nearing the door.

Aja stood. "Am I to follow you?"

"If you would like a tour of the ship you should," he teased with a wink as the gold doors slid open. "So, if you're finished coupling with my sofa..."

Aja took her time to join him. "Envious?" she asked.

Anansi looked down at Aja as she stood before him. "Why do you like to tempt me?" he asked huskily, his black eyes searching hers.

And there it was, that potent energy they created whenever they were near each other.

She pursed her lips and released a stream of air meant to diffuse the pressure she felt to have him. She failed. "I could ask you the same thing," she said, her eyes falling to his supple mouth.

Aja stepped closer to him boldly and raised one hand to lightly caress his chin before eased her hand up to grip the back of his neck. With a tug, she bent his upper body and rose on her toes to kiss him softly. She was about to step back when his strong hands quickly rose to grasp her waist and lifted her body up against his.

"You and I can't seem to keep our hands—or anything else, off one another," he whispered in the electrified air between them as his head lowered towards her.

"I know," she agreed just before he captured her mouth in a far deeper kiss. There were tongue-dancing, deep-breathing, and tight clutches while their heads shifted back and forth from left to right. They kissed as if they had forever. With passion. No urgency. Slowness.

They both moaned as Aja gently sucked the tip of his tongue into her mouth, lightly teasing it with her own as her hands tightly grabbed the lapels of his jacket. "I don't want to want you so much," she breathed into his mouth.

He opened his flushed and heated eyes to gaze down at her. "Neither do I...but I can't fight it."

Aja tilted her head back to meet his stare. She wanted him. With a life that was lacking so much, she wanted some pleasure. She deserved it.

Anansi nodded. "Last night was—"

"Amazing," she finished for him.

"Yes," he agreed thickly, shifting his hands under her dress to dig his fingers into her fleshy buttocks.

"I'm beginning to forget it, though, maybe I need a quick reminder," she breathed against his lips.

The thought of being inside her tested his reasoning. "I can't right now," he said, amazed that he found the will to deny her. "After the tour, I have some tasks to oversee as captain."

"Well, if we don't get out of each other's face and space I am going to strip you of that uniform and make the lower parts of your body salute *me*."

Anansi's eyes smoldered, but he cleared his throat before setting her down on her feet and holding his hand out towards the portal.

Aja laughed as she stepped out into an expansive white corridor lined with silver. She looked around as she waited for Anansi, but there was nothing to see. Everything was nondescript, unlike the beauty of Anansi's *mana*. Still, she was fascinated. Her *abbaa* had passed on tales of supersized spaceships able to soar through different vast galaxies.

Previously, she'd had only her imagination to envision one.

She looked up and gasped a little in surprise at the glass ceiling showing an *urjii* shooting across the ship.

"The quarters for the officers of the ship are located on this level," he explained to her as they came to a large metal door.

"It's not as luxurious as your *mana*," she said, continuing to look around at the unadorned floors and walls.

Anansi laughed. "Welcome to the militia."

The metal door rose, revealing a tall and wide box.

Aja bent forward to peek in before she allowed

Anansi to guide her inside with one of his hands to the small of her back. "And this is?" she asked, her nervousness apparent.

"A *kaasuu*," he explained as the door lowered. "It will take us from one level to the next."

"No XR-2 to pop you in and out of rooms aboard the ship?" she asked with a sly glance up at him.

Anansi chuckled. "That type of expense is not in the Council's coffers."

"It's good to be *giiftiin*," she mused, her body relaxing where she stood beside him.

"I sacrifice for that cost, believe me," he said darkly, his tone tinged with anger.

Aja glanced over at him, noticing the stern set of his jaw as he entered a code on the touchpad to the left of the door. She squinted. Never once had she questioned that the weight of the power he was to inherit was heavy. She was surprised by the compassion she felt for him. It shook her. She fought the urge to wrap his hand in hers to offer him comfort.

"You seemed very upset by the *bwa kasuwa*," Anansi said suddenly.

Aja thought of Juuba and shook her head to free it of the horrible image of him on display. "I'm sure you understand why," she expressed in a husky tone.

"Is he significant to you?" Anansi asked.

"He was well-loved by all in our *olla*," Aja said, her sadness rising as she speculated on his fate.

The door opened, and they stepped into another gold room, this one with a large domed ceiling. A massive *komputara* covered one entire wall. Bright red automatons were lined before it as hundred or more neon graphs were displayed. In the center of the room hovered a giant bubble-shaped container with a *qanddii* in the center.

"This is the curative division," Anansi advised. "The technology is not as advanced as Erised with our advanced medical recovery, but the staff onboard is highly skilled with the basic for healing therapies."

Aja nodded as they walked deeper into the room.

"Like the removal of the microchip that is blocking you from using your powers," he said.

Aja paused, and she looked up to find his eyes on her. She gripped his arm and felt his strength. "A microchip? It's inside me? What is it? Is it harmful to me?"

"Not at all," Anansi assured her. "It's a small device, hardly larger than a hair that was implanted by an injection."

Aja felt Anansi's warm hand pressed against her back, and she welcomed his touch as she tried to process yet another effect of the war on her life. *When will enough be enough?*

"Aja—"

"Will I have my powers back once it's taken out? Is the procedure painful?" she asked, her voice tinged with her fear.

"I think I can answer that."

They both turned.

Aja quickly held her composure at the sight of a petite feminine with glowing white skin and wide eyes that were a mosaic of bright colors. Her hair was bright pink and piled atop her head in an intricate topknot. Even in her oddity, Aja found her beautiful. Distractingly so. *What is she?*

She saluted Anansi and then turned to Aja with an outstretched hand. "I'm the medic Chli. It's nice to meet you, Aja."

Aja accepted her hand, trying not to stare at her talon-like nails that were bright pink as well. "You know me?" she asked.

Chli smiled. "The captain told me about you when he contacted me this morning. And if you're all set we can get that microchip out."

Aja cast Anansi a nervous glance over her shoulder before looking back at the medic. "No prep time?" she joked, her heart racing in her chest.

Chli reached out and warmly grasped her hand. "With the help of the captain's XR-2, I already know exactly where the chip is located. The incision and any sign of that chip will be gone soon after were done."

"No pain?" Aja asked with clear doubt.

Chli shook her head.

"No scar?"

"Welcome to the wonderful world of technology," Anansi drawled dryly from behind her.

"Reparative regeneration," Chli explained, pointing to the bubble in the center of the room.

"Similar to the powers I use to have," Aja said slowly, trying to make sense of it all.

"That you will have again," Anansi insisted.

"And this isn't some weird experiment where you dissect Empaths for research?" she asked, some of her old mistrust rising in her like a tide.

Anansi gave Chli a look. She nodded before her body elevated inches from the floor and she floated away.

Aja's mouth gaped as she turned to watch.

Anansi pressed his hands to hers. "Aja, the choice is yours. I understand your fear, but I want to give you back as much of your old life as I can."

She looked up at him.

"I would never hurt you, Aja," he promised, raising his hand to stroke her bottom lip gently.

His eyes comforted her.

Aja pushed aside her fears, her thumb stroking his palm. "Okay," she agreed softly.

∞

Anansi was worried.

He paced the length of the glass room in his mana, barely taking in the surrounding views as he anxiously awaited news that Aja's surgery was complete. Taking her aboard ship for the operation, instead of a treatment center on Erised, had been an attempt to conceal her presence. Although he was confident in Chli's capabilities, his concern would ease once he brought Aja back to his mana and XR-2 scanned her.

He hadn't waited in his quarters, not wanting to reveal his presence on board. With Daryan on

Planet Earth leading an exploratory mission, his second mate, Tyn Zyn, had command of the spaceship and Anansi didn't want to undermine him.

And, he wanted nothing more than to be back in his mana with Aja. Barely a *torbaan* had passed since Aja was gifted to him and now everything about his life revolved her. Her wants. Her needs. Her desires.

Before Aja, his missions traveling the distant galaxies exploring new worlds and fighting those species that compromised the safety of The Council had been all he wanted. Life onboard the spaceship, even though the luxuries of his mana far surpassed it, had been sufficient. He hadn't wanted anything more.

Until Aja.

Anansi paced some more, rubbing his hands together anxiously as he tried not to think of anything going wrong as Chli removed the microchip from the surface of Aja's *surrii*. *Will I forever be changed when she's gone?*

Lately, he didn't like to think about it.

He paused in his pacing at the passion they shared last night. It was like nothing he had ever experienced before. For the first time in a long time, he felt complete. Sated.

Aja had fed a hunger in him that he didn't know existed.

And once she was gone from his life he would be starved again.

"Incoming communication from *Spaceship Infinite*," XR-2 said.

Anansi frowned. By his own design, the glass room was not equipped to accept transmissions. The room was his solace.

He thought of his office and in an instant XR-2 transported him from one room to the other. "Connect," he ordered, moving over to stand before the *komputara*.

An image of Chli filled the display.

His breath caught as his eyes went past her to the background. Aja's prone body was levitating in the center of the giant glass bubble. There was a soft golden glow around her body as she lay nude beneath a red *huccuu* sheet. She looked peaceful as she lay there with her hands at her side and her waist length hair floating to the floor. Thousands of illuminated molecules bounced off each other around her like flakes of *cabhii*, healing her.

The site was remarkable.

His heart pounded.

"It's all done, sir," Chli said, with a smile. "Aja is doing excellent."

Anansi was flooded with relief. "I'm on my way," he said.

In an instant, XR-2 transported him inside the transference chamber, anxious to be back by Aja's side.

∞

"Aja...Aja. Wake up."

As she stirred and opened her gold-flecked eyes, Aja felt more invigorated than she ever had before. The twinkling lights that surrounded her began to fade, but not before she marveled at their brilliance. Raising her hand to poke her finger into the middle of a cluster, she then noticed the golden glow framing her.

"Aja, I need you to breathe in and out of your mouth, slowly and deeply."

Aja looked around at the sound of the voice filling the bubble. Her eyes filled with alarm at being eye level with the top of the massive *komputara*. She looked down. Chli was standing outside the balloon looking up at her. She shrieked.

"Aja," Chli called out with calm. "Please relax. You're safe. You will not fall."

Aja closed her eyes and tried her best to obey.

"Now take deep breaths," Chli added.

Aja nodded and licked her lips before inhaling and exhaling deeply. In truth, as she focused more on her body than her fear she felt energized as if she was plugged into a power source. Stronger. Better.

She took a breath so deep that her back arched.

She held it for a bit before releasing it slowly.

And again. In. Then out.

And once more. In. Out.

"You can sit up now. You're all done."

Aja turned her head to the side to look out at Chli smiling at her as she stood just outside the bubble. "I'm okay?" she asked, her body now lowered back onto the slender *qanddii*. The last of the tiny lights disappeared, and the golden glow framing her body faded away.

"Yes, you are," the medic reassured her.

Holding the sheet to her body, Aja swung her legs over the side and sat up. With her free hand, she eased her fingers through her hair to rub her entire scalp.

There was a smooth patch at the base where her hair had been shaven, but no scar. No pain. The hair would grow back.

The door to the round chamber opened. Chli floated in carrying Aja's clothing. "Follow me. You can get dressed in my quarters. Captain Nyame is on the way," she said.

Aja wrapped the *huccuu* sheet around her body thoroughly and quickly followed behind the floating feminine. To a small room of gold in the rear of the curative division. As soon as the door slid down to a close, Aja barely wasted time to dress.

She was still amazed at the total lack of a scar, but she was also disappointed because every effort she made to use her powers failed.

What if it's gone forever?

She swallowed back her disappointed and walked to the door, pleased when it opened. Pausing in the entrance, she closed her eyes as she took deep calming breaths. She just wanted to feel something. *Anything.*

Releasing a heavy breath, Aja left the private quarters of Chli.

"Aja?"

She stopped and looked to her right down a short hall. Her name had echoed from there. It was a male voice. "Anansi?" she asked, wanting to throw her arms around his neck and be held close by him as she struggled with her disappointment.

Without hesitation, she rushed to the entrance.

Her words trailed off at the sight of Juuba Huuntu standing before her instead of Anansi. Shock took words from her for a moment before she propelled herself forward to run into his open and waiting arms. He symbolized everything for which she missed and yearned.

Home. Familiarity. Friendship.

"Oh, Juuba, they're all dead," Aja whispered, her tears wetting his neck.

"I know. I know." His deep voice seemed to echo and boom inside his large frame.

As his arms wrapped around her with strength, she tried to hone in on those amorous feelings he once had for her. She even pressed her lips to his neck, closing her eyes as she tried so valiantly to connect with his emotions.

Nothing.

Aja opened her eyes to find Anansi standing off in the distance watching them. Her gaze locked with his and she found herself releasing Juuba and stepping back out of his embrace. She felt as if she betrayed him, but that was ludicrous because one night of passion did not make a relationship.

Anansi turned his attention to Chli.

Aja looked up at Juuba's handsome face. "I saw you auctioned and sold at the bwa kasuwa as it was airing. I wondered what became of you."

She was surprised when his eyes turned bitterly cold. "Your captain was kind enough to purchase me from the winner of the auction," he chewed out in anger.

Aja's eyes cut past Juuba's broad shoulder to find Anansi was gone. "When? Where? How?" she asked.

Juuba's hands tightly clenched into fists at his sides. His eyes became distant before he turned away from her. "Your captain purchased me for a million warqee, and I was delivered here early this morning."

Aja frowned as she crossed her arms over her chest. "Why do you keep referring to him as my captain?"

Juuba turned and looked her up and down. "You smell of him. You wear the Erisedians' expensive garments. He saved me because of you. Are you his feminine?"

"Why are you so angry at him?" she asked, purposefully avoiding his question.

"Why do you care if I am?" he volleyed back.

Aja remained silent.

He saved me because of you.

She felt light-headed.

Juuba strode away from her. "Our people have been killed or enslaved. I have been enslaved and then sold, beaten, shamed..."

Aja went to him and lightly touched his arm. "Juuba, my life after the war was not easy. I was held captive by Kyl Diasi's own daughter, Oduda, and made to live in filth. Barely fed. Ridiculed. Not sure of my future. Gifted as a *gumna* at her whim."

Juuba turned and looked down at her with sad eyes. "I didn't think before I spoke. I never asked you about your well-being. I'm sorry."

She offered him a smile with no emotion behind it. "We both have seen and experienced a lot," she said, reaching to squeeze his hand.

Juuba snorted in contempt.

"When can you leave here? Where will you go?" she asked.

"Juuba Huuntu is a guest aboard the *Spaceship Infinite*," Chli said as she drifted over to them. "That is per the captain's orders, of course."

"Of course," Juuba drawled sarcastically.

"Here?" Aja asked in astonishment.

Chli nodded. "Yes, it is for his own safety," she explained. "Aja, the captain has requested I escort you to his quarters now."

Aja turned back to Juuba to hug him close as Chli floated away. "All of this will be over soon," she whispered to him.

"I am no freer aboard this ship than I was when

they auctioned me at the *bwa kasuwa*." Juuba looked down into her eyes with a steady intensity that disturbed her. "First chance I get to escape I will. I will be owned by no one no matter the intention."

Aja squeezed his hands one last time and turned to walk over to Chli. She was anxious to speak to Anansi. *What does this all mean?*

Juuba hollered out suddenly behind them, and she whirled to see him bent over clutching his hand. "What happened?" she asked, headed back towards him.

Chli put a restraining hand on Aja's arm. "It's a temporary and very mild shock. There is an invisible force field around this area of the unit that Juuba cannot penetrate. He has been warned of this, and he insists on trying to escape."

"Why?" Aja asked as Juuba stood up straight and glared at Chli like he wanted to tear her limb-from-limb.

"We did a psychological profile of him even down to his subconscious, and it is clear that he will kill any masculine or feminine on the ship if he believes it will help him gain his freedom." Chli used the same soft hand to guide an apparently reluctant Aja out of the curative division unit. "Captain Nyame is to be respected for saving Juuba from the uncertainty and brutality of being a gabra, but it would have been reckless to this ship and everyone aboard to allow Juuba Huuntu to roam freely."

Aja frowned as she and Chli came to the kaasuu and the door rose. She had no doubt Juuba would strike anyone in his way. She'd had the same rage before the kindness of Anansi. She stepped aboard the *kaasuu* and stood at Chli's side.

"Are you and Juuba intimately acquainted?" Chli asked, casting Aja a sidelong glance.

Aja caught the look. "We are friends and nothing else," she said, aware that her tone was short.

Chli fell silent beside her.

Aja felt overwhelmed by everything. The

surgery. Her powers not returning. Juuba's freedom. Anansi's cost for it.

She raised her hand to press her fingertips against the closed lids of her eyes. The grunt she released was but a small sign of the confusion and frustration swirling inside of her.

∞

Anansi ran his long fingers through the length of his dreads as he hung his head between his knees. He grimaced as his stomach felt lit with fire. It was jealousy he could not deny. The emotion had gripped him from the moment he watched Aja jump into Juuba Huuntu's arms. Finally, he forced himself to retreat to his quarters to avoid witnessing their reunion or giving in to a desire to tear her from Juuba's embrace.

He swore under his breath as he sat up straight and pushed his locs back from his face. He had instructed Chli to bring Aja to him. His patience was thin.

For a moment, he regretted interfering with Juuba Huuntu's fate. Shame filled him. Jealousy did not suit who he was raised to be. In an instant, his integrity had vanished because he hated the thought of Aja being with this other masculine. Or any other for that matter.

Relax.

He didn't like being without reason.

I have nothing more to offer her than her freedom...and that comes at the cost of my gaa'ila *to another feminine.*

The door to his quarters slid upward. Anansi looked up as Aja entered. His eyes took in how beautiful she looked in her bright red tunic before raising to search hers. "We have to get back to my *mana*. The ship is preparing for a mission—"

His heart slammed against his chest as Aja walked up to him and lifted one leg over his lap to straddle him. He fought his desire to press his hands to her waist.

"*Galatoomaa*, Anansi," she whispered huskily

into the slight distance between them before she lowered her head to kiss him with a slow and deliberate passion.

His resistance broke as finally gripped her hips and slid his hands beneath the edge of the tunic to massage her buttocks.

They moaned in unison as the kiss deepened and their intensity heightened. She lifted her tunic over her head and flung it away before guiding his head forward until his mouth latched onto one of her nipples and sucked deeply on it. He used one strong arm around her waist to lift her from his lap just enough to jerk his pants down and slide her down upon his throbbing hard dick. She cried out, flinging her head back in abandon as they both worked their hips in fiery unison.

Anansi held her tightly, pressing his face to her cleavage and closing his eyes, wondering if he would ever get his fill of her or if the time would come when he would even want to.

X

Oduda released a satisfied moan as she pushed Huung's naked frame off her in the center of her *qanddii*. She gasped for air as she lay sprawled naked on her back. Huung had just ravished her like he was crazed with desire for her. Which of course he was, her special concoction made sure of that.

In the last two days, she had been poked, stroked, prodded, sucked and licked more than ever. Everything that was decidedly feminine about her body was tender and sore from her nipples to her core. Sometimes pleasure was a pain.

Oduda was relieved to hear his snores. Her thoughts were full. In truth, Huung's betrayal hurt her in a way she hated to admit. She delayed her *qaadhimamuu* to the heir of the powerful throne of Erised for him, and he chose to mate with a servant?

She glanced back over her shoulder at him, and her eyes burned with rage as her lips snarled. She felt foolish for those moments where she thought of running from her obligation to her people to be with him. Hurt replaced the hate, but she pushed it away. She wondered if he weren't under her spell, would he search for his precious LeeToo on Planet Whoor. "Would you pay for what she offered for free as you both betrayed me in my domain?" she mouthed before a malicious glint filled her eyes as she smiled with bitterness.

Huung was scheduled to leave in two or three days, and she was prepared for their time together to end. Her *abbaa*, Kyl Diasi, had allowed her the *torbaan* of reprieve from meeting with Anansi Nyame, but no more, of that she was sure. He was anxious to begin trading the *nkume* he pirated from the foolish Empaths.

No, the time was near, and she needed to prepare.

Oduda sat up on the side of the *qanddii* and swiped her hand across a small pad atop the table. A small komputara rose at an angle and illuminated.

"Locate Reeock Jhyun," she said aloud, rolling her eyes as Huung began to stir beside her.

As her communication system worked to obey her command, she pulled a rod from the drawer.

"Reeock Jhyun located on Planet Whoor."

"Of course, he would be," she drawled in disgust as she reached back and pressed the rod to Huung. She didn't know, nor did she care, where the implement landed on his frame.

Oduda stood up and quickly snatched up her robe from the floor to pull on. "Connect," she ordered sharply.

Modesty was never an issue for her, but she did draw the line at broadcasting her wares to the oddities and weirdos on Planet Whoor—especially Reeock Jhyun, the biggest of them all.

Huung's snores deepened in resonance. She would be free from his desires for hours.

"*Giiftiin* Oduda Diasi, it has been a long time since we last spoke, beautiful one."

Oduda cringed a bit at the sight of Reeock Jhyun on the *komputara*. As were all Uhitans, his skin was a pale, iridescent blue with large green circles over his bald and lumpy head. His tongue was long, thin and black with a split in the tip that gave him a lisp when he spoke. His teeth were rotten, and the few that he had left were so yellow they looked golden-brown. That, coupled with being short and obese with the worst body odor and breath she ever had the misfortune to swallow, made him truly revolting.

"I need your investigative services, Reeock," Oduda said, her eyes focusing on the background of his dark and gloomy surroundings. The small room was dingy and barely lit. She could just make out the lower half of the feminine behind where he sat on the edge of the *qanddii*. Her legs were spread wide and her feet tied to the posts. Her torn and ragged dress was pushed up around her waist exposing reddish bruises on her inner thighs and the lips of her intimacy. Both she and the sheets looked in need of washing.

Reeock's tongue wiggled out past his thin lips excitedly. "Dare I hope that payment is a night with you? I would be more than happy to do whatever you wish."

Uhitans' sex organs were their mouths, and the thought of his head between her thighs licking away at her clit with his foul tongue made her sick. She tried to hide her revulsion at his words, which were drawn out and seemed to be surrounded by spittle. "I am not a sex worker on Planet Whoor, Reeock."

"Pity because this tongue works wonders," he said, as he stood to his full four-foot height and moved to the foot of the *qanddii* to crawl between her thighs.

Oduda grimaced as he opened his mouth and unfurled his tongue. It grew in length, and the split tip seemed to have a life all its own as it latched onto her clit. She turned her head and pressed her eyes close as the *gumna* hollered out.

She deserves a bonus.

Oduda looked at the *komputara* again. "Reeock!" she snapped. "My patience with you is wearing thin."

He chuckled as he extracted his tongue and shifted his mucus-colored eyes to stare at the display. "It is my pleasure to serve you as well, *Giiftiin*."

"Payment of ten thousand *warqee* for anything not commonly known about *Giiftiin* Anansi Nyame," she said.

"May I ask why this request is being made?" he asked.

"No."

He fell silent as he stroked his fingers together.

"Your *gumna* is waiting," she said snidely.

"For digging into the secrets of the descendant of the most powerful ruler in the Acirfa Galaxy, my nonrefundable fee is fifty thousand *warqee*."

Anansi Nyame was an influential masculine, and she was to be his mate for life. Oduda needed ammunition to ensure she maintained some power in the relationship. If there were secrets to be discovered, Reeock moved in the right circles to uncover it.

"Twenty-five thousand. Half now and half when I receive my report," Oduda answered coldly.

"Thirty thousand."

"Deal." Oduda raised her hand to end the call.

"By the way, *giiftiin*, I see that your servant LeeToo was working here on Planet Whoor." Reeock moved to the head of the dingy *qanddii* and jerked down the top of the *gumna's* tunic to expose her breasts. He unfurled his tongue again. The ends split further with each latching onto her nipples.

Oduda ignored them. "Was?" she asked.

"She killed herself."

Oduda shifted on the bed to turn and look down into Huung's face as he slept. "If only I cared, Reeock."

"Same old Oduda."

"Just get what I need, Reeock," she told him coldly before turning back to press the button and end the communication.

∞

The sight of his parent's imperial *mana* was impressive. Anansi eyed it through the front window of his self-driven *xiyyaara*. Its four levels sat atop the highest mountain in the northern region of Erised. Its metal and glass glistened under the three *aduus*. The tips reached the skies. Automaton guards lined the gold gates surrounding the property. It was grandeur. Pomp and circumstance. A testament to the reign of his parents, *Moticha* Hwosi Kan Nyame and *Giiftii* Mondi Nyame.

And he was their heritor.

Anansi was grateful for the nanotechnological advances that led to the average life span for most Erisedians being well over a *jaarraa*. His time to ascend the throne was not upon him.

The gates opened as soon as his *xiyyaara* approached it. As soon as he entered the security zones surround the *mana* his vehicle had long since been scanned for the identity of all occupants. He traveled with four automatons programmed to protect him at all costs. It would have been much quicker and easier to use his transport dock but decided instead to enjoy the trip and take a look at the planet over which he'd rule one day.

The sleek *xiyyaara*, in black reinforced metal impenetrable to lasers, lowered to the large pad in front of the *mana*. Anansi and his guards exited, with them flanking his sides. He smiled a bit as soon as they jogged up the palatial stairs and reached the double doors that were three times his eight-foot height. As soon as he crossed the threshold into the reception area, he stood akimbo and waited.

His body disappeared and then appeared in the official office of the *moticha*. Anansi's smile faded, and he stiffened his relaxed stance, at the stern look his *abbaa* cast him.

"What do you plan to do about your missing intended?" Hwosi asked as he settled his large frame in his high-back chair behind a desk as wide as the length of two Erisedian masculines. The bright light from the *aduus* filled the floor to ceiling windows with light, outlining the ruler with a glow, his silvery locs seeming on fire.

The *moticha* was irate. That was evident.

Anansi opened his mouth to speak but closed it when his *abbaa* continued without allowing an answer to his question. He folded his tall frame to sit down on one of the floating seats.

"While Oduda Diasi is playing hide-and-seek, lives are being affected daily as Empaths are enslaved, and trade relations are halted concerning the *nkumes*." Hwosi Kan Nyame slammed his hand on top of his massive desk as he glared at his son. "Enough is enough."

Anansi nodded, but he hesitated to speak. What should he say? The truth? Should he tell him he had not made one attempt to contact Oduda? Should he tell him that he was also pleased Oduda had not arrived because he was enjoying his time at his mana with his beautiful Empath *gabra*?

Anansi thought of her, laying beneath him, her

hair spread on the pillow, her legs around her waist, her face lit with passion as he stroked deeply inside her.

"Give me more, Anansi," he imagined her whispering up to him.

A small smile touched his supple lips.

"What is funny?" Hwosi roared his white eyebrows seeming to become one angry slash across his forehead.

Anansi made his expression blank as he rose and walked over to stand behind the desk to look out the window. His *da'ee*, Mondi, was in the garden below, her feet bare as she walked along the lush yellow grass and bent to smell the florae. None of it was real. The land was far to parched to produce such vegetation. The *gennii* of Erised had long since invented lifelike virtuality reality zones near major landmarks and the *manas* of wealthy and prominent Erisedians. Like his *zwodriu* and his own outdoor oasis at his mana, it all seemed real and kept Erisedians from feeling the actual effects of a planet beat down upon three *aduus*.

"Anansi?" his *abbaa* said, prompting him.

"Oduda was to travel to Erised," Anansi began, easing his hands into the pockets of his pant. "She changed the plan, not me. I was—I *am*—ready to make the sacrifice."

Hwosi remained silent as he gave a bow of his regal head.

Anansi glanced over his broad shoulder at his abbaa's stern profile. Love and respect for him filled his chest, but there was also a longing for him to want more for him than an arranged *gaa'ila*. "Oduda taking a few days to handle some business is not going to throw the plan off enough for it to matter. Besides, didn't you say the Kordis have now at least agreed to better treatment of their *gabras* in the interim?"

"And your point?" Hwosi asked, turning in his chair to look at him.

I think I have found the love of my life and I will never have the time to know.

The words came, but he didn't mouth them. Instead, Anansi released a heavy breath as he shifted his black eyes to the floor. "My *qaadhimamuu* will become formally announced at the end of the torbaan, and the *cidha* ceremony will follow soon after that. The treaty will be signed immediately following the ceremony." Anansi said this very simply, even as his heart ached with his regrets.

Hwosi leaned back in a stone chair with a back that had to be every bit of ten-feet-tall—it went well with the ostentatious thirty-foot ceilings. He surveyed his son with wise eyes. "How is the Empath?" he asked suddenly.

Anansi gut clenched. "She is well."

Hwosi nodded. "I understand that you also purchased a masculine Empath—a Juuba Huuntu—who is now aboard the *Infinite*."

"Correct."

"I presume he will remain there until the treaty is signed?"

"Correct."

Two glasses of *alkoolii* appeared on the desk. Hwosi picked up one and wave his hand to the other in an offer to Anansi. "Will Aja Drakar be joining him onboard the *Infinite* or will she remain in the *mana* of a masculine who happens to be the *giiftiin* of Erised and the future lifemate of another?" he asked before taking a deep sip.

Anansi walked over to pick up the tumbler, drinking from it as he met his *abbaa's* gaze over the bejeweled rim. "Aja was presented to me as my *gabra*, and she will remain under my personal protection at my *mana*," he finally answered.

Hwosi tapped the bottom of his glass against the top of his desk. "And you believe that is wise?"

"It's what I want."

"I disagree with your choice."

Anansi heart beat a little faster. His disapproval was evident. It was a significant moment between them. His *abbaa's* censure and Anansi's defiance. They locked stares. "In a world where suddenly it is demanded that I enter into a union with a feminine I don't know for the rest of my life, I am inclined to enjoy my own choices in every other area."

Hwosi's eyes steeled over. "Is that your way of telling me to mind my own business?"

Anansi's eyes never wavered. "With all due respect, yes it is."

The *moticha* brought the glass down on the desk hard enough to break it into shards. Bright white blood poured from the cuts on his palms.

"*Abbaa!*" Anansi exclaimed coming over to cradle his injured hand in his own. He put pressure on the wound with his fingers.

The glass disappeared and was replaced with medical supplies.

"I'm alright," Hwosi balked, his tone gruff even as he winced in pain.

"You really should calm down," Anansi joked, trying to lighten the mood as he made sure no shards were embedded in the flesh before he tightly wrapped it with a bandage.

"Do not jeopardize this treaty and all it will mean for your people, the Empaths, and the Kordis," Hwosi said, his voice low but very clear.

Anansi swallowed hard. "You have my word," he swore, meaning it even as a piece of his heart shattered.

∞

"Aja. Aja? Wake up."

She stirred lightly before she pulled herself up to a sitting position on the *qanddii* and rubbed her eyes as she yawned. "Anansi?"

"Yes, I just got back, and here you are in my *diinqa*," he teased as he smiled down at her.

"I'm naked too," Aja said whipping the *huccuu* covers back to reveal her nudity against the seductive radiance of the burning fireplace.

Anansi's eyes slowly traveled over her smooth round shoulders, full breasts, the plump vee, and long shapely legs as Aja tossed her thick hair over her shoulder.

"Your body is beautiful, Aja," he said thickly as

the seat of his pants suddenly felt as if it needed to be let out.

"As beautiful as mine, my *giiftiin*?"

Aja screamed out and pulled the covers to her chin at the nude golden siren suddenly stretched across the *qanddii*, her breasts high and firm with pointy dark metallic gold nipples and full hips with thick shapely legs. Her eyes widened as the golden nymph spread her legs wide to offer Anansi an intimate look between her thighs. "What the...?"

"Sasha off," he barked as he sprung to his feet.

The sexy gold feminine disappeared.

"Sasha?" Aja asked with attitude, reaching out to pat the now empty area where the other feminine had just been laying. Her eyes cut to Anansi's at his continued silence. She looked at him pointedly in question.

"Sasha isn't real."

Aja's eyebrow arched higher.

"She's a computer generated animated lover," he told her, taking a deep sip from the snifter of *alkoolii* that suddenly appeared in his hand.

Aja pulled her knees to her chest as she cocked her head to the side and studied him by the firelight. She bit back a smile. Anansi watched her out the corner of his eye as he tilted his head back to drain the glass. "So, I presume Sasha would be the feminine of your dreams. She would be made to have just the body you desire and to be all too willing—and probably eager— to fulfill your every sexual desire?" Aja asked as she watched Anansi remove the leather jacket of his uniform.

"Something like that," was all he replied, sounding elusive.

"So why did she suddenly appear while I'm laying here naked with a body you also desire and also willing to fulfill your every sexual desire?" Aja asked coquettishly.

Anansi remained silent as he removed his uniform.

Aja enjoyed the sight of his hard muscled body being revealed to her with each layer of clothing he removed. When he turned to face her, she allowed her eyes to take in the length of him. She felt her body temperature rise. "XR-2 hard at work fulfilling your every spoken word and thought's desire again?" she asked.

His eyes smoldered as he watched her peel back the covers again. "I thought that Sasha had nothing on you," he answered truthfully, coming to stand by the *qanddii* as it levitated. He took his dick into one of his hands and stroked the length of it as he watched her intensely.

"I think you wanted both of us in your *qanddii*," Aja said, watching him closely. "Make her come back."

Anansi's face became stunned and both his brows rose. "You're okay with the three of us—"

"I don't need help to please you." Aja grabbed a feather sac to fling at him playfully. "Just bring her back."

He dodged the pillow with ease and laughed. "Sasha on," he ordered.

She appeared this time on all fours with her golden rear towards Aja as she climbed towards the foot of the *qanddii* where Anansi stood. "I've missed you, Anansi," she purred.

Aja calmly kicked away the covers, arching her back so that her breasts were high as she spread her legs wide and rotated her hips clockwise and then counterclockwise like she was trying to hypnotize him. She licked her lips with a soft moan and pressed her fingers between her thighs to open the folds shielding her plump clit.

Through half-closed lids, she saw Anansi's eyes go right past the golden siren to watch her. His dick hardened in his hand. It was her body that drew his heated gaze, and it was her body that he wanted.

"Bye-bye, Sasha," Aja mocked huskily just as golden fingers began to stroke Anansi's rising erection.

"Sasha off," he ordered, diving over Sasha's image just as it disappeared. He wrapped his arms around Aja's soft, warm and all too real form.

She welcomed the pressure of his body atop hers with a sigh of triumph and satisfaction.

Anansi watched the fire flicker in the depths of her honey eyes as he lowered his head to hers. "We're not supposed to do this, Aja," he whispered against her mouth before he kissed her tenderly.

"But we can't stop," she whispered back as she traced his mouth with her fingertip.

"This was supposed to be for one night only."

Aja pushed back onto the sacs to look up at him as the chemistry between them crackled with the same energy of the fire. "Do you want me to go, Anansi?" she asked.

Her eyes flickered over his face remembering everything and forgetting nothing as he pushed her hands above her head, thrusting her breasts forward.

He shook his head no as he lowered his head to taste her lips again and again and again.

The *qanddii* landed in front of the fireplace.

Aja deepened the kiss with a moan, caressing his leg with her own as she offered Anansi her tongue. He worked his hips bringing his hard dick against her. Slowly. Wickedly. Passionately.

"Yes, Anansi, yes," Aja sighed as his hands shifted down to massage her breasts, his thick fingers lightly rolling her nipples.

He shivered as Aja's hands pressed deep circles into his shoulders before easing down the hard contours of his back to cup his buttocks. He shifted his body down hers and gently pushed her breasts up to her chin as he kissed and suckled the smooth area under her breast leaving a love bite there.

Aja gasped sharply and arched her back. "Anansi," she moaned, her fingers twisting in his locs.

He sucked her nipples deeply before shifting back up her body to nuzzle her neck with his mouth. "Uhm, you smell good."

"It's one of the new fragrances you gave me."

"Do you have it everywhere?" he asked thickly.

"*Everywhere*," she answered.

He growled.

"I can't wait, Anansi. Fill me," she pleaded huskily as she unwrapped her legs from his back and spread them wide beneath him. She felt the tip of his thick dick pressing with strength and heat against the moist lips of her core and with one upward lift of her hips she brought him deeply with him.

They both gasped at the feel of one another.

"Oh yes," Aja sighed as she trembled from the very feel of him pressing against her walls.

"Aja," Anansi cried out with no shame as she sheathed him tightly. Perfectly.

He lifted up to look down into her face as he slowly began to work his hips pushing his hardness inside her and against her walls in a wicked clockwise motion. He felt his heart swell in his chest as he studied the emotions clearly etched on her face. Somehow in these short days, this feminine had become as integral to his life as food and water. The physical was becoming deeply entwined with the emotional and Anansi ached at the thought of their parting. "What will I do without you?" he asked not caring that he exposed himself.

Aja brought her hands up to stroke his face. She felt his emotions so strongly at that moment. Her eyes felt sensitive to the fire's light, and she recognized that familiar tingling of her body whenever she honed in on someone's feelings and emotions.

Anansi's eyes widened as the pale metallic gold moles on her chin and on her forehead deepened in color. She gasped harshly, and her fingernails dug deeply into the muscles of his arms as her honey colored eyes flashed bright white.

Her powers were back, and he knew there was nothing he could hide from her. And he did not care. He held her tighter, stroking deeply inside her as she matched his tempo and rhythm.

He loves me.

She felt it. She absorbed it. It made her intoxicated. She felt able to soar. It was magnificent. Never had she felt desire, passion, and love. Never.

She lightly kissed his lips as tears filled her

eyes. "You will miss me as much as I will miss you," she told him softly. "And you will never forget me just like I will...*never*...forget you."

As a tear raced down her cheek, he lowered his head to capture it with his lips.

"No one masculine can or will ever compete. He will forever fall short of this. He will forever chase a losing battle." Aja's voice broke with all the emotion swelling between them like a rising tide that eventually washed over them, taking them under.

Anansi felt sweat coat his body as his nut rose with an intensity that shook him. He stopped his strokes and held his body still as he waited for it to subside. He felt her hips shift downward, pulling on his hardness, and shook his head. "Please...do not move. I'm not ready to cum. I'm not ready to be out of you."

She kissed him as Anansi rested his forehead against hers.

He grunted lightly as he allowed a tiny bit of his release to fill her. "Feel that?" he asked thickly as his dick pulsed.

Aja worked her walls to lightly clamp and then release his tool. "Feel that?" she countered.

Anansi visibly shivered as he nodded.

Slowly he began that wicked grind of his hips, feeling his dick slide in and out of her. Pulling himself out of her enough to stroke her quivering clit before he stroked inside of her again. He felt core became hotter, wetter, and just loosened enough for him to stroke harder, but not hurt her with his size.

"I feel like every day could be our last," he admitted with honesty as he stroked them both to mindless pleasure. "I hate that. I hate it, Aja."

"Then let's enjoy what we have while we have it."

Anansi shifted his hands up to hold her face. "No other feminine can or will ever compete. She will forever fall short of this right here. She will forever chase a losing battle," he whispered into her mouth as he felt Aja's wall rhythmically clutch and release his dick as she coated him with her juices. She cried out in passion, and he swallowed it with a kiss as his own climax made everything from his toes upward tingle with anticipation before he filled her with his seed.

They kissed as they slowly mated to a special rhythm all their own. They held each other tightly as they seemed to float and drift in their own galaxy, lost in the tumultuous waves and blinding white-hot spasms of their releases.

XI

Aja stared out the window of the planetary cruiser amazed by being so close to the *urjiis*. She splayed her hand against the glass, her excitement and wonder unbridled. "When I was little I used to lay on the top of our *goojjoo* and count them and down there on our planet they look like tiny white dots," she told Anansi, the vastness of the dark galaxy reflected in her eyes. "But up here, up close, they are so large and bright. It's just amazing."

She felt Anansi's eyes on her as he rubbed her back where they sat in the rear of the cruiser. It sat still amid the inky vastness because he honored her request to slow the vehicle down so that she could take in being in space. Initially, when the vessel left the bay of the *Spaceship Infinite,* it had moved at such high speed that everything around them was a blur.

"And I used to love to mate under the *urjiis*," Aja admitted, her breath fanning against the window as her eyes darted, taking in everything.

Anansi said nothing. He didn't have to.

She turned and smiled as she leaned back against his chest, snuggling her arm through his. "Don't be jealous, Anansi," she teased lightly as she nuzzled his cheek.

"Jealous? I'm not jealous," he balked.

Aja cleared her throat and looked up at him.

He chuckled as he lowered his head to taste her lips. "Did I tell you I'm beginning to regret having your powers restored?" he joked, his black eyes bright and dancing with humor.

"Never be afraid of your true feelings, Anansi," she said, squeezing his arm one last time before she released him and turned back to the window.

"Okay," he began. "I am feeling impatient and would like to increase speed to finish our journey."

She smiled at her reflection in the glass and allowed herself one last perusal of space before she sat back, tucked her feet beneath herself and eyed him. "I'm done. Thank you," she said.

He maneuvered his fingers above a transparent tablet on the console by his arm without ever touching his tips to it. Moments later, the cruiser launched forward, and the galaxy outside was a blur again.

She looked around at the interior of the sizable cruiser. Although it had been docked aboard the spaceship, it belonged to Anansi. Like his *diinqa*, the entire interior was black and sleek with enough room and height for its occupants to walk around during the journey.

Aja eyed the four automatons traveling with them. Her first interaction with the lifelike creations had scared her when she happened upon a collection of them in the lowest level of Anansi's mana. Like then, they stood at ease with their eyes wide open and unblinking, dressed in dark blue uniforms, with nothing but a silver barcode branded on their chin to distinguish them as artificial beings.

In the very brief time since she been on Planet Erised, Aja had seen firsthand how different life was on her planet and Anansi's. She had experienced things only told to them by the *abuturoos* and things perhaps even they couldn't even imagine had developed since they left to establish themselves on Nede.

Like lifespans reaching two *jaarraas*.

Aja had never realized just what they lacked on Nede, how far behind they were. But she'd never had anything to compare it to before. She wasn't saying Erised was flawless, but she was coming to ponder if some of the advances wouldn't benefit Nede.

Or what is left of our ollaa.

Sadness overwhelmed her, but she made the concerted effort to distract herself. "Where are we going?" she asked, looking at Anansi's profile.

"Nice try," he teased. "You'll see where we're going when we get there."

Aja just smiled as she turned to look out at the universe. She felt Anansi's warmth and her eyes focused on his reflection as he shifted over to sit close beside her. One of his hands rested on her hip.

"Erised is scheduled for a rare nightfall in two days, and I would love to meet you on my rooftop to make love under the *urjiis*," he said, before pressing a kiss to her bare shoulder in the white strapless tunic she wore.

Her body trembled as she leaned back against his muscular chest and clasped his hand to draw his arm around her waist. "I look forward to that," she said, her body warming as she sensed his intense desire for her.

∞

Anansi stroked Aja's hair as she napped with her head in his lap. He was glad she was asleep because he didn't trust his thoughts or emotions around her now that her empathic powers had been fully restored.

The chief emotion plaguing him was guilt. He wanted to tell Aja about his upcoming *qaadhimamuu* to Oduda Diasi—the very feminine she hated and wanted to punish with deliberate slowness.

Time was running out. Plans had to be made. The truth would soon be revealed whether he was prepared for it or not.

Just as he had to ready himself for losing Aja Drakar from his life.

He swore and took a deep breath before wiping his hand over his mouth as he tilted his head back against his seat. He never knew that so very quickly the things between him and Aja would become so serious, so deep and so emotional. Their rule was to enjoy what they had while they had it. They were supposed to be prepared to let go of each other.

He never expected to fall in love.

He looked down at her sleeping face, her soft mouth slightly ajar. *I love her, and I am going to lose her.*

That was hard to accept.

Anansi looked down at the console. The

planetary cruiser was navigated by an automaton, although he was equipped to do so, and he was able to see the same advanced view of the path they voyaged as the pilot.

He felt excitement at the sight of the small blue and purple planet looming before them. Minutes later the vessel landed with ease in a large open field with grass of the deepest purple. They had arrived with no fanfare just the way he wanted. This wasn't about publicity for the *Giiftiin* of Erised visiting the war-torn Nede planet with a native.

"Aja, wake up."

"I'm awake. All closed eyes aren't asleep, Anansi."

He laughed as she sat up and stretched. He kept his eyes locked on her as she looked out at the landscape. He missed no detail when her expression went from curiosity to doubt to surprise.

"It's Nede," she said without question as she placed her hand against the glass.

Anansi rose and held his hand out to her. "Yes. I want you to show me your world," he said as his gut wrenched at the sadness she tried to keep from her eyes.

He squeezed her hand as she slipped it into his.

"Has the treaty been signed? Are your returning me back to Nede?" she asked as the guards escorted them off the space cruiser.

Her eagerness to get away from him sparked anger. "No. The Kordis have officially evacuated the planet, but the country is still unsafe for Empaths with the *gabra* market in full swing."

Aja tugged on Anansi's hand as he watched one of the guards unload a *xiyyaara* from the rear of the cruiser. He turned his head and looked off into the distance. "You cover it well, but I feel your anger," she said. "Just like I have felt the guilt you have because you are holding something back?"

"Such as?" he asked as he squinted his eyes against a sudden gust of wind as they stood in the center of the field.

"I don't know. You tell me, Anansi."

"You seem to know everything, so you tell me," he shot back at her, his ire making him irrational.

Aja licked her lips as she met his dark and brooding look. "Am I wrong for wanting to return to Nede and resume my own life? Am I wrong for being uncomfortable knowing I am owned by you or anyone else? Am I crazy to hope that this madness can go back to normal?"

Anansi knew she spoke the truth. There was no permanent place in his life for her, and there was nothing he could do about it. It was wise of her to stay focused on her goal of returning to Nede. His anger dissipated.

"Thank you for understanding," she said, completely zoned in on his feelings.

"Do you understand why you will be returning to my *mana* and not remaining here on Nede?" he asked, easing his hand from her grasp.

"Do you promise to tell me what is going on with this treaty and what your role is in it all?" she countered as she held a hand up to block the wind and the *aduu* from her eyes.

Anansi and Aja squared off as he looked down at her and she met his long glare.

"Fine, Anansi. Keep your secrets and that guilt that's eating you up but don't get upset because I don't like living my life in the dark. I like to be in control just as much as you do." Aja turned and ignored him as she surveyed the land.

"If you try to escape I will have to use every measure to ensure you fail," he warned her.

Aja whirled around, and her eyes flashed as her hair was caught in a turbulent air stream. "Say what, say who?" she snapped.

Anansi never thought she looked more beautiful.

"Why ruin what could've been a nice day? I wasn't going to try to escape, Anansi. Seeing Juuba on sale at the *bwa kasuwa* and cured me of that."

He made the wrong move, and he regretted it. "I—"

She held up her hand as she turned from him.

"Don't bother. I accept your apology."

Anansi took two large steps forward to lightly grab her wrist and whip her back around into his arms. "Let me tell you how I feel even if you know it before I do," he said wryly. "I'm masculine enough to admit when I'm wrong and I apologize for that."

Aja just shrugged.

He offered her his hand again.

"The truth will always step into the light, Anansi," she told him even as she slid her hand into his warm grasp.

∞

Surrounded by the guards Anansi and Aja climbed into the rear of the *xiyyaara*. As it rose to the air under the guidance of the ooftuu, they settled into the back. Aja twisted her hair up into a loose top knot as she looked down at what was left of Nede. "The ollaa was set up on the southern side of the planet. It was more conducive to farming and our simplistic way of life," she said aloud to no one in particular. "We always have had respect, reverence even, for the land, the sky, the water, and fire."

She was nervous about her first sight of their *ollaa*. She didn't know how much more loss she could bear.

The *xiyyaara* soared above the crimson trees.

Aja frowned as she spotted smoke in the distance. It had been nearly two *torbaans* since the Kordi invasion. *Is our* ollaa *still burning?*

They soared over the hill. She fell silent as she took in the scorched remains of *goojjoos* and the long stretches of land where lives had been destroyed. The Kordi lasers had burned holes in the grass and cracked the trunk of trees, sending them falling over onto their sides. One lay across the irrigation system and another through the field of crops.

The Nede people were either dead or *gabras*.

No laughter. No activity. No work. No sign of life.

The *ollaa* was a wasteland.

There was nothing but loss.

She allowed him to pull her back into his embrace, feeling comforted as he kissed the top of her head and stroked her back. "I promise you that things for the Nede people are already on track for getting better. We will all settle into a galaxy of peace and co-existence. My people are aiding in that as are the entire coalition."

"I believe you, Anansi. I know that you speak the truth and I look forward to this peaceful coexistence although I know I will *never* forgive the Kordis—particularly Oduda Diasi." She wiped away her tears and stiffened her back with a determination not to wallow in her pain.

"We're here," Anansi said.

Aja felt pain spread across her chest. Memories of the night her family was killed by Kordis came back in a rush. Her eyes darted to the exact spot where their bodies fell.

Her eyes clouded as she recalled the Kordi's thirst for blood. "We had nowhere to run or hide. They killed innocent people, Anansi."

The *xiyyaara* lowered to the ground just outside the communal area bordered with rocks. As the vehicle lowered to the ground, swirls of black dust rose to lightly coat the windows.

Anansi pressed his large hand to the small of her back. "Aja—"

"Ssshhh." She was so lost in absorbing being back on her home planet that she barely registered the doors automatically opening and the seats rotating outwards with ease.

Without hesitation, she exited, pausing just long enough to kick off her footwear and press her toes into the warm black dirt before she raced the short distance to the circle of rocks. She took a deep breath of air before falling to the spot where her brother fell to his death. She winced at the clear memory of that fatal moment. "Llor," she whispered, missing him with an intensity that shook her.

Her tears wet the dirt as she frantically crawled

on her knees over to where the strike of a single laser struck down her parents at one time when her *da'ee* had wrapped her arms around the masculine she loved.

Anansi came up beside her. "It's not safe to enter that, Aja," he warned her as she headed closer to the remains.

She paused feeling his concern for her. "You're right," she said, turning back to face him. She released a tortured cry, digging her fingers into the dirt and balling her hands into fists as the pace of her tears quickened. Her back arched with each deep heave.

"Aja."

She felt Anansi's warmth as he knelt beside her. Blindly, she reached out and clasped his hand, squeezing it tightly. "Leave me be," she begged, lowering her head to the dirt. "Please."

He pressed a kiss to her hand. Seconds later he released her and was gone from beside her.

Aja was glad for the solace as she allowed herself to grieve.

Her tears burned her eyes.

Her sorrow aggrieved her soul.

It was overwhelming, but she pushed through, feeling every bit of her grief. Her Empath powers intensified it all. The pain was visceral.

With dirt still clutched in her fists, Aja sat up slowly and tilted her head back as she deeply inhaled and exhaled through her open mouth. She focused on inner balance of her emotions as she counted slowly, mouthing, "*Tokko, lama, sadi, afur, shan...*"

Aja continued counting until her body went still, and she felt disconnected from her emotions. She spread her arms wide and opened her hand, allowing the rich black dirt to seep through her splayed fingers.

She was at peace. Calm. Still.

It took her years to perfect the technique taught to her by her *da'ee* whenever her Empath powers left her feeling overwhelmed. At that moment, she was grateful for her perseverance.

She lowered her hands to the top of her thighs and opened her eyes as she looked forward.

Anansi stood there, looking down at her his black eyes filled with concern and curiosity.

Aja offered him a smile and extended her arm to him.

He stepped forward and grasped her wrist to gently pull her to her bare feet. "You okay?" he asked.

She nodded, looking up at him briefly. "I know that this all seems outdated in comparison to your world," she began, moving around his large frame to look at the tattered remains of the *ollaa*. "But this place represented decades upon decades of hard work to even advance us this far."

Aja turned to Anansi, shaking her head in disbelief. "My *abuturoos* came to this planet with nothing but a desire to live in peace. Everything we had was built from scratch," she continued. "*Everything.*"

Anansi remained quiet.

"Our irrigation system," she said, waving her hand towards the ruins.

She turned. "Our farms."

She turned again. "Our *goojjoos*. Each one built by hands. Piece by piece."

Aja turned once more and began walking up the middle of the wide dirt-packed path. "Those of us who get to return here to *our* world will rebuild," she swore, her strength and confidence in that were obvious in her tone.

Anansi and his automaton guards followed behind her as she came to stand in front of the remains of Pintar Neek's *goojjoo*. "Our leaders will return," she said.

I hope.

They continued up the path, stepping over debris, and taking in the destruction. Aja gasped at the sight of the charred remnants of her family *goojjoo*. The red door and a portion of the front walls were all that still stood. The rest of the structure was in blackened and smoky heaps behind it.

Everything was lost.

Her eyes leveled on where her *diinqa* once sat, and she thought of the many nights she lay in her *qanddii* after a hard day of work toting water, picking *mkpu̱ru̱*, or teaching younger Empaths how to home in and use their powers the way she was guided by her *da'ee*.

Her eyes darted from the space where room once stood, and memories were made. And now nothing remained but her recollections. "I see nothing but destruction, *but* this is my home, my heritage, my past and my future," she stressed, perhaps to remind herself even more than Anansi.

Silence reigned.

Anansi was the first to break it.

"Aja, there is something I need you to do."

She turned to face him. "Yes, Anansi?" she asked, her voice soft.

He stepped closer to her. "I sent an exploratory team ahead, and the bodies of the deceased have been collected and preserved at the burial ground."

Aja eyed him.

"Come," he said, holding out his hand to her.

She took it as the fast and hard pounding of heart nearly deafened her. They moved past the last of the *goojjoos* and came to a grove of sprawling crimson trees. Just through a break in the wide trunks, she spotted rows of long and clear pods floating above open graves. Each was aglow, but she wasn't sure if it was lit from within or if the glare of the *aduu* reflected off of them. Her gut clenched and her steps faltered a bit.

"It won't be easy, Aja, but it's necessary for the bodies to be identified," Anansi said tightening his hand around hers.

She tugged her hand from his and took off at a full run to eat up the distance to reach the pods. Her feet left deep indentations in the soft dirt as she moved in a zig-zag pattern between the trees. Out of the corner of her eye, she spotted one of the automatons fly past the edge of the grove like a bullet. As soon as she broke through the trees, it hovered beside her as she came to the first pod, almost sliding in the dirt beneath the pod and into the grave.

"Aja?" Anansi yelled out in alarm coming to run up beside her.

Aja pressed her hands to the pod and looked down into the face of Manteek Naneen. There were no visible injuries, and the light from within the pod made him look peaceful, the kind found only during restful sleep or death. Her heart ached that it was the latter.

"All the bodies were collected?" she asked, glancing back over her shoulder.

"Yes," Anansi answered with a nod.

Then the bodies of my family are here as well. She looked down the long length of illuminated pods, steeling herself for the moment when she would look down into the face of her deceased loved ones.

"Say their name clearly to be recorded and we'll make sure it's inscribed on a headstone," Anansi explained, coming to stand by her side with his hands crossed behind his wide back.

His presence blocked some of the rays of *aduu* from beaming directly down upon her.

"Can you be sure to also mark the grave with the role they played in the survival of our people," she requested. "It's important...especially with all our written records possibly destroyed."

With a long exhale of breath that she hoped would steady her, Aja rose to her feet. "Manteek Naneen," she said clearly. "A dedicated farmer and thus one of the providers of nourishment for our people."

Aja looked on in curiosity as, and an innate protection of her people as Anansi pressed a hand to the top of the pod. The light faded, shrouding the preserved body in darkness before it lowered into the open grave.

She moved to each pod, spoke their name

aloud, gave the name of their lifemate or children, acknowledged their position in the *ollaa*, and always ended with a request to the *waaqa* of resurrection that the spirits found new bodies.

One by one. Men. Women. Children. She'd lost count but knew it close to a hundred if not more.

Aja paused. Only three remained. She didn't dare look. Not yet. "How did you know?" she asked with a softness that revealed her resolved had weakened.

Anansi looked down at her with those black eyes of his. "I remember you telling me about the Kordi invasion, and your description was so clear that when I surveilled the *ollaa*, I knew right away from the positioning of the bodies that it was your parents and your brother."

She took that all too important step to look down into the pod. Her eyes glistened with tears. She swallowed over a lump in her throat. "Llor Drakar," she said, clearing her throat. "Farmer."

Anansi nodded.

"Shia Drakar, lifemate of Malc, and life giver of Llor and Aja," she said, smiling a little as she let eyes flit over her *da'ee's* face. "Teacher and singer."

She moved on. "Malc Drakar, lifemate of Shia, sire of Llor and Aja," she finished, stroking the pod and hungering to feel the warmth of her *abbaa's* skin. "Historian. Elder. Researcher. Inventor."

Anansi stepped back from her. She was thankful he allowed her time alone with them. She said nothing because the Empaths believed in the afterlife and she felt their spiritual presences very strong around her.

Aja had no idea how long she sat there, but Anansi patiently waited for her.

With one final touch to each of their pods, Aja stepped back as each darkened and lowered into the grave. She turned and rushed into Anansi's arms. "How can I tell you how much it means to me to know they all were properly buried together here on the land that we all loved and cherished so much? How can I repay you?" she asked, her words muffled against his chest.

Anansi raised one strong and masculine hand to stroke her cheek. "Consider it all said and done."

She allowed him to pull her to his side as they made their way back to the *xiyyaara* in silence.

∞

"Don't do this to me! You can't. What am I supposed to do without you?"

Oduda turned mocking violet eyes on Huung as he knelt at her feet. His desperation was pungent. "Your business in Kordi is complete and returning home a day early should not be *this* big of a problem. Our time together is over."

Huung rose to grab her body to his as he tried to plant kisses on her face and press his erection against her bared belly. "Be my lifemate?" he pleaded. "I love you. I want you. I *need* you, Oduda."

She tried to struggle out of his tight oppressive grasp, wishing she had decreased his dosage of the concoction she gave him. "I have to take care of some business," she lied with ease.

"I'll go with you," Huung asserted.

It became clear she underestimated the power of her brew.

Unease flooded her.

"No, that's not possible."

Huung's eyes darkened in disappointment. "I can't be away from you, Oduda. I *can't,*" he stressed, his voice frantic and his skin sweat-soaked as he looked at her with crazed eyes.

Oduda futilely pressed her hand against his shoulders, feeling the pressure of his arms against her ribs. "Huung, you're hurting me."

"And if you leave it...will...HURT...ME!" he roared. "I WILL NOT LET YOU LEAVE ME!"

"Okay," she lied.

He looked down at her. "Okay?" he asked with child-like hope.

"Yes, I won't go."

Oduda breathed a sigh of relief when he

released her. She moved over to the table beside her *qanddii*, taking rapid breaths through her mouth.

"And will you be my lifemate?" Huung asked as he walked over to her with his male hood swinging like an arm between his legs.

As soon as he stood before her, Oduda reached out with the infuser she removed from the drawer and pressed it to his neck in one fluid movement. His eyes had widened in shock before he fell to his knees. He swung an arm out towards her, but she hopped up onto the *qanddii* just before he fell face forward onto the floor with an echoing thud.

Oduda climbed down and stepped over his prone body before she double clapped her hands. Moments later there was a brief knock on the door of her *diinqa*. "Enter," she called out, not bothering to hide her nakedness as her new servant walked into the room.

Bhula was every bit of seventy *baras*, and as wide as she was short with hair as white as *cabbii*. "I have taken your *shaanxtaa* to the *xiyyaara*. How else may I help you, *Giiftiin* Oduda?"

She stepped into a strapless lilac *huccuu* gown. Bhula immediately stepped forward to assist her.

"Guards," Oduda yelled out as she dramatically flung a matching cloak over her shoulders and pulled the elaborately decorated hood over her sensitive bald head.

Two leather dressed guards stepped into the *diinqa*. "Make sure Huung is returned to his planet...immediately," she coldly ordered.

As her servants scurried to do her bidding and avoid her wrath, Oduda turned on her mini *komputara* that fit the palm of her hand. "Locate Reeock Jhyun."

"Reeock Jhyun located."

"Connect," she said, sliding her free hand into one of the deep pockets of her cape.

"*Giiftiin* Oduda, I've been anxiously awaiting your communication," he said, his long, thin, and black forked tongue slithering from his open mouth. with a split in the tip

"I've received your report, and I must say I was disappointed," she told him as she headed out of her *diinqa* and towards the transportation berth on the lower level of her mana. "Hardly worth the price we discussed, Reeock."

"Is it my fault the masculine has no real secrets?" Reeock asked, his lisp pronounced.

"Is it my fault I am not transferring any additional *warqee* to you," she said, descending the stone stairs before she climbed into the back of her waiting *xiyyaara*.

The green splotches on Reeock's iridescent blue head deepened in color. "We had a deal, Oduda Diasi," he lisped, as he brought his fist down on the wooden table where he sat.

"*Nagaya*, Reeock." She ended the communication without a second thought and then pulled up the electronic report he sent to her. The handsome and chiseled face of Captain *Giiftiin* Anansi Nyame filled the screen.

Oduda slid her hand beneath her hood and stroked her scalp.

If she had known *this* was the masculine she was to spend her life with she would have never made him wait or sent that *badaa* Aja Drakar to him. She thought of her future lifemate pleasuring the Empath and anger gripped her as she felt irrationally duped. "Hurry to my space cruiser," she shouted as she looked out the darkened glass window at the cold winds whipping outside the *xiyyaara*.

"I have to get to Planet Erised."

XII

"Are you sure you're not afraid?" Anansi asked Aja. "I know it's so long and wide."

"Trust me; I'm built to handle it, Anansi."

"It's quite a ride, and you shouldn't hop on it if you're scared."

"I could say the same for you."

"I bet you'll scream as you go down on it."

"Careful *you're* not the one screaming, Anansi."

Aja gave him one last look over her shoulder before she pushed off and went whooshing down the slide leading from the rear of his *mana* to the pool awaiting her at the base. She threw her hands up as her body skimmed across the thin layer of water as it spiraled, twisted and turned. She took a deep breath and held it just moments before her body broke through the water and plunged like a missile. She kicked her feet to propel her body back upward.

Just as she emerged, she felt the splash of water against her face as Anansi landed. Moments later his arms surrounded her waist as he lifted her high above his head beneath the three Erisedian *aduus*.

"No, Anansi, don't," she cried out, covering her face with her hands.

He eased her back down into the water to pull her body close to his. "Are you okay?" he asked with concern as she buried her face against his neck.

Aja nodded and snaked her arms around his waist. "With the return of my powers, my eyes are sensitive to the constant light here on Erised," she admitted.

"Do you want to go in?" he asked, assessing her with his fathomless black eyes.

She shook her head. "I just can't stare directly into the light when I'm outside," she said, taking in the beauty of his face with his dreadlocks piled high above his head emphasizing his square jawline and high cheekbones.

Anansi nodded in understanding.

"Besides, this is the best I've felt in a long time,

Anansi," she told him with a smile as she blessed him with a kiss before she brought her knees up and pressed her feet against his hard chest to push off. She waved as she went swimming away from him backward, enjoying the feel of the warm water and the exotic surroundings. She still was trying to understand how it all was a visage conjured by the beloved technology that dominated the planet.

Aja made her way over to the waterfall and lifted her head high above the water to inhale the sweet scent of the flowers that bloomed in shades of reds, purples, whites and deep blues with enough greenery to make her feel she was in a forest and not Anansi's backyard.

It reminded her of the best of Nede.

Aja pushed away the sadness that crept up on her. The time she and Anansi shared the past few days were special to her. It was way more than she had been looking for when she seduced him in that steamy *dhiqata* that day, but how could she deny her feelings for him? She knew as an Empath she was more aware and in touch with her feelings. She was in love with Anansi Nyame. She loved him. Plain and simple. To think she once tried to kill him and now she knew she would die for him.

She watched him take his time to swim over to her, and her heart swelled with love for him. She dove under the water and quickly removed her gold two-piece before she reemerged, using her hands to push the wet strands of her hair from her face.

"I have to go in and handle some business, Aja," Anansi said as he reached for her. His eyes smoldered when she lightly wiggled her bare breasts against her chest.

Aja sighed at the feel of his curly chest hair tickling her nipples. "You have business to handle right here," she whispered against his neck before she bit him playfully as she used her hands to jerk his trunks down his narrow hips. As her hands came up, they brushed against his erection.

Anansi steered her towards the waterfall, letting the cascade pour down on them lightly as they shared a tender kiss that quickly deepened. The water around them seemed to become as steamy as a hot tub.

Aja leaned backward a bit enjoying the feel of the water pounding down against her full breasts and dripping from the tips of her hard nipples. She gasped when she felt his mouth latch onto one as he circled it with his tongue. A sigh escaped her mouth as she brought one hand up to massage the back of his neck.

"Let's go in the cavern," she huskily suggested as she massaged his hardness in the water, pulling *it* and him towards the small cave behind the waterfall.

Aja climbed out of the water first and laid her nude body back against the cool base of the grotto as Anansi climbed out behind her. Her eyes missed nothing about him as the water cascaded from the hard contours of his body to drip from the tip of his dick. The light of the *aduus* framing the entrance and highlighted him. His broad square shoulders and lean muscular branded arms, strong chest and ridged abdomen with a small jagged scar on his hip. His legs were like that of a powerful animal, flexing and tensing as he walked to her with his tool swinging like a heavy pendulum. Back and forth.

Aja's was hot with anticipation and aching for that deep-down fulfillment only he seemed built to deliver. "It's a shame for one masculine to be so beautiful," she told him without disgrace or pause as she tossed her hair over her shoulders and spread her legs before him.

Anansi dick rose up. Hard. Curving. Wanting.

She spread her legs wider and brought her knees up to her shoulders.

"It's a shame for one feminine to be so beautiful... *everywhere*," he stressed as he dropped to his knees to crawl the rest of the way to her. He kissed a fiery trail from her toes to the thighs.

Aja shivered.

When his mouth reached the plump lips shielding her femininity, she felt his breath caress her clit, and she gasped in anticipation. His tongue stroked the plump bud first. "Yes," she panted, closing her eyes as her heart raced.

The tip of her his clever tongue fluttered against the swollen flesh with the speed of butterfly wings.

She cried out, arching her back.

His lips suckled her.

She spread her legs to the limit as she moaned from deep in her gut, feeling the wicked blur between reality and fantasy.

He groaned in mindless pleasure as he tastes her from the crease of her buttocks up to dip inside her before he shifted up to circle her clit.

"I'm gonna cum, Anansi," she cried out, her entire body alive with desire.

Quickly, he moved his toned frame to probe her warm and moist opening with the tip of his dick before he arched his back and flexed his hips to fill her tight heat with his hardness. "Aja," he moaned against her throat, sucking that little dip above her clavicle as he stroked inside her with speed and fiery determination to feel her climax against his dick.

She obliged. Her cries echoed around them in the cavern as heat exploded within her as his rigid length slid back and forth against her walls. Over and over. "Anansi," she gasped, trembling with each wave of her release as she coated his dick with her juices and her walls clenched and released his hardness, pushing them both over the edge.

Giiftiin Nyame, there is a communication from The Spaceship Infinite *and a request for permission to transport.*

They both swore at the sound of XR-2's mellow voice echoing inside the grotto.

Aja froze, but Anansi shook his head as he looked down into her eyes with hot determination. "I'm not stopping," he promised her, his voice thick. "No way."

She reached up to free his locs and entwined some in her fingers as she worked his hips to match his. "No way," she parroted him, biting her bottom lips as she worked her inner muscles to prime his dick.

He swore and looked down in wonder, moments before his dick hardened even more inside of her and his body froze above her as he coated her walls with his explosive release.

She took over and worked her hips up and down to drain him.

Anansi bit the inside of his cheek to keep from hollering out as rode the waves until his body slackened and he wrapped an arm around her waist to carry her body with him as he rolled over onto his back.

Giiftiin Nyame, there is a communication from The Spaceship Infinite *and a request for permission to transport.*

"Is he everywhere?" Aja snapped in exasperation.

"At moments like this, the answer to that is an unfortunate yes." Anansi playfully swatted her bottom for her to rise before he rose to his feet.

"You go ahead. I'm going to try and cool off," Aja said, before diving into the water and allowed herself to enjoy the feel of the warm water pressing against her body. She swam until her arms and legs, leaving the water to wrap a thick furry cloth around her nude body before she raced onto the small *kaasuu* that carried her back to the rear opening of the *mana*.

Hoping he was done with his business so they could enjoy dinner, Aja headed to his office. "Anansi—"

"Well, isn't this...*something*." Oduda Diasi's amethyst-tinted eyes were cold as they raked up and down Aja's shapely form with obvious derision and scorn.

Surprise froze Aja at Oduda's presence at first. That quickly boiled into anger. She fed on Oduda's own turbulent and hateful emotions as she let out a barbaric scream and flew across the room. She dug her fingernails into Oduda's neck as she forcefully knocked the other feminine to the floor under her weight. She slapped Oduda's cheek in rapid succession.

Whap-whap-whap-whap-whap!

Even as Anansi wrapped his arm around Aja's waist and lifted her off Oduda, Aja continued to swing, kick and swear wildly.

Oduda gripped the edge of his desk to rise to her feet. Her lip was split, and blood spotted her disheveled lilac cloak. "This is no way for a gabra to treat the future lifemate of the *Giiftiin* of Erised, Anansi."

Aja's eyes widened as he carried her out of the office. "Put me down, Anansi," she coldly ordered as her chest heaved and she pressed her nails into her palm until she thought she'd draw blood.

"Hurry back, Anansi, we have so much lost time to make up," Oduda called from the doorway of his office.

"Put me down. Put me down. Put...me...down!" Aja beat on his arm around her waist. It was as strong as a band of pure steel.

He didn't release her until the door to her *diinqa* closed securely behind them. Aja turned and pushed him hard in the chest with both her hands. He didn't budge one inch, and that frustrated her more.

"What did she mean?" Aja roared, her emotions raging as she paced like a caged wild animal. She stopped and faced him. "Tell me something, Anansi. Tell me something *now*."

"Will you calm down?" he asked. His face was unreadable.

"Calm down? Calm...down?" Aja stepped close to him and looked up at his face.

His eyes softened as he stared down at her. "Aja," he said.

She swallowed over a lump in her throat as she reached out pressed her palm to his bare chest. His regret, guilt, and his pain flooded her. It was true. He was to belong to her mortal enemy. "I'm nothing but your *gabra*, but I ask you to please leave me be Anansi. Your future lifemate awaits you."

His pain filled his face. "Aja, you don't understand—"

"I understand that what we had was nothing special. It was a nice way to pass the time, but let's be clear, Anansi, that *that* time has passed." Aja turned from him as she intensely felt the loss of all they shared recently. The pain of her heartbreak was so intense that she doubled over and clutched at her chest. Everything she thought they built was slipping from under her like sand in an hourglass.

All of it meant nothing now. Nothing.

Why, Anansi. Why?

She felt him walk up behind her as she forced herself to stand tall and not shed one of the tears nearly strangling her.

What am I to do now? What will happen to me? Will I be sent to the bwa kasuwa?

She turned to look up at him. "*Galatoomaa*, Anansi, for helping Juuba Huuntu and for all you did to properly bury my people. To give me the last chance to see my family," she said, her pain softening her tone. "You have treated me as anything but a *gabra* while I was here, but I do not appreciate you deceiving me about your relationship with *her*."

Anansi reached for her, and she shook her head, denying him. His hands fell to his sides. "I never lied to you, Aja. I told you there were things I couldn't discuss with you. Trust me, if I could change this, I would, but there is so much that is out of my hands."

Tears clouded her vision. "But what she said is true, right?" she asked softly as her eyes locked on the brilliant trio of *aduus* through the window.

"In all probability, Oduda Diasi will be my lifemate."

Aja felt her knees give out, but she refused to fall from the pain of him saying the words. Her mouth quivered as she sniffed back the tears she couldn't keep from filling her long lashes before they raced down her cheeks.

Anansi touched her arms, but she shook away his touch. "I never should have let this happen between us."

Aja closed her eyes against a wave of pain. "No,

we're both adults. We both agreed it was a dalliance. Your *badaa* awaits you, *master*," she hissed as she turned to face him.

Anansi placed his hands on her face.

She closed her eyes. His emotions flooded her. It confused her. The love she hoped for was there in his eyes and felt by her through his touch.

"Do you love her?" she asked, pressing her hands atop his, seeking the truth.

"No," he admitted, with a shake of his head. "I barely know her, and this is the first time I've seen her in so many *baras*."

Then why?

"No other feminine can or will ever compete. She will forever fall short to this right here. She will forever chase a losing battle," he huskily whispered as he kept his eyes locked with hers.

"Anansi, don't," Aja said, stepping out of his embrace. "I know this is your *mana* and I am your *gabra*, but I beg you to please leave me be."

He stood there for long a time before he finally turned and left. As soon as the curtain slid closed behind him, Aja fell in a heap on the floor. Her body heaved with hot, painful tears.

∞

Oduda's lip curled in hatred as she wiped the blood from her lip. She still could not believe that Empath gabra had attacked her. *For that, she will be punished.*

Her eyes lit with pleasure as she weighed presenting the *gabra* to Reeock or to just kill her and be done with it. Regardless, the *badaa* had to pay for her insolence.

Oduda turned as the door to his office slid open. She was disappointed to see that Anansi was now fully dressed in his military uniform sans the jacket. "This is a rather awkward situation, Anansi," she began as he moved past her to sit at his desk. "One that I feel you should correct immediately. She must go."

"Let's introduce ourselves and make some small

talk before you try to run my *mana*," Anansi said, as a chair rose from the floor for her use. He waved his hand towards it. "The *qaadhimamuu* is not official yet."

Oduda removed her cape and let it drape over the back of the chair to reveal the sheer lilac strapless gown she wore. It revealed her small but plump breasts and her large round areolas. When his eyes darted down, she pushed her chest forward a bit. "Can you imagine how it will look when our *qaadhimamuu* is announced, and it is discovered you keep your *gumna* right here in your *mana*? I doubt that will please either of our parents or The Council."

"First, she's not a *gumna* and second, I doubt they would be any more pleased to know you doped her up on *extos* and sent her to me naked as the day she was born."

Oduda eyes caressed his fine features as she crossed her legs and pulled the hem of her dress high up on her thigh. "I think it's clear today that you didn't oppose the gift."

"I was disappointed to discover your use of her as a sexual object. Once I discovered her system was filled with *extos,* I sedated her until the next morning." Anansi pierced her with hard black eyes. "I hope that type of conduct was a detour from your normal behavior."

Oduda's eyes flashed and deepened in color. "The Erisedian's treatment of the Empaths was enough for them to flee and set up a colony. Judge not the Kordi way of handling *gabras*, Anansi."

"That was *jaarraas* ago and thus hardly relevant as the Kordis terrorizing an entire race before forcing them to be *gabras*," Anansi said as he watched Oduda with quiet intensity.

"If you so obviously disdain my ways then why are we to be lifemates?" she asked, feigning hurt.

"I do not disdain you. I just acknowledge that our ways are different." Anansi held up his hands. "Thankfully with our *gaa'ila,* we will all learn to coexist in this galaxy. I look forward to the signing of the treaty. Don't you?"

Oduda laughed. "I look forward to one day being the *Giiftii* of Erised with all of the wealth and power it will afford me," she said with honesty.

Anansi leaned back in his chair and studied her with his ebony eyes. She was undoubtedly a beautiful woman, but it was clear the beauty was only on the surface. She would have never been his choice as a lifemate. "I do hope there is more to you than what I am seeing."

"Much...much more," Oduda told him huskily with a slow lick of her lips.

Anansi cleared his throat. "Aja is now under my protection. Once the *cidha* is performed, and the treaty signed she will be free to return to Nede. Until that time, she will remain under my protection."

"Here?" Oduda asked incredulously as she felt her jealousy rise about his obvious buttressing of the Empath.

Anansi frowned. "You sent her here."

"Okay, now I want to send her somewhere else," she insisted.

"Impossible. You gifted Aja to me, and legally that makes her my property and thus mine to do as I see fit."

Oduda felt a volatile rage build inside her even though she kept it masked well. This little exchange with Anansi was very revealing. She was used to being in control, and she wasn't going to get used to otherwise. This masculine was strong, confident, honorable, outspoken and used to being a leader. She would have to conjure something potent to break him down so that he bent to her will and not the other way around.

When she thought he was still overweight the thought of him having a concubine had been to her liking. Now she didn't want to share the fine masculine specimen at all.

"We're supposed to be seen publicly for the next *torbaan*," Anansi said averting his eyes from her body.

"My security and I will be staying here during the next *torhaan* or two...of course," she said, stroking her collarbone with the tip of her finger.

"If you wish," he said with obvious reluctance.

"I have *many* wishes you can fulfill, *Giiftiin*," she purred as she crossed and then uncrossed her legs offering him a long peek of her intimacy sans undergarments.

She hid her disappointment as he ignored her indecent exposure. Oduda could smell a virile masculine a mile away, and everything about Anansi Nyame—from the build of his body to the way he walked—said he was an excellent lover. She knew she was quite adept at pleasing a masculine—with or without her herbal assistance. He obviously needed a taste of her skill to realize the treasure with which he was being blessed. "I think we will be a good match, Anansi."

He nodded. "It certainly is a lifelong match," he said, being evasive.

"You sound disappointed," Oduda said with her voice clearly laced with irritation as she rose to her feet and reached behind her to unzip her dress. It fell with a whisper to the floor. "I'm sure you can see disappointment is something I'm not equipped to deal with."

Anansi's eyes perused her body leisurely once before his black eyes locked with her own. "You are a very beautiful feminine. I'm sorry if you feel insulted. Please don't. I have a lot on my mind, and I was in the middle of communication with my ship when you arrived unexpectedly."

"Of course, I understand. We have plenty of time to get better acquainted." Oduda smiled, but inwardly her chest was hot with anger at his rejection as she eased her dress back up on her gleaming brown body.

He rose to his feet, dismissing her. "I will activate one of my servant automatons for your use, and it will lead you to your room and help you to unpack."

'One of my brews will set him straight,' Oduda

thought as she gave him a false smile.

∞

Anansi felt trapped, and he knew he had no one to blame but himself. When Oduda Diasi sent Aja Drakar to him, he should have kept his distance from her. He should have resisted that instant pull he had towards her. Fought his desires for her. Ignored their chemistry. Sent her to another safe place until the treaty had been signed.

There was a line he crossed, because although he loved her—and he *did* love her—his priority had to be his responsibility as the heir to a powerful throne. He had to put the freedom of all the *gabras* over his feelings for one. To do otherwise would be selfish. He *had* to wed Oduda Diasi, and he was sworn by his duties as a captain for the coalition not to reveal the truth of his relationship with Oduda.

But it is Aja I love.

Anansi's heart ached at the thought of the day he would never see her again.

He had his future lifemate unpacking in a *diinqa* in a wing of his *mana* to the right of him and the feminine he loved, desired and wanted in a room down the hall to the left of him.

In a perfect world, the Kordis would sign the agreement without him aligning himself to Oduda for the rest of his life. Then he could let his feelings for Aja grow so that they had a future together. It was just over a *torbaan* since they first met and he felt like he could love her forever.

Anansi smiled at the image of a small baby with Aja's honey eyes feeding at her breasts as she rocked the babe to sleep.

But that would never happen. There would be no beautiful brown babies with Aja. No days filled with comfort and happiness. No more long nights of passion.

No more love.

Anansi tightened his hand into a fist and lightly pounded it on his knee.

Oduda Diasi was royalty, but she was not Aja.

He immediately surmised the *giiftiin* was cold and calculating. Oduda was a beautiful woman, but he didn't desire her. *Maybe* one day his desire for her would appear, but right now at this moment in his life, there was no feminine who could compete Aja. Oduda truly would be fighting a losing battle.

Anansi made his way to his diinqa, but he paused to look down the long and wide hall to the door of Aja's *diinqa*. He stood there for countless long moments debating whether to follow her wishes and leave her alone or give in to his desire to check on her.

Eventually, after pacing halfway between her door and his, he entered his *diinqa*. He had contacted his parents to let them know Oduda had arrived and they had immediately invited them over for dinner. His military dress uniform appeared at the foot of his *qanddii*. Needing to be cleaned he began to undress to use the *dhiqata*.

He was bending down to remove his boots when his eyes caught sight of the transport docking station. He rose slowly as his face went from curiosity to alarm at the body slumped down inside the vertical tube.

Anansi's heart slammed against his chest as he raced over to it. "Unlock transport dock," he ordered. As soon as the door slowly slid open, he pushed his fingers into the widening crack and forcefully pushed it out of the way.

Aja fell in a heap at his feet, and he knelt to scoop her up into his arms. He already knew she was unconscious. Once the transporter failed to identify her during the scan, she had been locked in and a drug released that rendered her unconscious.

He sat down on the *qanddii* and held her in his arms, his hands rising under the folds of her hair to massage her nape as he pressed her head to his shoulder. "Scan her XR-2."

"Subject is heavily sedated but in no imminent need for medic attention."

His heart ached as he kissed the top of her hair and inhaled deeply of her sweet scent as he rose with her still in his strong arms. "Transport us to her *diinqa*, XR-2," he said as his heart continued to race with concern for her.

In her *diinqa*, Anansi laid her on the *qanddii* and removed her boots before he pulled the covers up around her body. He ordered XR-2 to shut the window covers and to turn on the lights at a dim level giving the room a relaxing and intimate glow. A plush leather chair appeared by the *qanddii*, and he sat down on the edge of it as he leaned forward to wipe her hair from her face. He entwined his fingers with hers as his black eyes studied her.

"XR-2, I want interval scans done on her," he demanded as he caressed the inside of her palm with her thumb.

Time slipped by slowly for Anansi as he sat there watching over Aja like a hawk over its prey. She never moved or stirred as she lay there breathing slowly and deeply.

He was not going to move until he was assured she was okay.

XR-2 alerted him twice that his parents wanted to communicate with him. He never responded.

He was sure Oduda was curious to his whereabouts, but he his mind was focused on Aja and how she had been so desperate to escape from his mana that she unknowingly put her life at risk. If she had stayed in the transport dock much longer, she would have slowly sunk into a coma.

Anansi leaned forward to plant a kiss on her brow. "I'm sorry, Aja," he whispered into the quiet.

'Escape to where?' he wondered suddenly.

"XR-2 what was the destination requested for the failed transport?" he asked.

"Planet Whoor."

Anansi frowned, causing deep lines in his forehead. "XR-2, power on the *komputara* in this room and replay activity in my *diinqa* before the failed transport."

He turned a bit as the curtains on the far walls slid open to reveal the screen on the wall. Soon the image of his *diinqa* filled the screen. His eyes hardened as he watched Oduda Diasi drag an obviously unconscious Aja by her feet.

"XR-2 what exactly made her unconscious?" he asked coldly as he watched Oduda roughly place Aja in the transport dock.

"There were large levels of an unknown drug in her system before the transport failure."

Anansi felt anger like he had never known nearly squeeze the air from his chest. He rose and picked up Aja into his arms. He strode out of the room carrying her in his arms. He would handle Oduda Diasi later, but for now, he was taking Aja somewhere safe and away from Oduda clutches.

∞

Oduda lifted her foot high and kicked the chair sitting before the wooden dressing table of her guest *diinqa*. The chair went flying across the room to land with a loud thud against the wall. The double doors to her room opened, and she whirled around to see her servant automaton, Poda, enter the room. Poda was thin and tall with a slightly muscular build. Its simulated skin was like that of the Earthling's Caucasian race with ash blonde hair that was pulled back into a ponytail. It wore a tight fitting black bodysuit that showed it was anatomically correct.

Oduda rolled her eyes in frustration.

"May I be of any assistance?" Poda asked as it looked down at her with a blank, emotionless stare.

"Where is Anansi?" she snapped as she watched the automaton move across the room to pick up the chair and carry it back to its place before the dressing table.

"He has left the *mana*," Poda reported.

Oduda raised her foot and kicked the chair across the room again with a frustrated grunt. "How...dare...he?" she roared at the top of her lungs. "I am here as his guest and his future lifemate, and he leaves me while we're supposed to go to his parents for dinner?"

"How may I be of assistance?" Poda asked, her expression blank.

"GET OUT!" Oduda screamed as she picked up a bottle of her most precious fragrance to fling at the automaton in a fit of rage. It flew over Poda's head and burst against the wall.

XIII

As Aja stirred from her sleep, she had the distinct feeling of déjà vu. Her eyes felt heavy. There was a bitter, metallic taste in her mouth. She felt unaware of the right time or place. Her head pounded like crazy.

"Good, you're awake. You have my son very worried."

Aja turned her head to the left and looked into the face of a middle aged feminine who made wearing a simple black dress appear regal. In her face, she saw hints of Anansi, and she instantly felt endeared to her.

"Where am I?" Aja asked, as she slowly pulled herself to a sitting position.

"You're in my *mana*," she said with a soft smile. "I am Anansi's *da'ee* Mondi Nyame, Giiftii of Erised."

Aja's eyes dulled at the mention of Anansi's name. "I am—"

"Aja Drakar, an Empath from the planet Nede," Mondi finished for her. "Anansi has told us all about you while he sat by your *qanddii* all night."

Her eyes widened a bit in surprise before she darted them around the luxurious *diinqa*.

"He's gone. His *abbaa* and I suggested he return to his *mana* to attend to his guest."

She shrugged even as pain radiated across her chest. "No disrespect intended, *Giiftii* Mondi, but Anansi Nyame's whereabouts are none of my business," she said, her voice husky.

"What am I missing?" Mondi asked, sitting back on her floating seat as she eyed her. "You do not hide your hurt or your anger well."

"It is not easy to hear that he is entertaining the same feminine who held me captive and nearly starved me to death before she doped me up on *extos* and presented me to Anansi as a sexual *gabra*."

Mondi slid to the edge of her seat. "Oduda Diasi did what?" she asked, her pretty face shocked.

"Seriously?"

"We Empaths are honest people," Aja said with a tinge of defensiveness.

Mondi crossed her legs as she nodded. "Anansi requested that we offer you our protection until such time it is completely safe for you to return to your planet. We have of course agreed," she said, her black eyes filled with concern.

Aja frowned in confusion. "My safety?" she asked.

Mondi nodded. "Yes, after Oduda's attempt to banish you to Planet Whoor—"

"Planet Whoor!" Aja gasped in horror before her eyes burned brilliantly with anger and hatred.

"I am beginning to wonder if this *cidha* is just a deal with the devil," Mondi said, almost to herself.

So, they will be lifemates.

Aja glanced up at the towering ceilings as tried to fight off her disappointment. She had truly believed there would be more for her and Anansi. She allowed herself to believe that. But as hurt and angry as she was, Anansi had never promised more and thus had never deceived her.

There was so much that bewildered her.

If Oduda loved Anansi why would she send another feminine to seduce him?

Even now, the thought of him mating with Oduda, sharing his body with her, made Aja's gut burn with jealousy.

"Their *cidha* is soon?" she asked, hating the need for more details.

Mondi "Yes, in one *ji'a*. I am already planning the festivities since Oduda's *da'ee* died at her birth."

Aja rapidly blinked away any more tears because crying would change nothing. Her future with Anansi was now a complete non-issue. The man she loved belonged to another.

Mondi reached over and gently held Aja's chin, locking their eyes. "Last night my son asked to be released from the agreement to have Oduda Diasi as his lifemate. Now I know that you are the reason."

Aja's heart seemed to leap into her throat in joy

until she saw the sad look in Mondi's warm eyes. "My husband, Hwosi, refused," she said regretfully, her thumb stroking Aja's chin. "The matter is out of his hands. Both he and Anansi have an obligation to the coalition."

"So, Anansi *has* to make Oduda his lifemate?" Aja asked, her heart pounding.

Mondi nodded. "Yes, their *gaa'ila* is arranged. On the day of the *cidha,* a treaty will be signed..."

"To free the *gabras,*" they finished in unison.

The truth hurt far more. That surprised Aja. All of his cryptic comments about protecting her and his obligation all made sense. The very thing that would take Anansi from her would also free her.

Her love and respect for him deepened. *Oh, Anansi.*

"Didn't he tell you?" Mondi asked, giving her chin one last soft pat before withdrawing her hand.

Aja shook her head. "He said there were things he could not explain like he was sworn to secrecy or something."

Mondi shrugged. "Well, I am in no one's militia, and under no one's rule, so I've told you. So be it."

"Thank you," Aja said.

When the *giiftii* innocently touched her, Aja felt the kindness of her. "There's so much goodness in you," she admitted. "No animosity to be found. You love your son, and you're concerned about his relationship with Oduda and curious about his relationship with me."

Mondi nodded, turning as a tray appeared on the *qanddii.* She picked up a clear carafe and filled one of the glasses with *inaba* juice. "So, there is something between my son and you?"

Aja remained silent as she took the glass she offered and sipped the drink.

"You love my son very much, don't you?"

Aja released a heavy breath. "Is it that obvious?"

"Yes," Mondi said with a nod. "I do not need your powers to see what is clearly expressed in your beautiful eyes, Aja."

A tear raced down her cheek as she tried to swallow down the waves of disappointment. "I don't know why it bothers me so much because we both agreed that whatever happened between us would never last," she admitted softly as she looked out the window.

Mondi held her palm up, and a white *huccuu* handkerchief appeared. "Please understand that I also see in my son that this is not easy for him," she said, handing the soft cloth to Aja.

"Yes, to be honest, I do know how much he loves me. I know very well, but it doesn't change the fact that he will soon be joined for life with my sworn enemy."

"Would it feel better if he was to wed someone else?" Mondi asked.

"Honestly?" Aja asked.

Mondi bowed her head. "Of course."

"No, it wouldn't matter because any other feminine would still not be me," Aja said with honesty.

∞

"Wake up, Anansi. Breakfast is served."

He frowned as he opened his ebon eyes. The scowl deepened at the sight of Oduda Diasi standing nude before him with one chocolate leg bent as she played in the folds of her intimacy. She purred in the back of her throat as she lifted one full breast up to tease her own thick nipple with her agile tongue.

He dropped his head back against his pillow sacs as he shook his head and wiped his eyes with his hand. "We need to go over some ground rules, Oduda."

Anansi opened his eyes and caught a flash of something metal in her hand. Sitting up he reached out with a steely strength and caught her wrist in his grasp to turn her hand over. He applied just enough pressure for her to release the tube with a gasp. It dropped onto his lap, and he picked it up as he cut his eyes up to her face.

"XR-2, scan the contents of this infuser," he ordered as he rose to his feet, making sure to pull the *huccuu* covers around his waist to cover his nakedness as he maintained his tight grasp on her wrist.

Oduda eyed him with coolness.

"The infuser is filled with high levels of extos and other unidentifiable herbs."

His grip tightened.

"Just a little something to add to our fun, Anansi, nothing more...nothing less," she said with simplicity.

Her nonchalance made him want to choke her.

"You know if I had to use concoctions to make a masculine want me I would have serious doubts about my abilities to please as a feminine," Anansi coldly told her as he released her with a slight push that sent her two steps back from him.

"*Unless* the masculine has the sexual appetite of a eunuch," she countered nastily.

Anansi looked down at her. "My prowess isn't lacking, but my desire for you is."

Oduda turned her nude body and slowly walked across the room to pick up her robe from the floor.

Anansi held the *huccuu* covers with one hand behind his back as he watched her pull on the robe with a flourish.

She paused as her eyes dropped.

Anansi followed her line of vision and scowled as the thickness of his dick against his thigh was clearly outlined. He loosened his hold on the cover so that it was not quite so clinging.

"Pity you're so enraptured with a stupid Empath *gabra* that you pass over all of this for memories of what you will never have with her," she said spitefully as she spun for his perusal. "That *badaa* is exactly where she belongs. Good...riddance."

Anansi opened his mouth and then closed it. "What have you done with her?" he asked, feigning ignorance.

Oduda reached up to run her hands lightly over her bald head. "I sent that no good *gumna* where she belongs. Don't try to locate her. It really will be a waste of time. By now she may be dead...or worse," she finished with a maniacal laugh.

"XR-2, what is the location of Aja Drakar in the mana?" he asked.

"Subject is nowhere on the premises."

"See. You might as well move on with life...with me." Oduda opened her arms wide, opening her robe wide and exposing her nudity as she turned. "Once I move in we really have to add some color to this room. Black is so...depressing."

He said nothing else as she finally took her leave.

"XR-2 restrict Oduda Diasi and her security to her wing," he ordered.

"Command completed."

Anansi hadn't bothered to correct the Kordi *giiftiin* as to Aja's true whereabouts. At the end of their farce of dating, falling deeply in love, and having a royal *cidha*, he planned to immediately return to duty aboard the *Spaceship Infinite*. At least now he didn't have to worry about Aja falling prey to Oduda Diasi's madness.

∞

Aja stood up in the tub, and the water dripped off her body as she wrapped a drying cloth around herself as she stepped down out of it and enjoyed the feel of the fur between her toes. She made her way to her diinqa, *pausing in the archway as the tiny hairs covering her body stood on end. Suddenly, she felt breathless.*

"I've missed you, Aja."

She turned at the sound of his voice just as Anansi stepped from the darkness. Her eyes clouded as it trailed from his locs down every bronzed inch of his nakedness. She smiled as his dick lengthened and then lifted as if to greet her. "I knew you would come," she said throatily, dropping the cloth as he took her hand in his and lead her to the qanddii.

He climbed up on it on his knees near the edge. His hands framed Aja's face before shifting down to massage her shoulders and then her breasts before continuing down to cup her buttocks. It was as if he was trying to put it all in his memory. "I can't do it. I won't do it. I will not have Oduda as my lifemate. You are the only feminine for me."

Aja's smile could rival the glimmer of a million nkumes as she stepped up to Anansi and allowed her body to be thrilled by his closeness. She kissed a trail from one broad shoulder to the next, moaning slightly as she paused to suckle his neck. He shivered as she pressed her soft breasts against the hardness of his chest as she slowly slid her hands down his back to deeply massage his buttocks.

Anansi lightly bit her bottom lip as Aja pressed one of her feet onto the qanddii. As if on cue he slid his hand down to play in the soft curls growing back on her fleshy mound. "I like it better with a little hair," he whispered against her cheek as he slid his middle finger deep inside of her. Wetness and heat made him ache to slide his dick inside instead.

Aja began to circle her hips when Anansi thumb pressed against her throbbing clit as his middle finger fluttered against her inner walls. "You on my spot," she gasped before she sucked his bottom lip deep into her mouth.

"Right here?" he asked as he leaned back to watch her face.

Aja nodded as she eyed him through half closed lids. "That feels...so good," she moaned, flinging her head back while her juices coated his hand. "But I'm ready for more."

Anansi wrapped his arm around her waist as he eased his finger from to suck before he kissed her deeply and fell back on the qanddii. "You missed that didn't you?" he asked thickly as Aja shifted down his body to kiss and lick his smooth tip.

His heart pounded madly, and he clenched his buttocks as his hips reared up. She sucked him into her mouth, and the tip of his hardness tickled the back of her throat as she hummed. The vibration plus the steady flicker of her tongue and the deep motion of her lips made him holler out roughly as he clutched the huccuu sheets.

Aja felt him go rigid as stone in her mouth. With one last lick, she released his dick with a smack of her lips.

"Don't stop, baby," he begged.

"If I didn't stop you would finish before I even began," she teased softly, kissing her way up to his abdomen and then chest to lightly trace circles around his nipples.

"You know how much I love that," he said in a deep voice.

"Sure do," she returned lightly before kissing a trail across his chest to trace the other hard nipple as well. She enjoyed the feel of the soft hairs on his chest against her tongue.

Aja shifted to her knees beside him as she continued to suck, lick and taste his nipples as she stroked his stiff shaft from the base to the tip in a fluid up and down motion.

"Damn that feels good," he moaned, licking his lips as he put his hands behind his head to enjoy her tricks with his treats.

Her clit thumped with life between her legs. Just knowing she turned Anansi excited Aja. She reached down with her free hand to play in the slick folds of her femininity. Her hips jerked as her finger stroked the sensitive bud. She gasped against his chest.

Anansi turned on his side to watch her as he deeply stroked his own hardness. "Lay down," he instructed her as he squeezed and released his smooth tip.

Aja did as he bid, letting her head fall back over the qanddii, causing her breasts to lift higher until the tips looked like twin peaks.

Anansi used his hand at the base of his hardness to slip the tip inside her glistening wet core. He loved how she hissed at the feel of him. He used his hips to give her inch after inch after delicious rock-hard inch until the soft hairs surrounding his thick base tickled her buttocks as he stroked her deeply.

"Aah," he hollered out as Aja began to circle her hips causing her tight walls to pull downward on *his dick as the heat of her core made his tip swell until he thought it would burst.*

"Like that?" she asked.

"Damn right, throw it back. Throw it. Throw it." Anansi slid his hand from her thigh to massage her breasts.

Aja worked her hips furiously, keeping the pattern that had Anansi's dick hardening inside her. She circled, circled, circled and stopped. Circle, circle, circle, and stop. Circle. Circle. Circle. Stop. She kept up the pace until a fine sheen of sweat coated her body.

Anansi reached down to massage her all too tempting clit in that same hypnotic and erotic pattern. Circle. Circle. Circle. Stop. Circle. Circle. Circle. Stop.

Together, caught up in a crazy rhythm that no other masculine or feminine could match or muster, Anansi and Aja brought each other to the climaxes they craved. The sounds of their sex echoed in the room until their cries of pleasure and ecstasy drowned out everything else as their bodies trembled and jerked with each spasm of their releases.

"I love you, Anansi," Aja cried out in wild abandon. "Say you love me. Say you love me."

"Aja...Aja...wake up you're dreaming."

At the firm pressure of a hand on her shoulder, Aja sprung up in the *qanddii* as the erotic images of her and Anansi hard at play faded away. She turned her head on the plush sac and flushed in embarrassment at the sight of Mondi looking down at her in amusement.

"He's here," she said.

Mondi's words dropped into the silence like a bomb.

Aja turned her face from the all too observant feminine to avoid her seeing the emotions she knew flittered across her face. She hadn't seen him in over a torbaan, and that felt like forever. Her heart soared to know he was near. *Will I ever get over him for good?*

"I don't want to see him. Please, Anansi has

gone on with his life, and I have to learn to go on with mine," she pleaded, rising from her *qanddii* to face the window.

"I just wanted to see *you* one last time."

Aja whirled and nearly collided with Anansi standing behind here dressed in his military uniform. Everything about him overwhelmed her and Aja bit her lip to keep from revealing the truth. Yes, she still missed him. Yes, she still loved and adored him. Yes, she still wanted him. Yes, if he said the word she would agree to be his for forever and a day.

Qorobu.

He reached for her, his hands pressed against her arms.

As his aura surrounded her and his emotions filled her she knew the truth of his own emotions clearly. Yes, he still missed her. Yes, he still loved and adored her. Yes, he still wanted her. And yes, if the choice were up to him he would be hers for forever and a day.

Qorobu.

She brushed away his touch and moved past him to walk across the room with her arms crossed over her chest. She noticed his *da'ee* had left them alone. She didn't miss the heavy breath he released, and she followed it with one of her own.

Aja laughed bitterly. "Oduda Diasi and Anansi Nyame, the new power couple. The perfect political match. The ones to watch. Oduda and Anansi photographed here and there. The people are all chanting and hoping for a love match between Oduda and Anansi. Oduda and Anansi reportedly secretly dating for *baatis*."

Anansi slid his hands into his pockets as he looked out the window. "You've seen the media."

"Oh yes, I've been lucky enough to watch your love bloom along with the rest of the galaxy," she snapped.

"I am returning to duty today...after the official announcement of my *qaadhimamuu* to *Giiftiin* Oduda."

Aja looked over her shoulder at him, and that was a mistake as he turned and their eyes met. "Then you have a lifetime with her to learn not to love me," she said, her sadness poignant.

The look he gave her made her shiver from the top of her head down to her toes.

"It is me you love, Anansi," she told him without hesitation or any doubt as she walked up to him and grabbed the front of his jacket to pull her body up close to his as she rose on the tip of her toes. She pressed her face against his chest and inhaled deeply as if she could absorb him into her body because he was already deeply implanted in her soul. "It is *me* you want."

He picked her body up until their face to face. "If I could change things I would," he whispered into the heat between them as his eyes locked on her mouth.

"Your *da'ee* told me everything," Aja admitted, running her hands over his thin waist-length locs and then pressing her palms to the sides of his face as she got lost in his black eyes. "The same truth you could have told me, Anansi. I know that the gaa'ila is arranged and the very basis for the treaty. Correct?"

"I cannot answer that, Aja," he told her.

His eyes revealed that it was fact.

"If you want to kiss me so badly, then just do it, Anansi," she told him, feeling his urge to do so.

He shook his head and lowered her to her feet, releasing her as he stepped back to put distance between them.

"I had to see you one last time," Anansi said, pushing his hands into the pocket of his pants as if to force himself not to reach for her again. "I won't return until..."

"Until your *cidha* in one *ji'a*, right?" she said bitterly. "Maybe while I am here I can help with the planning. I want this sham to be just perfect for you."

"Aja," he said a bit sternly.

"I cannot believe you are going through with

this. There has to be another way."

Anansi strode across the room to pull her into his tight embrace. "I..."

Aja leaned back. "If you say that you have no choice one more time I'm going to scream."

Anansi pulled her back into his arms as he lifted her hair to bury his face against her neck and give her one final squeeze. He held her for the longest time. Countless moments.

"Aja, I do love you," he told her fiercely with a final kiss to her neck before he quickly turned and strode out of the room.

She reached out towards his retreating figure but forced herself to pull her hand back as her heart crashed into a million pieces. She touched her neck to find it was wet from his tears.

XIV

Three torbaans *later*

Oduda smoothed her hands over the rich, shiny material as she twirled in her elaborate gown for her *cidha*. It was a deep purple of a simple form fitting strapless design. The luxury was in the matching headpiece—as per the custom of the Kordis. It was shaped to her head and encrusted with jewels with thin strings of rare *nkumes* that framed her face as it draped down past her breasts.

Oduda spun in the looking glass as she studied herself. She was more than pleased with her reflection. Every eye would be on her during the cidha, and she wanted to ensure that she left them breathless with her Kordi beauty.

The union of Oduda Diasi and Anansi Nyame wasn't a love match by any means, but it would make Oduda one of the most powerful females in the Acirfa Galaxy, and for that, she was anxious for their union.

She paused in her inspection.

She hadn't seen Anansi since the night the *qaadhimamuu* was officially announced. That very evening she returned to planet Kordi, and he boarded his precious spaceship. Their façade was over.

It was obvious he was pining away for that *gabra*.

Oduda smiled in delight at the thought of a legion of males with the looks and scent of Reeock Jhyun mating Aja Drakar. "Hopefully she has killed herself like that no good Leetoo," Oduda said aloud with obvious pleasure.

"Did you say something, *Giiftiin*?" Bhula asked from across the room where she was making Oduda's *qanddii*.

"Shut up," she snapped, her eyes flashing with her ire. "Did I call your name?"

"No, my *giiftin*."

"Then I'm not talking to you," she said snidely. "Now come help me out of my gown."

"Right away," she said, quickly moving across the *diinqa* to undo the ties.

"Guard!" Oduda yelled as she stepped out of her gown.

Bhula immediately gathered the precious garment up into her arms.

The double doors immediately opened. Oduda eyed the guard as she pulled on a sheer black robe, not bothering to close it. "Get out," she ordered Bhula coldly.

"But I must pack away your gown—"

Oduda whirled and slapped the old feminine across her withered mouth.

WHAP!

Bhula fell to the floor and cowered as Oduda towered over her. "Get...out!"

As the servant got to her feet as quickly as she could and scurried from the room in fear, Oduda turned and strode up to the guard whose face was hidden beneath a leather mask like all the rest. She identified them by the numeral code on their chest. She reached for his strong hands and placed them on her breasts. She sighed in pleasure at their warmth.

"Welcome back," she sighed as his fingers gripped and tightly twisted her nipples the way she liked.

When his leather clad head dipped as if to kiss her, Oduda stepped back from him. "I do hope you took notes, Muzi."

"I can't wait to show you everything I learned," he said, as he unzipped the leather hood.

"Strip," she ordered, eyeing him with impatience.

Recently she had taken the young guard as her lover. With nothing brewing between her and Anansi but animosity, Muzi had caught her attention during her time on Erised. Unfortunately, she discovered he was well-equipped but inexperienced with using it well. She sent him to Planet Whoor to learn the tricks to be a better lover. She didn't have the time nor patience to teach a masculine how to make her climax.

"You do know that Aja Drakar never arrived on Planet Whoor?" he asked casually as he climbed his naked frame onto the *qanddii* between her open legs.

Oduda was pulling his bald head towards her center but froze at his words. "What?" she snapped.

"She is not on Planet Whoor and never was," he said, leaning in to place a kiss on her inner thigh.

"And how do you know this?" Oduda asked as she closed her legs, entrapping his bald head.

He pushed her legs open to free himself. "A friend of mine who works to the *Moticha's mana* was enjoying a night of fun on Planet Whoor, and he told me of the beautiful Empath residing there."

Oduda made herself breathe deeply as she felt her body tremble with rage. "This friend of yours has seen Aja Drakar at the *mana* of Moticha Hwosi Kan Nyame?" she asked through clenched teeth as she tightly clutched his thigh.

He winced at the tension in her clasp. "Yes."

Oduda's clutch tightened, and her fingernails pierced his skin until she drew blood.

"*Giiftiin*!" Muzi cried out sharply.

Oduda's crazed eyes cut to his face. She released him as she wiped her mouth with trembling hands. "Get out," she said in a low, menacing voice.

He sat up to place a kiss to her nipple. "Don't you mean get in," he teased, oblivious to her rage.

In a flash, Oduda had one of her infusers and pressed it to his thigh. His eyes widened slightly before he slumped back against the *qanddii*. She turned and used her feet to kick his naked body. He tumbled to the floor noisily, but she could care less.

Thinking quickly, she turned and opened her communicator. "Locate Reeock Jhyun."

"*Reeock Jhyun located. Location blocked.*"

His disgusting image soon filled the screen, and she was glad to see it. "Reeock, I need—"

His lizard-like forked tongue circled his mouth

quickly. "You *need* to pay me my *warqee*," he snapped angrily causing spittle to fly against the screen.

Oduda recoiled in disgust. "I will pay you that and much more," she told him, feeling desperation claw at her. "How does one hundred thousand *warqee* sound to you?"

"Paid in advance? It sounds like we're ready to do business," he said, as the green spots on his head deepened in color.

"Good. I have a little problem I need you to dispose of."

∞

"I love you so much, Anansi," Aja said as she stood before him in a flowing white gown and reached out with her soft hand to caress his cheek. *"I love you."*

Anansi awakened with a start, sitting up in his *qanddii* as he looked around his darkly lit quarters aboard *Spaceship Infinite*. He breathed deeply as he pushed his locs back from his face before wiping away the sweat with both of his hands.

Aja.

Try as he might Anansi couldn't shake her. He couldn't stop loving her. He couldn't forget her. And he tried everything including working himself ragged aboard the ship doing tasks usually assigned to his crew. He couldn't eat. He couldn't sleep. He felt like a drug addict going through withdrawals and Aja was his fix.

This was not just about sex. He missed her laughter and her sassy mouth. He missed holding her body close to his as they slept. He missed waking up to her in his arms, his *qanddii*, his *mana*, and his life.

During their time apart his love for her had deepened and grown.

Does she still love me?

The thought of that both pleased and plagued him. He wanted Aja to get over him and move on with her life. When he spoke with his parents he made them swear not to mention her. Perhaps she would find the love she deserved, the love he was unable to give her.

No other masculine can or will ever compete. He will forever fall short to this right here. He will forever chase a losing battle.

Those words shouldn't please and comfort him...but they did.

Next *torbaan* his *cidha* would forever seal him to a feminine he didn't even like. After all the stunts Oduda had pulled, Anansi had long since decided to keep his distance from the Kordi *giiftiin*. If he had to permanently live aboard the spaceship to avoid her, then he would. He wasn't even willing to try and make their *gaa'ila* work.

Anansi lay back on the *qanddii* and placed his forearm across his closed eyes. Instantly he saw images of Aja, and he wished he could just reach out to touch her.

He finally fell in love and fate was delivering him a terrible blow as he was obligated to vow his life to another. "*Qorobu*," he swore.

When the memory of Aja's buttocks quivering as she rode him backward caused his penis to tent the covers, Anansi jumped up to his feet. He covered his nudity with thin sleep pants and a T-shirt before he grabbed the wooden box holding the physical version of the *morkii* game and a bottle of *alkoolii*.

Following an impulse, and needing a distraction, Anansi left his quarters and made his way down the hall to the *kaasuu*. He rode it down to the spaceship's curative division. The lights of the spacious gold room were dimmed with only the large bubble-shaped restorative chamber brightly illuminated. Even the massive *komputara* covering one entire wall and the unit's bright red automatons were in sleep mode.

Anansi made his way over to Juuba Huuntu knowing the Empath rarely slept.

Juuba was sitting in a chair beside the floor to ceiling wall looking out at the inky universe. He turned to watch as Anansi pulled a chair up to the other side of the invisible one-way force field keeping Juuba contained to a large area of the unit.

"Do you normally roam your ship late at night in your *qanddii* clothes, Captain?" Juuba asked as swiveled in the chair to face him.

Anansi rolled an empty surgical tray over to push half in through the force field and half out. He sat the *alkoolii* and the board game on it. "Try to be me for a day, and you'll do more than that."

Juuba looked around at his surroundings with a wry expression. "Try my life. It is not an easy fit either," he drawled sarcastically.

Anansi nodded, and he turned his lips downward. "True," he agreed as he retrieved two pill cups to fill with alkoolii. "Come drink with me."

He watched Juuba eye him suspiciously before he rolled the chair closer. "And the reason for this visit?"

"Loneliness, Juuba, plain and simple." Anansi tilted his head back to empty the contents of the cup. He winced as it slightly burned the back of his throat. "I felt you couldn't be much better down here than me...although I'm sure, you would prefer Chli's presence to my own."

Anansi poured himself another cup as Juuba sipped gingerly from his. "Do you play?" he asked as he set up the board game.

Juuba nodded. "Yes, and I play to win."

"So do I, so this should be good."

Juuba actually laughed as he drained his cup. "Chli taught me how to play."

Anansi set up the board before he reached beyond the force field to pour more *alkoolii* into Juuba's cup. "Chli, huh?" he teased lightly.

Juuba's face filled with anger. "Is it improper for a *gabra* to address an officer by her first name?"

Anansi emptied another cup as he shook his head. "No. First off, you're not in the militia, and thus do not fall under its rules. Second, you're no longer a *gabra*."

"Am I free to leave here?" he countered as the

angry set of his broad shoulders faded.

"Would you like to face uncertainty or the bwa *kasuwa* again?" Anansi returned.

Juuba snorted in derision.

"In fact, I have a question for you," Anansi said, leveling his all black eyes on the other masculine. "Once your people are reunited would you stand as their leader?"

Juuba frowned and shook his head. "Our leaders are the *abuturoos* and our *dawaa*, Pintar Neek," he said without hesitation.

Anansi remained quiet. Pintar's name was not on the list of fatalities Aja identified. *But that doesn't mean he is alive.*

The Empath's would need to appoint official leadership to sign the peace treaty and join the Acirfa Galaxy's coalition. That was hard to do with the entire race enslaved and spread out over the galaxy. He had paid attention to the Empath while he was onboard, and Anansi found him to smart and level-headed. He knew Aja thought very well of him.

"But if necessary, until Pintar Neek or any of the *abuturoos* are located," Anansi said, keeping his tone calm. "Would you step up and make decisions that affect your people for the better?"

Juuba eyed him, assessing him.

Anansi arched a brow. "Listen, the only way to ensure peace for Empaths is a peace treaty," he finally admitted. "By joining the coalition and having a leader sit on ruling Council, your planet would fall under its protection. Your people will never suffer such loss again and with the right direction—at the speed desirable to your people—advancements can be made."

Juuba's eyes shifted to the restorative chamber. "I have seen firsthand the good technology can do," he said. "But—"

Anansi tensed.

"What is in this for the Council and the Kordis?" he asked.

Anansi took a sip of his *alkooli*, admiring Juuba's intuitiveness and gauging just how much to reveal. "I am not at liberty to reveal more at this time," he said. "But I will not lie that there is a lot to gain for us all."

Juuba eyed him again before reaching out his hand and turning it palm up.

Anansi looked at it warily.

"You want me to trust you," he said. "Now I ask you to do the same."

Like Aja, his powers had been returned to him. Anansi sat his cup down and took a deep breath as he slid one of his hands pass the force field.

Juuba took it into his grasp. The gold dots on his forehead and chin glistened and his eyes flashed with a white glow that covered the brown of his irises. The moment came and went so quickly before he freed Anansi. "You feel frustrated by the secret you keep, but you show hope for a better future for my people."

"That sounds right," Anansi admitted. "I would never do anything to hurt Aja."

Juuba's eyes hardened. "I would hope not," he warned.

He refilled their cups.

"This seems like a very powerful position," Juuba observed.

"It is," he admitted.

"Here is for the advancement and the freedom of my people for our return to Nede," Juuba said.

Anansi released a heavy breath. "Do all Empaths have a one-track mind?" he asked as Juuba made his first move on the board.

"Are all Erisedians in need of control?"

Anansi laughed as he made his move and then held his cup up. "Here's to a better world for all people with no discriminations and no pre-judgments."

Juuba begrudgingly lifted his cup as well. "To a better world."

∞

With every day that brought the *cidha* of Anansi and Oduda closer, Aja wanted away from his parent's palatial *mana*. Sitting back as the plans were made and the entire staff buzzed with the excitement of the upcoming event was painful. Mocking even.

She spent most days in her *diinqa*, but idle time on her hands kept her mind filled with memories of her time with Anansi. Jealousy burned her at the thought of another feminine loving him, kissing him, touching him, laughing with him, mating him, and living with him day to day. Having him or a lifetime.

Anansi Nyame was a good masculine. An honorable masculine. *Her* masculine.

Oduda Diasi was not good enough for him. The evil in her rain deep.

I love him.

I should be the one with the one excited to have him. I should be the one to wear the bands sealing us together for eternity. I should carry his children.

Nothing in this world could make her believe that Anansi Nyame was not made just for her, and three *torbaans* later she loved him even more. Each day got worse before it got better. To think that she would be here on the property as *her* Anansi married another feminine. She dreaded the day. Not even the solace of knowing she soon would be allowed to travel back to Nede eased the ache in her soul.

She knew she had to get over Anansi, but it was easier said than done.

Aja flipped over onto her back in the darkness as she struggled to find either sleep or peace of mind. Both escaped her.

The door to her *diinqa* suddenly slid open. Aja sat up in *qanddii* as Xhione, the *Giiftii's* personal servant, slipped in. The darkness nearly shielded her. "Xhione, what are you doing in here?" Aja asked.

The plump feminine with skin the color of biscuits froze as Aja waved her hand over the switch to turn the lights on.

"*Giiftii* Mondi wanted to see you in her quarters and sent me for you," she said as she neared the *qanddii* still in her nightclothes.

Aja frowned. "This late at night?" she asked in confusion. "She's never sent you in my *diinqa* before."

"I think there is something wrong with *Giiftiin* Anansi," she said as she moved closer.

Aja's heart hammered at the thought of Anansi being injured. "What happened?" she asked as she flung the covers back and reached for her robe.

"Nothing."

Aja turned to look at Xhione just in time to see the feminine spray a fine mist into her face. Aja coughed as her eyelids suddenly felt heavy. She remembered thinking, 'Not again,' just before she fell back onto the *qanddii*.

∞

Huung was a nuisance.

As she had done since she banished him, Oduda ignored his attempts to contact her. Several times he traveled back from planet Zheen and tried to gain entrance to her fort. Each time she looked on from a distance as her faithful guards physically escorted him from the property.

Twelve inches or not he was creeping her out with his intensity and his inability to understand that no means no. She'd thought her incantation over him would have lessened its grip on him.

"Incoming communication from Reeock Jhyun."

Oduda passed aside any thoughts of Huung as her thirst for revenge reigned. "Connect," she said from her bath as Bhula bathed her back. His image filled the *komputara* on the stone wall of her *kutaa dhiqannaa*. "Is it done?"

The screen soon filled with the image of Aja Drakar on a dirty floor with her wrists and ankles tied before it swung back to Reeock's face. "It is done."

She smiled in satisfaction. "Good work. Enjoy her before you sell her to one of the brothels."

Reeock's repulsive tongue quickly licked his lips. "I plan to," he said with a grin.

Oduda ended the call and sat back in the tub to

rub her scalp in satisfaction. She giggled as she imagined Aja's face when she awakened to find Reeock Jhyun rutting away inside of her. The giggle soon turned to laughter that was maniacal.

∞

Aja was now familiar with the after effects of being rendered unconscious. As she struggled to awaken from the influence of being drugged, she realized her hands and feet were tied and her mouth taped. Her eyes widened in panic as she struggled against her ties. She tried to lift her head but the pounding hurt worst with the movement.

She heard a door open behind her and struggled to turn over. A horrible stench filled the room. She frowned and shook her head as if to clear her offended nostrils. She felt herself wretch, but she kept it down for fear she would choke.

Aja held her breath as a pair of grungy boots came to a stop beside her. Her eyes widened as they lit on the face of her newest captor. Fear and repulsion assailed her as she looked up at the short and obese masculine with pale blue skin and large green circles on his odd shaped head.

He smiled at her revealing a mouth filled with rotted teeth and horrid breath that reached her on the floor. "This is her," he said with a lisp as his tongue slithered out of his mouth.

Terror seized her as she looked up at a Kordi guard in a leather hood. Oduda Diasi!

The guard scooped her up before he tossed her over a shoulder. She tried to struggle as she was carried out into the hall of the *mana* and she looked around at the scantily clad *gumnas* leading their customers into *diinqas*. The walls were made of blue tinted glass, and lascivious acts were on display beneath flashing lights. Bass-driven music filled the air. The smell of sex was thick. The moans and cries of pleasure echoed.

"Are you sure I can't make you an offer? Empath *gumnas* fetch a high price."

Aja looked over her shoulder at a buxom and

beautiful feminine with porcelain-like ebony skin and floor-length jet-black hair that she wore pulled over one shoulder. She was wearing nothing but thigh-high boots and assessed Aja with bright white eyes with plush black lashes.

The Kordi guard didn't answer as he pushed past her and left the house.

Aja shrieked when the sound of a whip crackled in the air.

It could only be Planet Whoor.

She barely had time to take in the brightly lit buildings with flashing neon signs with dark gray skies as their backdrop. The Kordi guard walked them onto a space cruiser and placed her a long bench. He disappeared, and soon she felt the space cruiser lift to the air.

She was left with her thoughts as she forced her body to relax so that the ties didn't hurt. It was hard to ignore that she was being hand delivered to a powerful feminine bent on her destruction. She was just as anxious to rid her life of Oduda, she just hadn't gotten the upper hand yet.

I thought I was safe.

The door leading to the next section of the space cruiser opened, and Aja swallowed over a sudden lump in her throat as the Kordi guard walked towards her. Each step echoed the beat of her heart.

He bent down beside her, and she forced any fear from her face as she glared at him angrily. When he reached towards her Aja forced her entire body back from him and released a string of expletives that were jumbled by the tape on her mouth. He shook his head as if frustrated with her.

"I was going to untie you. If I had known you liked to be tied up, I would have mated you that way."

Aja's froze as she tilted her head to the side and looked up at the Kordi guard. Slowly he unzipped the leather hood and flung it away. She looked up into the smiling and handsome face of Anansi and went weak with relief as her heart raced with love.

∞

Anansi felt nervous in Aja's presence.

He fought so long to stay away from her and not think of her. Now here they were aboard the space cruiser together. Their chemistry was ever present and made the spacious vessel seemed much smaller.

Anansi saw the disappointment in her eyes when he failed to kiss her. It wasn't for lack of desire. In fact, he made himself busy doing useless tasks aboard the cruiser to keep himself from pulling her to the floor to crush beneath his weight as he buried his heat deep within the walls for which he longed.

"So that awful masculine back on Planet Whoor contacted you to let you know that Oduda Diasi contacted him to kidnap me," Aja said as she sat with her legs pulled to her chest.

"Yes, seems Oduda double crossed him, so he was looking for a little revenge of his own. With the *warqee* she paid him up front, and what I paid him for his help this little con made him a tiny sum." Anansi sat on the plush leather seat adjacent to where she sat. His strong hands were folded in the space between his knees as he looked over at her.

Their eyes met and held for just a few precious moments before they both looked away.

"So Xhione was in on it, too?" Aja asked, obviously struggling to fill the awkward silence.

"Reeock used her. My parents should have sent her on her way by now," he told her as he stretched his legs out in front of him to cross at the ankles.

"She won't be arrested?"

Anansi shook his head, his black eyes resting on her. "I would have to involve Reeock to do that."

"Thank you for saving me...again," she told him softly as she crossed her arms over her chest and looked over at him with those gold flecked eyes.

She is so beautiful.

"I would never do anything to hurt you, Aja," he said, shifting his eyes from her as his love for her swelled in his chest.

"Well almost anything," she added before she rose to walk over to the large glass windows of the space cruiser.

Anansi said nothing because he had nothing new to offer her concerning his *gaa'ila*.

"Where am I going now in this mad race to avoid Oduda Diasi?"

"You will stay aboard the spaceship with me."

She turned and leaned her back against the window as she watched him. "In your quarters?" she asked.

"No, Aja."

"Your loyalty to your lifemate-to-be is admirable," she said.

Anansi fought the urge to rise and pull her into his arms. "You know that has nothing to with it."

"You're right, Anansi, I do know."

His chest ached because he knew she was in pain. He hurt, too. He rose and took two steps towards her before he turned and walked through the door leading to the next section of the space cruiser.

∞

Aja bit her bottom lips as she stared at the door he just walked through. When she saw that it was Anansi that rescued her, she had hope for the happily ever after. How perfect it would've been if he whipped off the mask, professed his undying love before pulling her into his arms and mated her sweetly while he swore that she would be his lifemate and no one else.

She turned and released a heavy breath as she looked out at outer space. She guessed her happily ever after was only for her dreams.

XV

One torbaan *later*

The *cidha* was complete.

The crowd down below roared in celebration as Anansi and Oduda turned beneath the stone arch adorned with florae. To all in attendance the union of *Giiftiin* Anansi Nyame and his *riti, Giiftii*n Oduda once Diasi now Nyame, was a beautiful event unifying the Acirfa galaxy.

A stunning charade.

Anansi paused as he looked out at the crowd comprised of sovereigns and commoners from each planet of the galaxy. Everything seemed to slow down, the noise faded, and the moment swelled with his heartache. He clenched his jaw as Oduda eased her arm through his.

At least my Aja is safe and free.

For that, he was happy.

He pressed a button and the disc on which they stood disconnected from the altar that was ten feet above the crowd. It lowered under it floated just above the *cidha* attendees and they both waved as florae were tossed up to them, landing against their bodies and onto their feet.

Oduda looked up at him as she trailed her hand down his arms to entwine their fingers. "Our first kiss was cold, Anansi. I hope tonight will be more heated," she whispered to him with a lick of her lips.

Anansi fought the urge to knock her hand away. "Actually, I will be returning to my military duties right after the festivities. We leave for a mission in the morning, and I must prepare the ship."

Her grip on his hand tightened. "Then I suppose I will find some other business to attend to," Oduda told him tightly before she released him.

"The choice is yours." Anansi slid his hands into the pocket of his pants as he watched his parent's XR-1 digitally transform the spacious room from a garden to a reception area complete with soft lighting and music. Chairs, tables and elegant floral decorations appeared.

A lot of the attendees sighed in surprise and delight.

All Anansi could do is wish it was Aja at his side so that he could truly enjoy the marvel before him.

"And this is the type of *gaa'ila* you want, Anansi?" Oduda asked, as the disc completed circling the room and floated high above the eight masculines and one feminine lined up before a large glass table top that levitated before them.

He finally looked down at her. "Oduda, there's no need to pretend that this anything more than a business arrangement. You may move into my *mana*, and I will grant you a stipend. I will attend important political functions and parties with you. I will smile and nod and pretend to be in love when asked, but that is all I will do."

Her violet eyes flashed with anger. "I hate you," she spat.

He shrugged one broad shoulder. "You don't even know me. You're just upset because you're spoiled and used to having your way and I'm not feeding into that."

"This is our life from here on out?" she asked, her voice incredulous.

"And from what I've learned recently, *riti*, may I remind you that the things you got away with in the past would now be punishable by law," he told her.

"You're a fool," Oduda snapped, nearly snarling in derision. "Do you know how many masculines would die to mate with me?"

Anansi locked his ebon eyes with hers. "I can accurately guess how many have already mated with you. Careful, dear, you'll wear yourself out if you don't slow down."

She shook her head even as she forced a smile, causing the *nkumes* to hit against each other and illuminate around her face from the contact.

Flutes of *alkoolii* appeared in their hands.

Anansi yearned for something much stronger as

he eyed his *abbaa*, *Moticha* Hwosi Kan Nyame, raise his hand to silence the room. The obedience was immediate.

"Let this be the first of a new day for the people of the Acirfa Galaxy, unified, as we celebrate the union of my son and newly appointed *gifftiin* of Erised, Oduda once Diasi now Nyame," he said his voice booming, seeming to vibrate against the bodies and the walls.

"To Anansi and Oduda," someone yelled from below.

"To Anansi and Oduda," the entire audience shouted in unison.

"Today we also celebrate the signing of a peace treaty ensuring the freedom of all *gabras* and the joining of both the Empaths and the Kordis into the coalition," Hwosi said.

Anansi eyed each one as his *abbaa* introduced them. Their physical characteristics and garb were indicative of each of their unique planets. They were the all-powerful Council, leaders of the Acirfa Galaxy. Kyl Diasi and Pintar Neek stood along with them as well.

Anansi barely spared his *abiyyuu* a glance as he took in Pintar Neek. He had made it his duty to find the Empath *abuturoo*. He had been sold to a wealthy family on Kordi who was more than happy to release him once Anansi compensated them for the *warqee* they spent.

Like Juuba, Aja had spoken of him as the leader of their people, and he wished he could be there to see her face when she saw Pintar for the first time.

Sadness and heartache assailed him again.

The peace treaty was digitally displayed in the air above the crowd. As each of The Council members signed the document, their signatures lit the sky in electric turquoise.

As the Principal of The Council, Hwosi stamped the document with his imperial seal making it immediate law. The Council all joined hands before raising them to the florae covered ceiling.

"Peace for all," Hwosi roared.

The crowd erupted in praise and applause that was deafening.

At that moments, as the signing of the treated was broadcast, as was the *cidha*, he knew *gabras* were freed and making use of the transport provided by The Council to return them to Nede. Pintar would leave the festivities to return along with his people to their world.

Knowing he made such a huge change in the life of Aja and her people gave him some pride and comfort. He had to hold on to that to finally began to adjust to his life without her.

For the last *torbaa*n they spent aboard the ship, he avoided her at all costs wanting to help her along in getting over him. He wondered if it worked because the distance only made him yearn for her more.

As The Council joined the festivities, the disc lowered to the floor as the table disappeared and was replaced with an arch heavy with florae with their own table beneath it.

Anansi held her hand to assist her to their table with the disc still levitating beside it. "Excuse me, Oduda," he said, once she was seated on her hovering seat.

He immediately crossed the room to Daryan. His best friend and first mate met him halfway through the dancing crowd. "It is done," Anansi said, shaking the hand he was offered. "I'm pleased you got back from your mission in time to be here."

Daryan smiled, but there was a tinge of sadness in his ebon eyes.

Anansi took note but didn't ask about it further. "Is everything in place on Nede?" he asked.

Daryan nodded. "Yes," he assured him.

"Good. I want the transition to go as smoothly as possible—"

"How could you, Oduda?"

At the loud yell, Anansi and Daryan whirled to see Oduda frozen in fear as a tall and broad masculine with disheveled blonde hair stood towering over her with a mix of rage and desperation in his blue eyes. Anansi raced over towards them just as the stranger reached out to grab Oduda's hand and roughly pulled her onto the disc. It rose high above the crowd.

"Hayyisa!" Daryan roughly called for the guards in their native tongue.

Anansi attempted to jump and catch the edge of the disc, but the crazed masculine pressed his boot against his face until his fingers slipped and he released it.

"Huung, what are you doing here?" Oduda asked, feeling fear as he wrapped an arm around her waist to try to pull her close. "Get off of me!"

He looked at her with pained eyes. "What about me? Us? I *can't* live without you, Oduda. I have to have you. I *will* have you."

Oduda looked down at them all. "Help," she shrieked.

Huung's eyes were crazed as they remained fixed on her face. "I can't eat. I can't sleep. I think of you constantly."

Oduda tried to break free of his hold as the music stopped and the people began to gasp and holler out as they looked up at the horrifying scene playing out above them. He tried to kiss her, placing a strong hand to her nape to pull her towards him. She jerked away, and her foot slipped off the disc.

Struggling for composure, Oduda's arms and legs flailed as she fell backward. The crowd's eyes widened in horror as her body zoomed downward past the circle of coalition guards that rose in the air with their radiation laser weapons drawn. Her screams echoed through the air.

Anansi pushed through the crowd valiantly trying to reach her. He flinched as her piercing screams ended abruptly with a loud thud.

The room became deathly quiet, and the throng parted to allow him into the circle surrounding her. Her body was twisted and obviously badly broken. Her violet eyes were wide and vacant of life. Anansi knelt beside her and used his fingers to close her eyes.

∞

Aja moved about the space cruiser stopping to hug or press her hand into that of her beleaguered people. Their numbers were lessened by the death of the race war, but they were free. Some were tired and hungry. Others' spirits had been defeated by being enslaved. *But we're free and going home.*

The Aja who just sat back and let others make her decisions and dictate her direction was not the Aja Drakar she was before the war. That Aja took matters into her owns hands. Allowed no questions of her decisions and asked for no opinions of the rules she made for her own life. This was her life, and for the last few ji'as she had not an iota of control over it. Not one bit. That was no more.

Everything was going to change once again.

And their freedom meant that Anansi and Oduda were lifemates. Deep down a piece of her didn't think he would do it. She longed for him to find a way to bring about peace without pledging his life to another. 'He *couldn't* do it,' she'd thought.

I was wrong.

They were leaving Planet Erised, and she would never see him again. The days of crying and bemoaning her life had to be over. Life would move on without her if she didn't deal with it.

Aja bent to press a kiss to the cheek of a babe before sharing a smile with its mother, Mova. "Thank God you two were not separated," she softly said to her, with one last squeeze of her thin shoulder in the torn top she wore.

She glanced out the window. There were six space cruisers lined up on the platform of the spaceship. It was a fry cry from the time her *abuturoos* had fled Erised more than a half a *jaarraa* ago in one battered *xiyyaara* that barely made the numerus trips needed to move everyone to their new world.

"Aja."

She turned, her heart already pounding. She smiled to hide her disappointment. For a second she thought it was Anansi come to claim her love.

"Yes, Juuba," she said, eyeing him where he stood at the entrance to the space cruiser.

He waved for her to follow and she did.

"We're riding back in this last one," Juuba said, looking pleased to finally be free of the confinement of the curative division.

"Is it time to depart?" she asked as military personnel continued with their duties around them.

"Yes, it is now."

Juuba stepped back and allowed Aja to step onto the space cruiser.

"*Dawaa!*" she gasped in surprise to see Pintar Neek sitting there.

She rushed over to kneel at his feet and pressed her face against his knee. Her tears were of joy and relief, and she could not stop them.

He patted her back. "Aja, all is well," he assured her.

Her eyes flashed white as she absorbed the hope he had for a brighter future for the Empaths.

Juuba walked up to them. "All went well with the signing of the treaty?" he asked.

"Yes, but..."

Aja gasped. She looked up at the leader. "There was a tragedy," she said.

He nodded.

"Who?" she asked, her feeling light-headed with fear for Anansi.

"Oduda Diasi."

Aja slowly rose to her feet, barely listening to the details of her demise as she dropped onto a seat. She hated herself for the hope she instantly felt. She was pleased, not because she felt revenge had been accurately exacted for the cruel treatment of her people but because it meant Anansi was free of her.

She felt ashamed of herself.

Still, as each space cruiser orbited into space, she wondered why he hadn't come to her. *Perhaps he is grieving.*

That made her jealous. Her shame returned.

During the entire voyage to Nede, Aja remained

in her seat with her bare feet tucked beneath her looking out at the inky blackness and the shooting *urjiis*. Her thoughts were filled with Anansi. Memories. Regrets. And yes, still, hope.

In time, their home planet grew in size as they neared it. No one had said many words during their travel. Aja looked at Juuba and Pintar over her shoulder.

"What are we returning to?" she asked.

They both turned gold flecked hazel eyes on her.

"I am willing to sleep on the ground as long as I am back on Nede soil," Juuba said.

"I was assured provisions have made," Pintar said, his hand closed into a loose fist as if he missed the feel of his intricately carved eight-foot staff. "Also, the Kordi agreed to financial sanctions for the *nkumes* they plundered from Nede."

"The *nkumes*?" Juuba asked, his face showing his confusion.

Pintar gave them a wide smile that showed his lone tooth. "It seems the stones we used for light are *very* valuable," he said, his eyes beaming.

Juuba smiled as well. "Then soon Nede will be back to normal again."

"With the allowance of *some* technological advances it will be even better," Aja assured him, thinking of XR-2 and all the luxuries of Anansi's *mana*. "There's something to be said for them."

She allowed herself to get lost in her sultry memories of her and Anansi in a floating *qanddii*.

Their view changed from outer space to the lavender and blue skies of the southern region of planet Nede. One by one the space cruisers landed in the same field as the day Anansi surprised her with the visit to Nede.

The Empaths who already landed were cheering and singing praises as their feet touched down on Nede ground. Even as the coalition guards escorted them into xiyyaaras for easier travel, their celebrating continued. Aja pushed away any sadness about Anansi and allowed herself the joy of knowing her people would thrive again.

As they neared their ollaa, her eyes widened to see temporary shelters erected. All signs of the carnage of the war were absent. Even in the distance, she could see the trees gone from their farm land and the water once again running freely in the repaired irrigation system.

Of those Empaths who had already left the xiyyaaras the mood shifted. The tone was more somber. There was dismay that all the goojjoos and their belongings were gone. There were memories of the war. Death. Loss.

Aja was grateful they had not seen the ruins as she had.

The vehicle lowered to a small clearing and the door rose.

"It is time to know who is here and who is gone," Pintar said, rising from his seat before he slowly made his way over to the exit.

She could hear the murmurs of surprise rush across the crowd as it set in that their beloved dawaa had survived the ordeal and had returned to lead them once again.

"Dawaa!" they cried out, rushing forward to encircle him.

He held up his rail arms. Silence reigned.

"First, we honor those who are gone, and then we celebrate those who made it back here," he said in their native tongue, his voice still strong although he appeared frail.

Juuba departed next and soon his sturdy frame was lost in the crowd.

Aja accepted the guard's hand as she climbed from the *xiyyaara* as well.

"This is from Captain *Giiftiin* Anansi Nyame," the guard told her as he pressed a medium-size metal box into her hand.

Her hair whipped around her as the guards climbed back into their *xiyyaara* and it rose into the air to fly away. She felt nervous and excited as she moved a distance from the crowd, sinking down to the black dirt with her back pressed against the broad trunk of a crimson tree.

Aja opened the box. She smiled and released a little breath to find a handwritten letter nestled behind a beautiful gold heart-shaped locket encrusted with *nkumes*. She sighed in pleasure as she removed the locket and chain to pull over her head. It nestled perfectly in her cleavage.

Her hand shook as she put the box under her arm before she opened the letter. She smiled at Anansi's slashing handwriting as she stroked his words with her fingertips and felt closer to him.

"Remember me always," she read aloud softly.

Her eyes glistened as she picked up the locket to press to her lips.

How could she *ever* forget him?

∞

"You can't go to her, son."

At the feel of his *abbaa's* hand on his shoulder, Anansi paused before climbing into the space cruiser. He turned and faced him. "So, my life is still not my own?" he asked.

"Oduda was your lifemate, and her death is too soon for you to be traipsing to another feminine." Hwosi rubbed his hand over his mouth as he eyed his son. "The proper Erisedian length of mourning is—"

"One *bara*," Anansi added. "I do not celebrate nor welcome Oduda's death, but this is hardly a normal situation. I didn't love her, nor did she love me. I love Aja."

Hwosi nodded his head, his white locs gently swaying. "I am well aware of that fact, son. Just as I know, she loves you just as much."

"Then don't ask me to wait for one *bara* before I can even speak to her," Anansi insisted, his voice serious and hard.

"What I ask is that you respect the customs of your people," Hwosi returned, his voice just as firm.

Anansi slid his hands inside the pockets of his pants. "And if I lose her in the process?"

"What better test of true love than time?"

Hwosi asked.

Anansi turned from the space cruiser and looked out the window. The three *aduus* were reflected in his troubled black eyes. "Our love has been tested enough, but no one nor anything—including time—can or will defeat it again."

∞

One bara *later*

Knock-knock.

Aja felt startled as someone knocked at the front door of her small *mana*. Her nerves had been frayed all day. She felt anxious, expectant, hopeful and fearful at varying moments of the day. At times, the back and forth was dizzying.

Her heart hammered wildly, and she took a deep breath as she walked to the door to pull it open. Her eyes dulled noticeably to find Juuba standing there.

He frowned. "Don't look so happy to see me," he kidded as he walked past Aja into the mana carrying a large wooden crate. "Were you expecting someone?"

Aja pinched the bridge of her nose. "No...yes...no..."

Juuba eyed her with an odd expression. "Which is it?"

She shifted her eyes from his. She was at a loss for words and didn't want to look foolish.

For the last *bara*, since she heard of Oduda's death at the hands of her crazed lover, Aja had thought there was no longer a reason for Anansi and her to be apart. As the days slipped into *torbaans* and then the *ji'as* began to stack up, her hope of reconciliation began to fade.

And then Medic Chli arrived on the developing planet for a visit, surprising both Aja and Juuba. She had been assigned by the coalition to offer supervision in the creation of a small medic clinic on Nede. Pintar Neek reluctantly accepted the offer, always mindful of keeping a delicate balance between their traditional ways and acclimating more modern technology onto their small world.

While there, Chli explained the Erisedian tradition of a one *bara* mourning period. An Erised widow or widower could not speak to any member of the opposite sex for any reason. Even Anansi's orders to feminine crew members had to be passed on thru another masculine except in the case of an emergency.

Aja's expectations began to change. Hope was renewed. She knew the type of love Anansi had for her, and she knew a love like theirs would never fade. She knew he would come to her in due time. She knew they would be together...one day.

So, Aja went on with her life. Alongside her people, she worked from morning to night to rebuild their *olla*. She eventually began teaching younger Empaths about the proper use of their powers in the same way her *da'ee* once taught her.

Sometimes she thought about Anansi daily. Other times days would pass, and it would take the littlest thing to make her think of him. Want him. Miss him.

Today his lengthy period of mourning was over. Faithfully, Aja waited to be able to hold him. Kiss him. Touch him. Mate him. Be with him. Love him.

He will come.

She tried her best not to think otherwise.

Of course there were times it would cross her mind that she was foolish to put her life on hold for a masculine when she had no guarantees that they would be together. In those moments she would instinctively reach inside her shirt to stroke her heart-shaped locket. Not once since she placed it around her neck had she taken it off.

What if he doesn't come?

She looked out the window as the darkness of night conquered the light of day.

"Then life goes on," Aja answered herself in a whisper with regret.

How much longer do I wait?

Love or no love she would not—could not—wait

forever. She refused to give up much more of her life waiting—not when there was nothing to hold them from being together any longer.

"Aja. Aja. Aja?"

She shifted her honey colored eyes to Juuba's face. "Huh?" she asked, still a little lost in her thoughts.

"Where do you want me to put this?" he asked, looking down at the crate.

"Right there by the window is fine," she said, remembering how much she had once yearned for one in their old *goojjoo*.

Their *manas* was not the scale of those on Erised but gone were drafts of winds of *ganna* or the sweltering heat of *bona* seeping through logs packed with dirt. "And *galatoomaa* for picking up the supplies for me."

Juuba nodded. "No problem at all."

Aja lightly rubbed her locket as she led him to the front door. "Be safe," she called out to him as he jogged down the stairs and went walking up the dirt-packed path while releasing a whistle into the air.

She leaned in the doorway and smiled at the line of *manas* with their round windows softly lit by their precious *nkumes*. In the distance, a feminine sang of love in their native tongue. The laughter and shouts of children still playing clung to the air. The masculines were on their way from a day's work in the fields and ready to rest their weary bodies and partake of the cooked food that scented the air.

All was well on Nede.

Even if all is not well with me.

Her loneliness echoed around her as she closed the door. There was no children or a lifemate to erase the emptiness. *No family at all.*

That fact would forever be painful.

As was her nightly ritual, Aja took a long bath before she dressed in nothing but a sheer *huccuu* caftan. She chose a black one, pulling the flowing garment over her nude frame. The feel of the soft material lightly breezing against her skin as she moved made her think of Anansi's touch.

On her breasts. Her nipples. Against her thighs. Between her legs.

Nothing could replace the warmth and electricity of his hands against her skin.

She stopped by her *alwaada* for a wooden cup of *alkoolii* and made her way up the metal stairs to the roof. As soon as she came up through the hatch, she seemed to be surrounded by the ebon darkness of night.

The thatched roof of the old *goojjoo* was replaced by a flat and sturdy rooftop garden. Aja sat her cup on the small wooden table next to lounging chair before taking her seat and tucking her bare feet beneath her. This was her place and hers alone. She would look up at the *urjiis* and think of her time up amongst them with Anansi.

"Where are you, Anansi?" she said aloud looking up at the sky and wishing for the lights of an arriving space cruise to appear in the distance. "Don't make me strangle you."

"Is that the only thing you have to say to me after an entire *bara*?"

Aja's breath caught in her throat as her cup slipped from her fingers and landed with a thud to the rooftop. She whirled in the lounge chair so quickly that it toppled on its side sending her rolling across the rooftop. When she stopped the hem of her caftan was twisted up around her face and the night air lightly raced across her exposed nude frame.

"Just as beautiful as I remember."

Aja felt familiar hands pull the material from her face as her body began to shake with laughter. "Not exactly the touching reunion scene I imagined," she joked just seconds before she was able to look up into the face of the masculine she irresistibly loved.

Anansi was squatted down beside her and smiled as he reached down to stroke her face. "*Nagaya*, Aja," he said.

"I knew you would come," she admitted as tears

filled her long lashes.

Anansi scooped her body up into his arms with ease, lowering his head to hers and causing his locs to fall forward to curtain their faces. "Right here in my arms is where you belong," he whispered fiercely against her parted mouth before his lips claimed hers.

"Yes," Aja sighed as she brought her hands up to grasp his handsome face. She kissed him back with all the passion and yearning she had for him.

"Nothing," he said before he kissed her.

"Or no one." He kissed her once more.

"Will come between us again." One last kiss to affirm his words.

With her arms wrapped around his strong neck, Aja leaned back to look up at him. "Not even this caftan?" she flirted shamelessly with a lick of her lips.

Anansi's eyes deepened. "*Definitely* not."

Aja gasped as he used one fluid motion to tear the front of the gown from her body. She raised one brow as she smiled sexily. "Well...well...well."

Anansi lowered their bodies to the rooftop. "We have a lot of time to make up for," he told her as he rolled over onto his back and pulled her atop him. "So much to talk about and catch up on."

Aja put a finger to his lips, looking down at the *urjiis* reflected in his eyes. "Sssh. We have all the time in the world for that. Right now, I want you to tell me you love me as much as I love and cherish you."

Anansi brought his hands up beneath the layers of her hair to massage her scalp as he licked his lips and locked his charismatic black eyes with hers. "Staying away from you has been the hardest thing I've ever done in my life. Every day that passed was a countdown to the day I could get to you. I have lived for this moment where I could just hold you and tell you how much I love you."

Aja felt breathless as emotions clutched wildly at her chest. She stroked the sides of his face as she looked down at him with tenderness and heat. She rose to sit astride his lap and felt a rush as his hands rose to grip her waist.

Anansi closed his eyes as she lowered her lips to his while he squeezed her buttocks deeply.

They undressed one another slowly until they could press their heated bodies together as their arms held the other tightly. Their moans echoed as they kissed each other with a passion and intensity that shook them.

Anansi used one strong arm around her waist to lift her up as he guided his hardness inside her.

Aja circled her hips atop him, slowly taking in all his inches.

She planted a dozen tiny kisses on his face as he worked hips in unison to hers. He swallowed her gasp of pleasure before he shifted his mouth down to suckle her throat, her collarbone, and then her warm sweetly scented cleavage.

Long into the night, they mated like it was their last night together. She rode him. He rode her. Their hearts beat wildly. Their breathing was ragged. The chemistry and love between them heightened their senses and awareness of one another. Aja's eyes and gold dots glowed. And when they reached their climax together, as they slowly mated to their own music, they shivered and held each other tightly until they both felt breathless and weak.

Aja lay atop Anansi listening to the beating of his heart as she played in the soft hair of his chest. "I have never been so happy, Anansi," she whispered into the surrounding night.

"I bet you I can top tonight," he said, twisting a strand of her hair around his finger.

"Impossible," she said, tracing the outlines of the black tribal markings on his strong arms.

He reached for her chin and tilted her face up so that her chin lightly rested on his chest and their eyes were locked. "Return to Erised with me and agree to be my lifemate?" Anansi asked.

Aja gasped in surprise, touched by the uncertainty she saw in the black depths of his eyes.

"I know how much you love Nede," Anansi

continued, his thumb stroking the gold dot on her chin. "And it would mean giving up so much of your way of life to be with me, but I cannot imagine my life without you any longer, Aja."

He's trying to convince me!

She thought it was adorable.

"The *Moticha* and *Giifftii* look forward to your return as well," he added.

I truly love him.

"And we can visit Nede as often as you please."

"Oh, Anansi," she chided him. "I was meant for you before you even knew it. Before *I* even knew it."

The doubt remained. "Is that a yes to my proposal of *gaa'ila*?" he asked.

"Yes, yes, yes," she promised, lowering her head to taste Anansi's lips, filled with pleasure that her destiny was truly filled.

All Romance Books by Niobia Bryant

Special 15th Anniversary eBook Reissues:
Admission of Love *
Three Times a Lady
Heavenly Match *
Can't Get Next to You
Let's Do It Again
Count on This

Strong Family Series:
Heated *
Hot Like Fire *
Gave Me Fever *
The Hot Spot *
Red Hot *
Strong Heat *
Just Say Yes * (Novella)

Make You Mine
Want, Need, Love *
Could It Be? (Novella)
More and More (Novella)

* *Books set in Holtsville, South Carolina*
(Hot Holtsville series)

All Mainstream Books by Niobia Bryant

Mistress Series:
Message from a Mistress
Mistress No More
Mistress, Inc.
The Pleasure Trap
Mistress for Hire

Friends & Sins Series:
Live and Learn
Show and Tell
Never Keeping Secret

All Urban Fiction Books by Niobia Bryant writing as Meesha Mink

Real Wifeys Trilogy
Real Wifeys: On the Grind
Real Wifeys: Get Money
Real Wifeys: Hustle Hard

Bentley Manor/Hoodwives Trilogy
Desperate Hoodwives
Shameless Hoodwives
The Hood Life

Queen Series (Crime Fiction)
Kiss the Ring
All Hail the Queen

All YA/Teen Fiction Books by Niobia Bryant writing as Simone Bryant

Pace Academy Novels/Pacesetters Series:
Fabulous
Famous

About the Author

Niobia Bryant is the award-winning and national bestselling author of more than thirty works of romance and commercial mainstream fiction. Twice she has won *RT Magazine's* Best African-American/Multicultural Romance Award, her most recent book written under the pseudonym of Meesha Mink was listed as one of the Library Journal's Best Books of 2014 (in the African-American fiction category), and her books have appeared in *Ebony, Essence, The New York Post, The Star Ledger, The Dallas Morning News* and many other national publications. Her bestselling book, Message from a Mistress, has been adapted to film.

"I am a writer, born and bred. I can't even fathom what else I would do besides creating stories and telling tales. When it comes to my writing I dabble in many genres, my ideas are unlimited, and the ink in my pen is infinite."
—Niobia Bryant

For more on me and my books, please visit:
www.NIOBIABRYANT.com
www.MEESHAMINK.com

or join my Official Facebook Fan Page:
Niobia Bryant | Meesha Mink

Made in the USA
Middletown, DE
06 February 2018